THE SA

OF

ABZU

ODIN

THE
SANDS OF ABZU

Nassim Odin

ODIN

2022

ISBN ebook: 978-1-954313-04-0
ISBN Paperback: 978-1-954313-05-7

Cover Design: Grigorri Gorshechnikov
Map: BMR Williams
Cover and map are protected under copyright 2022

Publisher: Odin Fantasy World

Dedication
Dedicated to Zoiya

Persian Soundtrack Musical Score

Odin Fantasy World - You Tube Channel

Foment Courage
Music Artist: Ivan Duch

Palace of King Kai Kobad (Kauui Kauuta)
Music Artist: Obaidas Guerra (obadiasharp)

The Simurgh Flight
Music Artist: Nun Silva

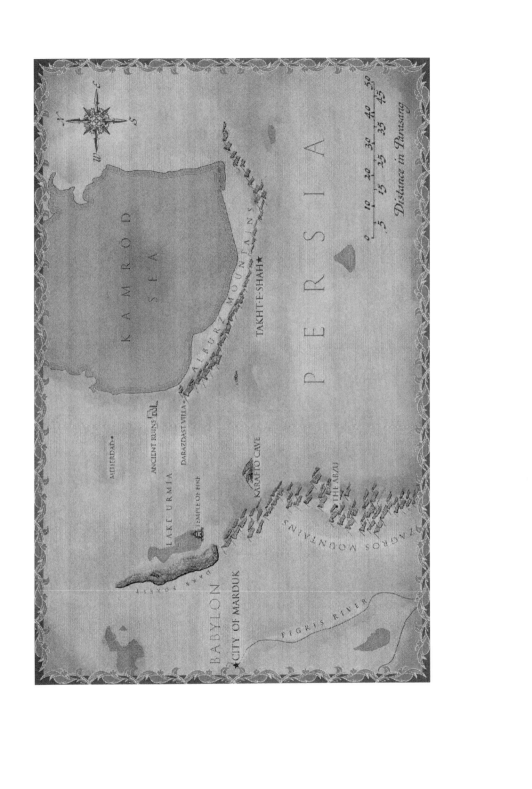

Contents

Chapter 1

The Calamity

THE thunder was so deafening that he couldn't hear anything else. It was not raining, but the lights were sweeping over his face from time to time, brightening up the thing he was doing in the vastness of the wilderness – alone and anxious.

Fardad dug into the earth with his bare hands. His nails were filled with dirt, and some even stuck on his fingers. The ground under his knees was soft, and his knees sank into the ground. He could feel the moisture of the soil seep up through the breathable linen of his clothes and onto the rough skin of his knees. Sometimes he looked up, beseeching Yazdan not to pour rain over him. Fardad didn't know what he was digging for, and he just knew why he was desperate. He felt that this was his calling, and something un-

CHAPTER 1.   THE CALAMITY

derneath was beckoning him, and he just had to dig deep.

His breath was fast and uneven. He was panting, and sweat dripped from his head. There was stress all over his face, and it was like he was in a race against time. He realized only a moment later that he was crying, too. The tears dropped on his hands, made the soil stick on them even more. Fardad realized how gross his hands looked and felt it too, but he had other matters, urgent matters, to take care of–what those matters were, he did not know. He just had to take care of those matters one step at a time. His heart was beating fast, and he tried to calm himself, but he couldn't. There was so much at stake, and it seemed like this was just the calm before the storm.

He knew he was looking for someone in his heart, but he didn't know who it was. Maybe he knew who it was but didn't want to acknowledge it. Perhaps the act of looking for someone, anyone, by digging the earth, especially in a place like this, scared him.

There are only hills and wind-sculpted rocks in the distance. Nobody here to witness his actions. The ground is soft and sandy, but he will feel it when he digs. The ground is still loose in places, and in others, it's firm.

Was it a graveyard? There was nothing but the flat ground around him, covered with a mixture of dirt and sand. Fardad hadn't looked at it at all, but he knew that was the case. His concern was only restricted to what lay six feet under. He was getting close.

The fear became too real for a moment. He felt as though a silhouette had moved in the distance. Fardad was scared to look up and look at it. He knew there was nobody around him. There couldn't be anyone around him, but he was sure there was someone there now. He didn't want to be distracted, but his mind kept wandering away from excavation to curiosity. Was there someone out there? Was he also here for the same thing that Fardad was? His mind kept asking a million questions but came up with zero answers. He just wanted to get this done and over with, but the silhouette was there quietly haunting him. He could feel the presence of someone or something near.

Fardad jolted from his sleep as a silhouette moved across the room.

"Who's there?" he asked, sitting upright.

There was a blur in his memory. The dream and the reality seemed not to have a boundary. They all became a whole, and nothing was left to the imagination when he heard a familiar voice. It was a voice that shook him to the core, and he shivered, surprised, and realized that it was none other than... "It's me, Son," said Kanisha, her voice breaking from all the sobbing.

"Are you weeping for Father?" asked Fardad.

He wanted to cry for his father, too.

"Yes...," she replied, her voice trailing off.

"Please don't cry, Mother," said Fardad. "I'm sure Father is fine and that he will be back soon. I can feel it in my heart that he is still alive." Kanisha held up the oil lamp in her hand. Fardad saw tears running

CHAPTER 1.   THE CALAMITY

down her cheeks as rivulets moved over the dunes in a desert. His father's disappearance had been quite disturbing, leaving him and his mother anxious. They both were hoping he was alive and perhaps captured or lost somewhere–anything but death. Fardad kept telling himself that they just had to see his father alive and on two feet.

"He has never been so late in returning," Kanisha said, sitting beside Fardad and putting the lamp beside his bed. "I can't help but worry about him, and I can't stop worrying about what we will eat tomorrow. We have sold what we could already. Son, what will we do now? Your father is missing, and we have nothing to eat!" "Are you sure, Mother? Is there nothing we can sell off? There must be something. Let's look back at the house after this, and I am sure we can find something," said Fardad. He became worried too.

"No, there's nothing except that silver cover, remember? What will get that us!" answered Kanisha.

"What silver cover?" asked Fardad.

"The one over the book that's placed on the niche close to the roof? You know about that, son, but that's the only thing we can sell, or we stay hungry." Kanisha explained.

"I don't know about that at all. You never told me before," said Fardad.

"I haven't seen it in a long time either. Whenever I try to take it, a black cobra comes out. I can never figure out what that means or why this happens. Something your father may know better. Either way, we need to do something about the snake before we could sell it," Kanisha further explained.

"I'll ask Ukund to come, and we will kill the snake. That should be no problem, Mother. I am here for you!" Fardad reassured his mother.

Kanisha smiled and replied, "My dear Fardad, that would be dangerous. Please be careful, and it means so much to know that you would risk your life for us to take out the snake!"

Fardad then looked up at her with his innocent eyes and said, "Mother, you mean everything to me. You are my world, and I would sacrifice my life without hesitation for you. We'll get the snake out and then can sell the silver cover. Even if I don't eat, I can't bear to see you hungry. Just take it easy!" "My Son, thank you so much. I just hope we find your father too, or at least he comes home. Don't you worry; my heart tells me he is still alive!" said Kanisha with blurred optimism.

"I feel the same way, Mother. I just hope we both are right. Our house is no home without him! I miss him so much!"

***

In the morning, Kanisha showed Fardad where the book was placed.

"Your Father placed it here," she told him as she pointed toward it.

Ukund arrived just then, a friend of Fardad and an apprentice of Fardad's father. Though Ukund was

5

CHAPTER 1.   THE CALAMITY

three years older than Fardad, the two were close friends. Ukund would not even think twice when asked by Fardad to help in any matter. Fardad's request was his command, and such was their friendship and loyalty to each other. It was so profound that none could ever break their bond.

Ukund was a friend's friend and will put his life on the line for them. To him, serving Fardad was an honor that he had always upheld. He had a long-standing history with Fardad's family that went back to generations; their grandparents and fathers were best friends. It was about protecting and honoring their bloodlines for both friends. This was why Ukund always considered Fardad's family as his own. Ukund would come to his aid at a moment's notice, and this time, he was there to help Fardad kill a snake that had come between them and the silver cover, which meant their livelihood.

Ukund saw the snake was there for protection and deciphered another exciting discovery. "Maybe your father put it here so nobody can steal his prized possession," commented Ukund.

Fardad's father, Aardburzin, was the only astrologer in the small town they lived in. The town was toward the southeastern shore of the Kamrod Sea but was surrounded by golden sands. He was a wise old man with a powerful personality. He was pretty distinguishable by his white beard and implausible knowledge sources. He was truly a man of honor, owning a truthful, impartial life. Tales of his adventures and his astrological knowledge were known throughout the lands of Persia. He was known as a living legend, and Fardad hoped to emulate his father someday. Aardbuzin's most prized possession was a silver-covered book, and this book's cover was going to get Fardad's family food on the table.

"I'll climb the ladder. Once I see the snake, I will clamp him and put him in this jute bag." Ukund explained his plan to Fardad. "If it attacks, then I will swing on my side and push it down. You'll have to be ready to smash its head then."

It seemed like a doable plan, but they were nervous. Fardad was relaxed to have his best friend by his side, even though it was not an effortless task for them, but it wouldn't be too hard for them not to accomplish.

Fardad held the hammer bolt in his hand, Ukund climbed the ladder. A black cobra came out as soon as Ukund tried to pick the book. The snake did exactly as Ukund had suspected; he moved on his side and pushed the snake out of the niche through his staff. As soon as the snake dropped on the floor, Fardad smashed its head with the hammer bolt. Kanisha screamed with joy. Finally, the snake was dead, and the silver cover became theirs to sell in the market. Ukund took the book and climbed down the ladder. He removed the dust, and the cobwebs stuck to it. He handed the book to Fardad, who broke the seal on the silver cover. However, the cover wasn't as important as the book's contents. There must have been something there that required protection, but from whom!

CHAPTER 1.   THE CALAMITY

That was the mystery Fardad was thinking about all this time.

They opened the book and found it a compendium of astrological knowledge and secrets. Being Fardad's father's student, Ukund was also well-versed in astrology and astronomy. The two boys spent a long time looking at different pages in the book. They both forgot they needed the food by selling the cover, but the knowledge inside fascinated them, and they wanted to uncover its secrets.

Also, Ukund had brought some food for Fardad and Kanisha. He didn't know they required food. For him, it was only a goodwill gesture toward his beloved master's family and his dear friend. Had he known that they needed food and the reason behind killing the snake was to sell the silver cover, he would have brought more food for them.

***

As Ukund was leaving, Fardad stepped out too. The two young men started walking toward Ukund's home.

"Ukund, I wanted to ask you something. . .," said Fardad, his voice trailing off in embarrassment. Ukund was bewildered, as Fardad was usually straightforward with questions and didn't ask like this. Something must be on his mind. They had gotten rid of the snake, but was something else bothering him? That was what Ukund kept thinking about.

"What is it?" Ukund asked, stopping in his tracks.

Fardad stopped too and looked around to see if there was anyone around. He needed to make sure no one listened to their conversation, and there was already too much going on in his mind.

Ukund could tell that Fardad was worried the minute they met this morning. Ukund was good at reading his friend's face, and this time, his expression was more than enough.

"How much would the silver cover on that book sell for?" said Fardad with a sigh.

"I don't know, really, but I'm sure it would bring a good amount. It's much heavy," replied Ukund, matter-of-factly. Ukund was shocked as the book's cover was precious and would make the book incomplete.

Fardad nodded his head understandingly.

"Okay," Fardad said in a small voice.

"What do you need, Fardad?" Ukund asked with much kindness, and he figured Fardad wasn't in the mood to sell it for food.

"Food," said Fardad and gulped.

"You don't need to worry about food," he replied.

"It would be too much Ukund...," said Fardad. The embarrassment in his voice had increased.

"It's just food, Fardad," Ukund reassured. "I'll tell my uncle to provide grains, meat, and fruits regularly. You and your mother will be taken care of. Listen, Fardad, your father was my mentor, and I am his protg. I want to honor him by serving you and your family the best way I can. Your family is my own, so I am happy to help. Don't worry about it, dear brother."

Ukund patted Fardad's shoulder.

"Thank you," said Fardad.

"You don't have to thank me. I just want a favor in return, though," Ukund replied.

"What is it?" asked Fardad, his voice filled with confusion now.

"You need to promise me one thing, old friend. And you have to honor this promise till death. You remember that a friend's promise is sacred in our lands, and you are aware of that, aren't you?" Ukund asked politely and as humble as he ever could.

Fardad knew he couldn't turn that request down. Therefore, he nodded his head and shook Ukund's hand.

"I don't want you ever to sell that silver cover," Ukund explained his deal. "I know that whatever your father owns belongs to you, but I don't want you to sell anything that belongs to my master; ever, please."

"I won't, ever. Promise," said Fardad.

"Thank you so much for this. He means a lot to me, and you are his son. I have sworn to protect you all my life, and today, I am shaking your hand, intending to keep this promise. I told your father that nothing will ever happen to his son as long as I am alive. I will never let even a scratch come onto you," said Ukund, smiling. Fardad smiled too. The two parted ways, and each walked back to his home. Fardad walked back with heavy sighs of relief that they didn't need to worry about food and that he had to keep his promise.

He would never sell the book or let anyone touch it without his permission.

***

That night, Fardad dreamed of his father; he was near the ancient ruins and in much agony. Fardad saw him in pain and crying for help, and there was nothing but dry sand around him. Fardad woke up from the disturbing dream, sweating all over.

His thoughts went to the dream he had dreamed of a night before. Could they be connected? He couldn't help but think and wish that wasn't the case. "No, they can't be connected," he whispered to himself in a barely audible voice. The ground in my first dream was covered with wet soil while Father seemed to be stranded in a deserted area with nothing but sand around, he thought. He kept thinking if that was a sign or a calling to find his father. Fardad knew that the ancient ruins were on the western shore of the Kamrod Sea, much further than that. The land was barren in that area, and nothing but pointy, prickly desert plants grew there. It would not be a peaceful journey by the slightest margin. He reiterated his dream to his mother in the morning–the one he had dreamed that night only and not the one before that. He didn't want to make his mother worried until he knew for sure that there was a need; even then, he wished he didn't have to make his poor mother worried. Fardad also told her he meant to look for his father. With his whereabouts

CHAPTER 1.   THE CALAMITY

unknown, something had to be done. He had to find his father and make sure he was alive.

Kanisha's heart felt as if being clutched in a tight fist, but she helped Fardad prepare for his journey. She packed some dried apricots and candied orange peels for him in a wrap made of wheat straws. She poured some water for his journey in a bottle made of sheepskin. She gave him a long and warm embrace while trying hard to hold back her tears.

She gave her son an important message: "Son, I understand you are traveling distances to seek your father and ensure he's alive. I don't know whether he is alive, but I want you back in one piece. I can't lose any more of my family. If your father has gone forever, and you disappear, whom will I have with me? Please, my boy, return to your mother. I love you so much; I will wait for you right here and pray for your well-being. I trust you will not engage with anyone. Keep a low profile, and I hope you find what you seek."

Fardad was also in tears because he felt it might be the last time he would see his mother. He was venturing a journey he may never return from, so he embraced her tightly and kept saying that he loved her. He had entrusted Ukund to stay and look after his mother in his absence. Fardad promised his mother. "Dear Mother, I promise you I will not disappoint you, and we will meet again. It may take some time, but I assure you I will return to you in one piece. Your prayers will help me and guide me through all the obstacles ahead. Ukund here will help you with whatever you require. He wanted to come with me, but I can't leave you alone. Our enemies could reach out to you if they have my father. At least, Ukund will make sure you're safe. I will see you soon, Mother, and I love you so much."

Ukund and Fardad exchanged a few words between them before the latter headed out searching for his father and whatever other truths he wanted to discover. Ukund said, "My brother, why don't you let me come with you. I will have one of my friends look after your mother. Otherwise, out there, you will be all alone with no one to watch your back. I want to come with you, and your mother will not be left alone to fend for herself. Please, let me come with you!"

Ukund's pleas weren't enough to convince his friend. Fardad said, "Ukund, my dear brother, you know I don't trust anyone but you with my mother. I understand you will worry about me, but her prayers will protect me. You know her prayers are powerful. They will never leave me, and I will meet all challenges. She can only keep praying for me if she is safe and looks after me. You are like her son, and my father would want no one but you by her side in my absence. Do it for him, if not for me. Do not worry about me. I will return here safe and sound."

Ukund was in tears and said, "I will miss you so much, my friend. You have mentioned your father's name and entrusted me with this responsibility, and I will uphold it and see she remains unharmed and looked after. Take care, my brother, and may you

13

CHAPTER 1.   THE CALAMITY

succeed!"

Both Fardad and Ukund embraced each other and shook each other's hands. Fardad gathered supplies for his expedition and ensured that he was well-stocked with everything he needed. He was feeling goosebumps the entire time because this would be the most arduous trip of his life. In every inch of his bones, he thought danger awaited him, but he also felt capable of handling the challenge. After all, his father's life was at stake. He knew his father would sacrifice his life for him, so he would do the same as his son if needed.

Fardad prepared his horse and left the same day.

***

Fardad headed toward the Alburz Mountains, a mountain range running at a distance of some kilometers away but along the entire length of the southern shore of the Kamrod (Caspian) Sea. Fardad rode his horse between the water's body and the mountain range. As the horse needed rest, he took a few breaks but quickly moved on ahead. There was no time to waste because he was very concerned about his father. He could feel the inner strength from his mother's prayers gushing through his veins. He would place his hand on his heart and could feel her mother praying for him. It was surreal for him, as he thought she was always with him in spirit. At night, he stopped close to the sea and dipped his toes in the water as he stood watching the reflection of the moon in the sea. It was a night of the half-moon. For a moment, Fardad felt he saw a reflection in the water of a giant bird. But as soon as he looked up at the sky, there was nothing but emptiness and a half-moon. There weren't even any stars that night. If it weren't for that half-moon, it would have been pitch black, almost as dark as his dreams of late. He knew he was getting very close to his destination. So far, he had been safe and faced no problems. He was ready to take on everything because he knew many prayers were with him. For the time being, it might just be the calm before the storm.

Later that following day, Fardad arrived at his destination. As he moved closer to the ancient ruins, he found himself at the same spot where his father was present in his dream. With every step he took toward the ruins, he felt an unearthly presence. Could it be his father sending some telepathic message? He couldn't guess but followed his instincts.

Once again, there was a blur in his memory. The dream and the reality seemed not to have a boundary.

Fardad found the ground exceptionally soft at that spot. His heart skipped a beat as he looked down and saw a specific area covered with dirt.

This time, there was a blur in his vision. Tears had welled his eyes, making it difficult for him to see. He knew something or someone was down there, and he was hoping it wasn't the dead body of his father. He would die the minute he saw that. He constantly prayed that his father was safe. He knew his mother would break down if she found out that her husband was no longer alive. Nonetheless, Fardad had to take his chances.

He had no shovel, so he got down on his knees and started digging with his bare hands. The dirt filled his nails and stuck to his hands, but Fardad carried on. He felt the moist soil beneath his knees. The moisture seeped up through the ground and onto the rough skin of his knees. As he dug deeper, he was getting more nervous. He was trying to hide negative thoughts and hoped to see his father alive and waiting to be rescued from wherever he had been left. Even if he were within an inch between life and death, Fardad would give his life for his father. He had not come this far for the bad news. The intensity of fear could be seen on his face, and he wished this was just a nightmare and not a reality. Unfortunately for him, he had seen all this before in his dream and now lived it. This was the moment of truth, and it beckoned him to dig deeper.

Fardad's heart was pounding. His thoughts rushed toward what the worst scenario could be, what it was. "No, no, it cannot be," Fardad told himself. But he couldn't help but remember his dreams–mixed images from both dreams. It was frightening and exciting at the same time. He was living his dream and perhaps minutes from making a discovery that might change his life as he knew it.

Fardad focused on digging the earth and pushed away all the unwanted thoughts with the hope he had in his heart, hoping he had carried with him from home and had survived on during all the time he had spent being away from his village and in search of his father.

He had come here on a mission, and he would not even think of going back without finding the truth about his father's whereabouts. Even if his father was potentially dead, he should know the truth, so he could find out who was responsible. He didn't even want to think that was a real possibility, but he kept digging for the truth. The time had arrived, and whatever he was searching for would finally be revealed. His dream didn't show him what he was supposed to find, but he knew something was there, and it was calling to him. He realized a moment later that he was screaming as he was digging. His eyes were red, and tears streamed down his face and on his hands, making the dirt stick on them even more. His screams echoed in ruins ahead and the surrounding emptiness. There was not a single being there beside him. Something inside told him he might just be digging out his father's lifeless body, but he didn't have the guts to feel that for sure. He knew he could be surprised, but he just wanted answers, and the more he would discover, the more he would be shocked.

Fardad's scream halted in a shock when he had come upon a torn piece of clothing. It was apparent that there was more of it underneath. Fardad dug further and faster. He had already recognized the piece of cloth as that of his father's tunic. Now he could also smell the rotten flesh. Fardad's hands began shaking, and his breath grew heavy and uneven. His heart was trembling with fear, and he had to get a hold of himself because his father might be buried underneath the rubble. To his shock, his eyes finally saw what he had wanted to see for a long time. There it was, the lifeless body of his father left like it was nobody's business. He broke down and screamed out so loud after seeing it. He could feel his mother crying, and he felt helpless. He wished he had never come there because this was too much for him to handle. He kept staring at it, hoping it was someone else, but it was his famed astrologer father, Aardbuzin. He was left to rot six feet under, and someone had to pay for it. He knew he would not return unless he found out what happened to his father and why. After staring at the body and crying for several minutes, he removed him from his apparent grave.

He finally dug out his father's body. The world revolved around him in circles as he dragged the body out of the mixture of dirt and sand.

***

After Fardad had cried and grieved by his father's side for a while, he noticed that the body was still recognizable because of the cold weather. He finally put the pieces together of how his father was killed. It was brutal, and it seemed like he had been buried only two nights ago. His father's neck was slit, and crusts of dried blood stuck to the wound. As he continued to examine the body, Fardad also noticed that his father's right hand was clenched in a fist. It seemed like he was hiding something within his fists. Fardad unclenched his father's fist and found a ring of gold. The ring looked expensive, but Fardad spent little time looking at it. He put it in his pocket and, after somehow placing his father's stiff body over his horse, pondered over the arduous journey that lay ahead of him. The trip wasn't over yet, and the road ahead had even more challenges. He wasn't returning home without answers. He thought about his mother and was satisfied that Ukund was there.

Those people who killed his father mercilessly could come after his mother and Ukund had been warned of this rare possibility. Hopefully, he was prepared to take any action if that happened and protected his mother. He was instructed to take his mother far if there was even a sense of danger. He was even thinking of how Ukund would react, knowing about his mentor's demise. He would break down just like Fardad did because they were very close. He wondered how he could send a message but knew it would not be possible. He had to move further to unravel the mystery behind his father's murder. Whoever was responsible had to pay for it, and he would make sure that the culprit paid it with their blood. Fardad would never forgive murderers because it took a lot inside you to take a life, and this was unacceptable beyond a measure. The ring might have meant something, and it was probably calling out to Fardad in his dream. That must be something his father wanted to protect, and now he made it his duty to protect it with his life.

The sun was setting in the distance. It was getting cold and dark, and Fardad wasn't feeling his best af-

CHAPTER 1.   THE CALAMITY

ter discovering that his beloved father was now dead. His father's body was dry, stiff, and cold and looked like a wooden log on the horse's back. This was too much to handle, and he never imagined not being able to say goodbye to his father but only saw him lying lifeless in a dirty grave. There was work to be done, and Fardad moved ahead. He searched the area for clues and spent a couple of hours surveying the ruins. He didn't know where else to go until he knew why his father was out here and what he was looking for. He didn't leave any stone unturned until he tired of looking for clues. Nothing was to be found, and he knew he couldn't go back home with any answers, but he decided that there was no point staying near the ruins. He wanted to share his findings with Ukund, no matter how heartbreaking it would be for him. His mother would be shocked beyond belief to see his father slain on his horse. Perhaps he was at peace but didn't leave behind any of that with his family. There was no point going elsewhere without figuring out his father's activities, and for that, he needed to talk to Ukund. Hence, he mounted his horse and made the trip home, knowing he was not bringing back good news. The truth needed to be told. He had to face the grief of his mother and best friend and let them process everything, just as he had.

Fardad galloped as fast as possible and reached back to his village by the following evening. His mother was waiting by the door as he rode his horse closer to it every moment. Her heart kept beating faster as he saw her son riding toward her. She was happy to see him alive, but what was he carrying with him? She pondered over this dilemma quite a lot.

She did not see anyone besides him, which meant that his father had not been found. If he was, then he might be captured or just missing. She kept hoping it was of the possibilities and intensified her praying. Soon, she realized that her deepest and darkest fears were being realized. The concerned face was dwelling into shock as she recognized the lifeless body strapped to the horse. Kanisha screamed a silent scream as she figured the dead body from afar. She broke down into tears. Fardad climbed down from the horse as soon as he got to his home and put the finger on his mother's lips. Fardad wasn't ready for everyone to know of the calamity that had befallen them. He whispered in his mother's ears, requesting her not to scream. She could grieve in silence because something was wrong. His father was murdered for a reason, and he needed to find answers. At this point, all that remained was putting more pieces of this puzzle together. For that, he needed his best friend Ukund, and he had to break the bad news to him.

Fardad visited Ukund later in the night. Ukund came back with Fardad to his home.

***

"We need to put his body in Dakhma (Tower of Silence) where vultures come," Kanisha said. Fardad

CHAPTER 1.   THE CALAMITY

was silent for a while, and then he looked at his mother and friend and said: "No, we can't do this."

"What are you talking about? Don't lose your mind." Ukund said cryingly. "I am fine. Don't worry." Fardad said.

"Murderers are out there. We do not know yet who had murdered whether he was alone or with a gang, whether he was a serial killer, a psychopath, or a friend. If we send the body to Dakhma, many questions would be asked by priests and people. Maybe, the people think we had committed the murder. We do not have any proof yet, and the murderer could be living in our village." Fardad said further.

"He is right!" Ukund endorsed.

"We need to inform the Satrap; only he has the resources to investigate the murder and get the culprit. Until then, we hide father in our house. We can decide what to do with the body later; once we get the answers, we need to put the pieces of the puzzle together."

Therefore, Ukund and Fardad buried Aardburzin in the house's corner. The tears would not stop falling from Ukund's eyes as he buried his beloved master with his best friend. However, he had to respect his friend's request and keep the death and subsequent burial a secret. Ukund, too, requested Kanisha not to reveal the death of her husband to anyone in the town. They all had to stay quiet until the mystery behind the astrologer's death was solved. He also needed to know the ring's purpose clenched in his father's fists.

Fardad showed Ukund the ring he had found clenched in his father's hand. Ukund examined it. It was a gold ring with a thick band and a large emerald stone fixed in its crown. There were also some numbers engraved on the inner side of the band.

Fardad looked closely and jotted down the numbers on a paper, and Ukund recognized them as a magic square sequence of Planet Saturn. They exchanged a look. They both knew the ring did not belong to Aardburzin. The things were getting muddled, and it seemed as if his father was on to something deeper and darker than he could imagine. There was a reason he was murdered in cold blood–he knew things that could not be let out in the open. It seemed like a web of lies was to be unfolded in front of Ukund and Fardad.

***

Fardad had never felt so lost before in his seventeen years of life. That night, the night he buried his father, he visited the local temple. Fardad sat in front of the sacred fire of Ahura Mazda. He asked for guidance to solve the mystery of his father's death. He also asked God to take care of his mother and help her as she grieved for her husband. This was a tough time for the family as they had lost the family's patriarch. Fardad looked up to his father and knew that he loved him and his mother very much. Did he give his life to protect his family? Fardad kept on wondering to himself. His father was someone who would go to any lengths to save them, and Fardad knew it.

Fardad took a stroll on the outskirts of the village afterward. He looked around and wondered what his purpose in life was. All his life, he had never asked about it before. He had expected his father to take him under his apprenticeship, but that was out of the question now. Instead of making him skilled in one specific field, his father had made sure that Fardad learned a bit of everything. Nobody had understood his father's thought behind the method he had applied to Fardad's schooling, and some had even criticized it, but Fardad knew his father saw for him. He trusted his father, but it was unfortunate that the man with the vision was now gone, and Fardad was left to his own devices with no guidance. No one better could mentor and guide him after his father had gone. Even Ukund didn't know everything from his father because he was also a student and an apprentice. Ukund was disappointed because his hero had gone, and there was so much more he desired to learn from him.

***

Fardad's father was a successor in a family that had given birth to some of the best astrologers of Persian history. Fardad, on the other hand, possessed no desire at all to dwell in the mystical realm of astrology as his father did. One of the major reasons to support this desire of Fardad was the simple fact that he had absolutely no inclination towards transcendental art.

However, a deeper reason behind it was that he did not want the stars to have any type of influence on his life whatsoever. He wanted to be the sole master of his life such that only his actions and decisions would decide upon the outcomes of his life. He was the last among his family, and he had married the daughter of one of the most excellent clairvoyants of his times. So Fardad's paternal family were all gifted astrologers, and his maternal family was expert clairvoyants. Fardad considered himself none of those, as he had not even reached the level of either of his parents. They were gifted individuals, and now he took care of his mother. He would die for her and make sure she lived on. His mission was to make sure she stayed protected at all costs.

Fardad went home late at night. His mother had fallen asleep already. He looked at her and felt immense sympathy for her in his heart. She was still young, and she was only fifteen years old when she married his father. She had her whole life ahead of her, but sadly, she would spend it all alone now. For this very reason, Fardad took an oath with himself that he would do whatever it took to keep his mother happy and ensure his father's legacy was secured for generations.

Fardad kissed her forehead and went to lie down on his bed. Sleep didn't come to him until late. As he tossed and turned in his bed, he wondered what he would do for the coming day. So much was going on in his mind, and he couldn't be comfortable. Even

CHAPTER 1. THE CALAMITY

though he was lying in the comfort of his bed, he was very uncomfortable knowing that his father's killer was out there. He knew he had to find out what had happened to his father. His father deserved justice, and revenge was a dish best served cold. Vengeance was on his mind, but he also worried about his mother. Both thoughts had left him very restless. Visions of his father's lifeless body kept haunting him. There was a purpose behind that dream and had more to do with recovering his father's body. Something was wrong, and he desperately wanted to understand it. He could not just let it slide and move on. The entity that took his father's life could also come after him and his mother. Both of them couldn't be on the run for the rest of their lives, so he wanted to face the enemy and make sure he got answers from him. There was a lot of work to be done, and time was running out.

***

In the morning, Fardad woke up with the decision to inform the region's Satrap of his father's death.

In the Persian region, Satraps were like governors responsible for looking over the everyday matters of their region's people. Darazdast, the Satrap of Persia's northeastern province, was a man who was very welcoming toward all the people in his region, or so Fardad had heard. Fardad hoped Darazdast would help him too. He could use all the help he could get.

Aardburzin was an important man, and the news of his death or at least that of his disappearance would spread, eventually. Fardad didn't want that news to reach the authorities through gossip, and he found it best to inform them himself and that too in person.

Fardad also wanted to catch his father's murderer by surprise. The murderer could be anyone from the village, even his neighbor or relative. As the villagers traded a lot, it was hard to keep a tab of everyone's movements. There was a lot of mystery surrounding the murder; someone must have answers. Fardad had to talk to the Satrap, hoping that he could reveal clues about the man who took his father's life.

Aardburzin wasn't the most famous man either; being honest with his work had earned him quite a few enemies. With great power comes great responsibility. And, with great responsibility comes great power and enemies. Fardad wanted to catch that one enemy of his father, who had gone above and beyond in his revenge, by surprise by involving the authorities.

***

Though Fardad knew his decision was for the best, he felt an uneasiness toward it in his heart. He made his way to the villa of Darazdast after a couple of days, at least. Maybe I'll dream a dream where it would become clear to me if I should go there or not, he thought. Doubts and fear were clouding up his mind as he kept searching for answers. Whoever wanted his father dead was hiding a dangerous secret. What that secret was, Fardad was very curious to find out. Fardad didn't consider himself a clairvoyant even though

CHAPTER 1.   THE CALAMITY

he had always had dreams that seemed to come true. He could see the future even though it was always very muddy, just like the one that led him to the ruins where his father lay buried. He never shared his dreams with anyone else either, and they were always too complex for him to decipher and understand. They never seemed about anything important either. If he couldn't understand them, it would be tough for anyone else to do the same.

As a kid, most of Fardad's dreams had been about the deaths of the pets of people he knew. He never explicitly saw anyone's pet die in his dream, but he would see them flying in the air, above the clouds. They'd be flying even if they weren't a bird. After seeing many dogs, cats, and sheep fly in the air, Fardad started ignoring his dreams after ruling them out as nothing but an absurd phenomenon. Even though he saw ruins in his dream, he never dreamed of his father buried under the dirt.

He dreamed of many structures too. One of these structures was a castle with eight gates. The gates were all black. These gates led to the same massive hall with an empty throne. The throne waited for Fardad. Though Fardad knew well in his heart that the throne was waiting for him to sit on it, he was always too scared to do it. Every time in his dream, he would look for his father to seek his approval to sit on the throne but never found his father to be there, or even anywhere. His father could become a ghost, and he never knew. As an astrologer, his father knew too much of things, and perhaps quite a lot of that knowledge might have been deemed too knowledgeable by one of his enemies, and that meant that his father had to pay the price for knowing a little too much. He dreamed of other tall structures too. One of these was a city as a tall tower. Arches as windows, one upon the other, were built upon as a tall tower. It seemed like a city carved inside a mountain.

Other structures seemed to be three-pointed when seen from a side or any of its four sides. These were three and varied in their heights. Fardad never understood that dream, and he had never seen such structures anywhere, nor had he heard of them.

The relatives on his mother's side of the family seemed to predict all sorts of future happenings, and that too so clearly. Fardad had only met them once or twice when he was a child. They were so confident in themselves, and it had much inspired Fardad. They talked too freely and with much conviction that so-and-so in the family would become rich or that so-and-so needs to sacrifice some lambs to Angra Mainyu to ward off the calamity that would strike them. However, his mother could not predict his father's demise despite having the ability to see the future. Despite having a clairvoyant mother, Fardad could not see it coming. This was a bit too uncomfortable for Fardad if he could see it. "Who knew what the future held?" he always asked himself. That would be too scary for him to comprehend, and that was why he decided not to overthink it. However, sometimes, he wished he could see the future in his dreams to stay prepared for all challenges that he would face in his life.

He remembered asking them how they knew what would happen, and they often replied, "We saw it in a dream."

"I want to see the future in my dreams too." Fardad had excitedly expressed his wish.

"If You will, you will," one of his mother's uncles had replied.

"How would I know its future and not something from the past?" Fardad had further probed to satisfy his curiosity.

"When you will, you'll know," that same uncle had answered with a smile.

Yet, Fardad had never known it. He had continued to dream absurd dreams but had never known if they were in the future or if it was something his mind made up on its own. Even when he had understood his dreams about the dying pets, he had not paid them much heed as he never wanted to appear a clairvoyant who gave grave information of pets dying instead of critical news. It wasn't an excellent quality to have, and Fardad had given up the whole idea and even his wish to become a clairvoyant. The dreams in which he had seen his father in pain and himself digging a grave were the only dreams Fardad had ever taken seriously, and they were also the only dreams he had paid the attention they deserved. He was in no mood to see visions of more people dying, except if the individual was responsible for his father's demise. Those dreams had brought discomfort to Fardad's heart. He had once wanted to be a clairvoyant, and he had tried to be one too, but his clairvoyance seemed to have only worked for something that had brought him an unexplainable amount of pain.

Fardad regretted having those dreams. He hadn't had them on purpose, but he wished he didn't have them at all.

If he hadn't had those dreams, then he would still be hopeful that his father lived, and he would still be optimistic about his father's return too. He wouldn't have to see his mother grieve, and he wouldn't be suffering himself, either.

Fardad sighed. This wasn't the time to indulge in what could have been or what should have been, he thought. What had happened had happened already, and it was time to decide what he should do now. He couldn't change the past, but he still had time to change the future.

Fardad waited to dream of any dreams that could guide him toward his course of action, but his sleep was as dark as his dreams of late. Maybe my heart is uneasy because I'm going to search for my father's murderer. Could it be that I'm scared for my own life? Fardad questioned himself. No matter what, I need to do what's right, and since I haven't had a bad dream about it, maybe this is the right thing to do, Fardad decided. He decided to leave the following day. He had to find answers as he had waited too long.

CHAPTER 1.   THE CALAMITY

***

Fardad made his way to the villa of Darazdast, the Satrap. It was located near the southern shores of the Kamrod Sea, between the Sea and Alburz mountain range. Fardad had passed by the nearby city on his way to the ancient ruins just a few days back. He reached the villa the same day he set out on his new journey. The villa was built on the hills. Fardad wondered when it was erected since he didn't remember it being there when he had visited the nearby city a couple of years back with his father. It didn't seem like an old villa, anyway.

It had huge wooden doors fastened by iron claddings. Two guards stood on each side of the gate, and there were guards stationed at every corner of the villa as well. As he reached the gate, which was at least three times as tall as Fardad was, he found them open for his welcome. Though the guards didn't ask him anything, Fardad still told them he was there to see Darazdast. The guards didn't seem to hear him, and they seemed to know already, though.

Fardad's jaw dropped, and his eyes bulged out of wonder as he set his sights on the majestic garden right at the entrance from the tall gates. Flowers of every color on the heavens and earth bloomed inside it. A narrow stream of water flowed through the garden over a path made up of glittering stones. An arrangement of trees and statues added another layer of glamour to the garden. The garden seemed to be constructed by

Parinaaz; it was too beautiful to be made by humans. The magnificence and beauty had engulfed him, and he was completely mesmerized by them.

The fragrance from the burning incense added a beautiful mistiness to the air over the garden. The fragrances from the incense mixed in with those of the flowers and created an overlap of fragrances that had the power to stun one's senses. Fardad's heart was jolted with the pleasing and intoxicating ambiance, so much so that for a moment, he forgot his purpose of traveling to Darazdast's villa. He would love to have a villa like this someday, he thought to himself. As soon as Fardad remembered his business in that place, he also realized that his purpose was, in fact, much bigger than he had initially thought. It wasn't just about his father's brutal murder; it was about the fact that a murderer was on the loose in the region and could harm other people too. He had been distracted by the beauty surrounding him, but he knew that this wasn't an ordinary visit. He was there to find answers and felt that the man he was about to meet knew them better than anyone else. He could lead him to the killer of his father and allow him to gain justice, even if it was bloody.

He looked at the garden longingly one more time, as if trying to take in all its beauty in his eyes, and walked toward the passage on the right side of the gate. He entered a narrow passage that led toward a big hall that Fardad thought could fit his entire village. The hall roof was covered in glittering mirrors and gems, with an enormous chandelier hanging from its center. The chandelier is more significant than my house for sure, Fardad thought. This man was living a life of luxury and perhaps deserved it. At that point, if this Satrap could provide him with the answers, he would be indebted to him. He wanted nothing more right now, and he hoped this visit would be very fruitful.

***

The Satrap, Darazdast, sat on the other side of the room on a throne. On both his left and right sides, bureaucrats sat on chairs of less grandeur with guards standing by behind them. Everyone's eyes were set on Fardad. They all waited anxiously to know what this young man was here for. They wondered what questions he was seeking answers for. There was an etiquette that Fardad had to follow as the Satrap was a well-respected individual of the land. Therefore, he had to be treated with the proper respect, and Fardad would do precisely that.

Fardad walked close to Darazdast and bowed to him. He had never been so close to someone so high in authority before, but Fardad was a man of manners. "May the glory of the Satrap, Darazdast, be high and his loftiness prevailing," he said. Darazdast smiled. He nodded his head ever so slightly.

Darazdast was a middle-aged man with a sturdy build and much of his face covered with a big mustache and a thick beard. Finally, words were spoken after the greetings were out of the way.

"What brings you here? What ails you? What pains you?" asked the man sitting to the left of Darazdast.

"Satrap Darazdast, my father has been murdered," Fardad stated.

Darazdast's expressions changed to that of somberness. He leaned forward while sitting on his throne. At that point, he turned into a sympathetic father figure to Fardad as he wanted to comfort him and help him find the answers.

"What happened, son?" he asked.

"My father was traveling on state duty. When he didn't return home for many days and didn't write to inform of his delay, I began my search for him. ..." Fardad's voice trailed off as his eyes scanned the room. He wanted to make sure nobody caught the harmless lie, and he had to reveal just enough so that he could get the answers he came for. He didn't want to appear someone who dreamed of actual events, and it was the first time it had happened to him. Nevertheless, all eyes were still on him. Darazdast brought his attention to Darazdast again.

"Go on." The man to the left of Darazdast urged him. "Continue your story. Tell us how we can help you."

"I found my father's dead body buried near the ancient ruins," added Fardad. "His throat was slit."

"Is there anyone you suspect?" asked Darazdast, leaning back on his throne again.

"No," replied Fardad, plainly. "However, I'm afraid

that there is a murderer on the loose who can harm others too. This is why I came to warn you because I don't want more of us to get hurt."

Darazdast seemed to understand and think over Fardad's words.

"Don't worry, son." He assured Fardad. "We will find that murderer and crucify him in the middle of the town center. Thanks for bringing this to our attention, and we will be on high alert from now on." The bureaucrats all nodded upon listening to Darazdast's words.

"What was your father's name, if I may ask?" asked Darazdast.

"He was Aardburzin, the famous astrologer," replied Fardad, lowering his gaze as he remembered his father.

He couldn't see the shadow that passed over Darazdast's face upon hearing Aardburzin's name, but Fardad didn't fail to notice as Darazdast's voice became heavier right afterward. His father was a widely known personality, and his loss would affect anyone, and someone of Darazdast's stature was feeling his loss too. His father was a man important to several people.

"Don't worry. . .son," said Darazdast.

He dismissed Fardad with a signal of his hand. Fardad took a seat in the area specified for civilians present in the court. From his seat, Fardad saw and heard the man on the left of Darazdast call the Pasbaans and ordered them to investigate the murder and look for the murderer. He also gave them some other instructions that Fardad couldn't hear.

The man on the left then got up from his chair and walked toward Fardad, and Fardad stood from his seat out of respect.

"Son, you're to stay here until the mystery around your father's death is resolved and the murderer caught," he said.

"But–" Fardad began but got interrupted.

"No buts. You're a guest of the Satrap himself, and his orders have to be obeyed. Your life could be in danger, young man, so it's best to accept his offer," the man added. Fardad wanted to speak again. He wanted to tell this man that his mother was all alone in the village, and her safety was more important than his, and he would feel more at peace if she was here too.

"It might take a while, but it doesn't matter. You're to stay here, and that's the Satrap's wish and order," said the man.

He briefly smiled and left without giving Fardad any chance to speak.

Fardad sighed. He had no other choice, it seemed. His mind kept wandering off to his mother because he didn't want to lose his only remaining parent.

Chapter 2

The Destiny

FARDAD walked around the Darazdast's villa. He was astounded by its beauty and glamour. The architecture included details that Fardad had never seen before, that he never even thought was possible. Fardad guessed that the exquisite materials used for the villa's decor had been sourced from all over the world.

While the village where Fardad came from houses was composed of clay, and other villas and castles were made of bricks, Darazdast's villa also had metal and wood infused in its structure. The many arched windows in all the rooms were draped with silk or net curtains, and the doors were mostly made of metal and had wooden door handles.

There were chandeliers as big as rooms encrusted with gems of different colors. Everything from chairs to food platters to the statues in the garden looked extravagant. Only a man of Darazdast's stature could live here or rather deserve to live here. Fardad was an ordinary man, despite being the son of a well-known astrologer. He was happy with non-material things, such as relationships. Beauty and grandeur fascinated him, but his loved ones mattered more to him. He would never abandon or forsake them for material wealth.

All the beautiful things around the villa soon became too overwhelming for Fardad. He went to his room. The room was lavishly furnished too. The bed frame was made of intricately carved wood. There was a side table by the bed with a beautiful gold-plated candle holder. The bed was of the finest ebony, the quilts patterned with silver. There was a lamp on the table with a beautiful glass shade of blue colors. The bed was covered in a top sheet of satin; the bed sheets were made of silk, the pillows were lined with a feather duvet. The bedroom was full of bowls filled with rose petals. The room smelled like a bouquet of roses and vanilla; the bath was filled with lavender water.

Right in front of the room was a large window with silk curtains draped over it. There were flecks of gold in the raw-white curtains, and Fardad wondered if it was gold or if they had somehow come up with a shade of it.

Placed under the window was a desk. The desk and the chair also had the same carved design on their edges as the bed frame. A set of scented, thick papers was placed over the desk under a heavy, round marble. Fardad's eyes could identify the thin strips of wildflowers placed randomly within the paper. Placed by the set of papers was a glass bottle full of ink and a couple of pigeon feathers with their tips sharpened for writing. It was all arranged in a simple but well-made wooden tray.

Fardad looked at it all and wondered how the Satrap was so rich. Persia was a prosperous land, yes, and the people were doing good. The trade sector had developed, and there was a boost in other industries, but everything about Darazdast's villa still seemed excessive to Fardad. To an extent, it even seemed pretentious to him. He kept wondering what made this man so important to deserve to live in so much luxury.

Darazdast was a Satrap, and it was his responsibility to solve the various issues of his people, but there was no way one wouldn't find more issues in their day-to-day life after spending a little time at Darazdast's villa. The opulence available at his villa was bound to make people feel unsatisfied with their own lives. Obviously, such grandeur could overwhelm anyone who's never lived in it, and the same was the case with Fardad. It was a little too much for the young man because his father's murder was the only thing bothering him, and nothing would keep his mind from that.

***

Fardad removed his attention from the villa's grandeur and directed his thoughts toward the matter that made him visit the villa. He hoped the Satrap would catch his father's murderer and soon get the verdict that he received. Justice had to be served because his father didn't deserve such a gruesome death. He tried to

41

come up with an action plan for himself. He knew that once his father's murder mystery was solved, he had to find some work to support himself and his mother. They couldn't live off Ukund's generosity and kindness all their lives; Fardad didn't want to, anyway. Fardad wasn't the type to take advantage of anyone's generosity. Ukund was his father's apprentice, but that never meant that Fardad would ask him to take care of him and his mother all their lives. He was happy to have such a thoughtful friend, who was always there for him and his family.

He paced around the room, thinking about what to pursue to earn the daily bread. They didn't have enough land to grow something on, and nor did Fardad specialize in a skill. Fardad wished he had specialized in some talent to become an educator, but it was too late for him to do that. He became a trader's apprentice if nothing else worked out. Perhaps he could team up with Ukund and trade to earn a living. He needed to have someone trustworthy by his side.

All the thinking about the future made Fardad feel tired. He lay on the bed, and he was already a little tired from roaming around the villa all day and getting some rest. The bed was comfortable and soft, the sheets were silky smooth, and the pillows were dense; he fell into a deep sleep after a few minutes of lying down.

***

It hadn't been long since Fardad had laid on the

silky sheets that he heard a knock on the door of the room in his occupancy. Fardad got up and opened the door. A guard, fully armored, stood outside.

"I have a message for you from the Satrap," said the guard. He took a pause.

Fardad said nothing. He waited for the guard to speak further.

"You're to join Darazdast, the magnificent Satrap, for dinner tonight," added the guard.

"I'll be there," said Fardad.

"The dinner will be held right after sunset, and you should be there when the sky has hues of orange and pink." The guard explained. Fardad nodded his head slightly. The guard left with swift but decisive footsteps. It had been just a day that he had stayed there, and he was invited for a grand dinner, all the while his mother was living in their humble home with Ukund's generosity.

Fardad lay on the bed again and watched the sky change its colors.

***

Fardad reached the dining hall on time, and he had already seen it earlier in the day.

A long table occupied almost the entire length of the room. It could seat at least thirty people at a time, Fardad deduced. Just like other standard rooms, the dining room had a large chandelier in the center as well. This chandelier didn't have any gems but had candle holders of various sizes. All the candle holders had candles in them, and their flames gave off enough light that every nook and corner of the room was well-lighted.

The chairs around the table had velvet cushions over them. The table itself was laid with delicacies and all kinds of meats and fruits.

Fardad was stunned at the lavish display. He had never seen so much food at the same time before; he had not even seen half the kinds of food and delicacies before either. He lived a very simple life for his family, despite his father being such a famous astrologer. He was happy with his way of life, and this luxury was just temporary. It never bothered him because he wanted to be with his mother once he found the answers.

Darazdast sat at one end of the table, and his dignitaries and bureaucrats sat on his right and left in the same arrangement that they sat beside his throne. Somewhere in between Darazdast's many men, Fardad noticed an empty chair.

The man seated on Darazdast's left in the enormous hall gestured toward the empty chair just as Fardad looked at him. Fardad had been granted a lofty place to sit, and he was a guest of honor at this table. Fardad silently walked toward the chair and took his place at the dinner table. He had never felt that important in his life. Days ago, he was in ruins, discovering his father's lifeless body, and now he was sitting and having dinner in complete luxury. He had been no one's guest of honor before this, but he cared little for it. He was here for answers and would take his leave once his work was completed. Only a few moments later, the table was full of men and women. Fardad had not seen many of those present at the table anywhere in the villa when he had roamed around it only earlier that day. He wondered where these people were then and, more so, who they were.

Darazdast looked at the table. Everyone sat quietly, waiting for him. He adjusted his hand. Everyone rolled their eyes away from Darazdast and sat straight. A line of servants moved swiftly and placed napkins in the lap of each guest. The guests started pouring helpings of food into wooden bowls set in front of them. Fardad was confused for a moment. He didn't know what to eat, and to see the enormous helpings of food had suppressed his hunger. The men on his right and left gauged his confusion and directed him toward the best of delicacies. Fardad tried a few morsels of the food they had recommended and found his appetite back. He made most of the occasion and sampled the different cuisines prepared for the grand dinner, of which he was a guest of honor.

He then tried various foods that he never even knew existed and found them all scrumptious and delicious. Soon, he found himself full.

As almost everyone on the table slowed down their consumption of food, Darazdast tapped a little spoon on glass twice to direct their attention toward him. The tinkering of glass made everyone slow down further, stop chatting, and look toward the Satrap.

"I've gathered you all here to share an important

CHAPTER 2.   THE DESTINY

piece of news." Darazdast began. "I received this news from the mighty Shahanshah, the Padshah, Kai Kobad." There was pin-drop silence in the dining room now. Everyone was keen to know the message from the great ruler of the lands they called home. Darazdast continued. "Our Shah has dreamed something which he could not understand. Yet, even without understanding, the dream has filled his heart with sorrow." The mood of the room became somber as well. Shah Kai Kobad was beloved by his people, after all.

"The royal astrologers and diviners have all failed to interpret Shah's dream, and so the Shah has called out to his people to interpret his dream," the Satrap added. The people in the room all looked at each other, and it was indeed surprising news to everyone.

Kai Kobad had been the Shahanshah of the lands of Persia for well over a decade now. He was a descendant of Manuchehr, who was the son of mighty Fereydun's brother. The monarchy over Persia had passed down from father to son in the Manuchehr family for the past couple hundred years. Unlike the rulers before them, the Manuchehr had brought the concepts of peace and sustenance to Persia. Instead of winning over other lands and forgetting their people, they had worked toward maintaining their lands and developing them, and had established themselves as peace-loving, progressed people.

The Kobad family had also boosted trading throughout the region, so much so that trading had become the primary occupation for many Persians. Shah Kai Kobad, following in his father's footsteps, had also promoted education among their people, especially the mystical knowledge. They had given esteemed positions in their courts to many astrologers and numerologists. "Legend says that in among our enemies – the Greeks, there were diviners so accomplished that they could decipher even the untold dreams," said Darazdast, "and who can forget the legend of Yousuf from Egypt? He was an expert interpreter of dreams, a skill gifted to him by the divine." Darazdast paused for a bit before concluding. "The Shah wishes to find someone similarly skilled, and I hope it can be one of you." The Satrap was hinting toward Fardad, but he made nothing clear. Though the Satrap was done speaking, nobody spoke anything at all. The pin-drop silence emerged again and enveloped the room. It was too big of news for everyone. After all, if the Shah had called out to his people, then it must be a grave matter. The Satrap gave his audience the time to digest the news as well. It seemed like Fardad's father's murder mystery had taken a backseat to the Shahanshah's troubles. Fardad felt a bit at peace because he wasn't the only one seeing disturbing dreams or having worries to deal with. For someone as opulent as the Shahanshah, one would wonder if he had any problems at all to deal with, but even men of majesty had their worries. Wealth and grandeur were never the answers to true happiness, and Fardad was very well aware of that.

CHAPTER 2.   THE DESTINY

***

Fardad looked around at the faces with whom he was sharing the table. Everyone looked puzzled, and they all wanted to say something but were too afraid to say it. It seemed as if everyone doubted their abilities.

Many of Darazdast's men were eminent astrologers and diviners, yet they too seemed too scared to get involved in a matter so delicate as the one their Satrap had just described.

Everyone seated at the dining table seemed to have many questions on their minds, yet no word came out of anyone's mouth. The silence in the room seemed to grow only louder and louder. Fardad was thinking of a lot of things, too, and was trying to connect the dots between his father's murder and the Shahanshah's dreams. There could be a relationship since the Satrap had mentioned that Fardad was the guest of honor at the dinner.

***

The news had presented everyone in the room a chance of winning the Shah's faith. However, of losing the ability to win his faith again and, worse, offending the Shahanshah. This opportunity presented itself as a double-edged sword, so anyone who would step forward would have to handle it with care. Besides, if the diviners and astrologists of the court had failed to interpret it, then it must be a very complex dream. Above all, there was no way of knowing the dream unless one presented themselves in front of the Shahanshah and told him they were there to interpret his dream.

***

The more Fardad thought about the matter, the more he understood the concern on people's faces at the dining table.

Darazdast had left shortly after, gauging that no other words would be said that night in that room. The guests at the table, too, had left after their Satrap. If anyone were eating before Darazdast's announcement, they had not even bothered to empty their bowl afterward. The news had shocked everyone, and thus all the guests had lost their appetite.

While sitting at the dinner table, Fardad had felt an urge inside of him to ask about the Shahanshah's dream. He hadn't taken acted upon this urge since nobody had asked anything either. Later, in his room alone, Fardad regretted not asking. He figured that there must be some connection between the dream and his father's murder. He was desperate to know what the dream was so he could connect the dots.

He knew for sure that he wanted to solve the riddle that the Shahanshah was trying to seek help for. He only had to gather enough courage to ask the Satrap of the contents of the king's dream. That would not be an effortless task as no one spoke a word last night to the Satrap, and now he would take the bold step to do so.

CHAPTER 2.   THE DESTINY

***

The mystery of the Shahanshah's dream had gotten hold of Fardad's mind, and he found himself unable to sleep. He left his room and walked through the empty but dimly lit corridors of the villa. There was nobody to be seen anywhere, yet every corner Fardad turned and every standard room he walked through, he felt as if someone had just walked out of it before he came in.

There was a strange presence everywhere, and it was empty, yet it felt occupied. There were voices echoing around, but they were only in Fardad's mind but not in his surroundings, despite seeming so.

Fardad made it to the tower that watched over the nearby city. The city was entirely enveloped by the darkness of the night, and it seemed to indulge in a deep sleep. Fardad wondered if that's how his village seemed at night as well. Following that thought came an overwhelming sense of nostalgia for his past days. Fardad missed his father. He remembered his mother, too, of what she would do all alone at home these days. Fardad knew she would miss his father more now that he wasn't there to console her. He was worried that his mother did not know where he was and didn't want to make his mother think that he was gone too for good. It was a callous place to be in, and Fardad knew that. Tears kept rolling down his eyes as he thought more about his mother and especially his father, who was no more.

To divert from feeling the sorrow, Fardad turned his back toward the city and faced the mountains. It began drizzling just then.

Fardad decided to stay despite getting wet. He stood watching the mountains, and they had many shades of grey. For a moment, they seemed like silhouettes of Parinaazs watching over the villa and its surroundings.

Fardad felt chilly in his bones. It was no doubt that there was an eeriness about the place, and he had thought it the moment he had stepped inside. From the shapes of the mountains to the intoxicating beauty of the garden to the extravagance about everything in the villa screamed the presence of something unusual. This uneasy feeling had come to him several times since he saw the dream of the ruins and then went to discover the place for himself.

Fardad began shivering, and he was suddenly too cold. Maybe it was because he had gotten wet in the rain, or perhaps because he had looked for too long into something that he wasn't even supposed to see.

Fardad climbed down the tower and passed the corridors to get to his room. The corridors felt warm, and the room felt a lot cozier than before. Fardad stripped down the wet clothes on his body, dried them up, and put on fresh clothes before getting into the bed. Sleep engulfed him in moments, and he passed out with his mind reverting to his parents. He prayed in his heart that his mother was safe and that he might return to her soon.

CHAPTER 2.   THE DESTINY

***

Fardad dreamed a strange dream. He was at the spot near the ancient ruins where his father was brutally murdered and buried. It was pretty weird to witness the same vision all over again, and something in ruins was still calling out to him.

In Fardad's dream, his father was still buried under the mixture of soil and sand. A torn piece of linen peeked out of the ground and fluttered in the blowing wind. The dining table at the Satrap's villa was near the spot, laden with all the meat, fruit, and delicacies Fardad had. He had a few hours before he slept. The guests, however, were not the same. Wild wolves instead of humans feasted on the table. They gorged all the food, and once it was all finished, they began fighting each other. He kept wondering what all this meant, as the symbolism was quite confusing.

Fardad stood at a distance and felt confused. He wanted to take out his father's body but didn't want to get the wolves' attention for both his and his father's body's sake. He felt as if he wanted all the wolves to die, but for what reason, he didn't know. Everything was so confusing, but he just waited with bated breath to see the outcome of all this. A few moments later, he went into some trance.

He began muttering this wish of his under his breath. "Die. Die," Fardad said.

The wolves didn't hear him, and they were too busy fighting each other.

The wind blew hard. The torn piece of tunic fluttered too fast to be even seen. Fardad kept muttering, "Die, die, die, die, die. ..."

Fardad woke up with a jolt. He saw another strange dream, which made him wonder what was going on. Something in the villa was making him see such scary and weird dreams. He now realized that all that glittered was not gold.

He thought he had heard someone say the word die' repetitively but realized only a moment later that it was his voice.

There was a blur in Fardad's memory. The images of wolves stuffing themselves mixed in with the images of guests at the dining table. Why were all the guests transformed into wolves and fighting with each other? These images kept rummaging in his mind, and he couldn't stop thinking about them. Fardad was covered in sweat. For a moment, he tried to remember if he had changed his clothes after getting wet in the rain. He didn't linger on that thought much. His attention, on its own, had been directed toward the surrounding silence. It was so deafening and became quite unbearable to him. Strange occurrences in a grand villa were something he had never thought of. It was quite possible and plausible that his mind was playing tricks on him. He had been thinking way too much about the Shah's dream and his father's murder and deciphering a connection that confused him and drove him insane.

Fardad didn't remember the night being so silent when he went to sleep. Fardad breathed silently too, and he inhaled and exhaled slow, deep breaths. He didn't want to disturb the surrounding silence, and it felt wrong to do so.

Fardad remembered the dream he had just seen. There was nothing blurred in it, and he could differentiate his dream from his reality.

Fardad kept breathing the slow, deep breaths. He was getting drowsy the more his breath slowed down. Somehow, he fell asleep again.

***

Fardad slipped into another vivid dream. It wasn't his mind playing tricks because he saw everything firsthand in his sleep.

He found himself standing on the top of the tower; he looked at the city and the mountains from there. He stood firmly, but the ground beneath him was soft, and it was like the mixture of soil and sand he had dug up his father's body from.

The ground, however, was as supportive as the other person in Fardad's dream. That other person was the Satrap, Darazdast. The Satrap seemed to be stuck in the ground as if it was a sinking hole. While dreaming, Fardad kept wondering if there was some connection between the Satrap and his father's murder. Could he know something that Fardad didn't, but how was it connecting with the Shah's dream.

Fardad was trying to help Darazdast, but Darazdast didn't seem to want his help. Instead, he was pushing Fardad's hands away from him. Fardad was confused for a moment, but he soon realized that he was, in fact, not helping the Satrap get up but was pushing him further into the sinkhole. This entire scenario freaked Fardad out the entire time. He was soon uttering the same words he had said in his earlier dream, where he saw the wolves at the dining table. Something seriously was messed up, but Fardad couldn't put his finger on it, yet he uttered those exact words again on repeat.

"...die, die, die, die, die...." Fardad said in his dream. That was getting too much for him, and soon, we woke up with a start.

***

Fardad woke up from his voice again.

He feared his voice and of his actions, too. He never thought he could harm anyone, not even in his dreams. He had learned to fight since his father had taught him that, but he had never really fought anyone.

Why was he actively trying to kill the man who was helping him find his father's murderer, that too, in his own house? Fardad wondered. More questions kept haunting him, and he needed to find answers.

Fardad decided not to fall asleep again. He got up from the bed and silently walked toward the small table in the corner. There was a large bowl of water placed there. Fardad splashed some water on his face in the little light coming from the moon and fully opened his eyes. He didn't want to see any crazier dreams because he had enough of them already. He had seen two in the same night, and that was more than enough for him.

Fardad wanted to go home. Suddenly, he didn't care about his father's murderer so much, and he just didn't want to become a murderer himself. He had never thought of taking a life and stooping to the level of the individual who took his father's life, and he could never live with that guilt.

He wanted to see his friend Ukund. Fardad knew he could interpret both the dreams that had disturbed his night's sleep. Ukund wasn't a diviner, but he had a strong intuition about things. He always knew the right thing to say, and Fardad hoped his friend could impart some of his wisdom on him.

Fardad realized that he just wanted to talk to his friend; he missed him, his mother, and his life in the village. What have I gotten myself into? Fardad wondered. He also wondered how important was it to catch his father's murderer. He kept wondering if it was more important than the welfare of his mother and his own. Ukund had to have the answers, but Fardad was stuck in the villa until he could leave by the Satrap.

Fardad paced around the room as he tried to make sense of his dreams and his reality. He had always had surreal but vivid dreams, but their frequency had increased in the recent past.

Fardad wondered why it had happened. His father's death had acted as a catalyst for his life to change completely, and Fardad wished none of it had happened. Fardad tried to rationalize the events that had taken place in his life. Maybe it was all happening because I had been feeling horrified and perplexed lately, he thought. His mother had often warned him against thinking of the future too much. Though she came from people who predicted the future, she was a stern believer that some things were best left unknown, including one's destiny. Fardad tried to remember his mother's warnings and words about how people wrote their destinies, yet he couldn't rationalize his father's dreams and how they turned into reality. He felt guilty that he had dreamed of his father's passing, which was why it happened in reality. This was one reason he had to give up his mission and resume a life of normalcy.

Fardad came up with a plan of action: as soon as the sun rose, he would pack his things and visit the Satrap. He would advise the Satrap to stay cautious about his safety and take his leave by apologizing that urgent matters at home needed his attention. He was hopeful the Satrap would understand, and he could leave. There was no point in staying in the villa now. The Satrap could call on him later if needed, but he had to go home back to his mother.

***

As Fardad quietly paced the floor of the room, he heard a faint click of turning off the doorknob. In one swift movement, he picked up his dagger from under his pillow and leaped toward the wall just by the door so he would be hidden when the door opened.

CHAPTER 2.   THE DESTINY

Fardad wondered who it could be. It was too early for anyone to come to see him. Besides, the secrecy with which the person had entered his room gave him an ill-feeling. He didn't know who it was, but he knew they did not carry good intentions toward him.

The moon had diminished and was now growing again since he had stood and reflected upon it on the night when he had left his home to search for his father. Moonlight from the thin crescent moon was already present in his room and had illuminated it enough for him to see who it was.

A tall man had entered Fardad's room. From his back, Fardad could make out the man's build and complexion. He seemed to be an African man. The man walked slowly and quietly toward the bed. From the way he was walking toward the bed, it is clear to Fardad that the man was sent to harm him. Fardad was wondering if this was another dream or reality. He kept pinching himself and realized this man was for real.

Before the man could figure out that Fardad wasn't lying on the bed, Fardad leaped at him from behind and took him by surprise. Though the man was large and robust, he was helpless with a dagger against his throat.

Since Fardad knew a little of everything, he knew a few fighting skills, too. He quickly thanked his father for teaching him the skill of taking a man out. The man dropped his dagger on the floor and raised his empty hands in the air as a sign of submission. Fardad hardened his grip on the man's throat. "What do you want?" whispered Fardad in the man's ear.

The man said nothing.

"I won't ask again," said Fardad. "Tell me the truth, or I will cut your throat."

The man gulped audibly.

"The Satrap has sent me to take your life," replied the man, his voice a whisper too.

"Why?" asked Fardad. There were a thousand questions in his head, but that's all he could ask.

"I'm a slave, merely following orders. I may not ask questions. We just do as we are told, and I have no personal reason to take you out," said the man.

Fardad thought for a moment before he quickly picked up the dropped dagger from the floor. With a dagger in each hand, he ordered the man to kneel.

"Knees on the ground, hands behind the head," said Fardad. The man did as he was told. He acted like a slave, asking no questions as if he had lived his entire life that way. Fardad then closed the room door and removed ordered the man to remove the sheets from the bed.

"Tie them both in a rope," added Fardad.

Once the man was done, Fardad went behind him and tied his hands with it.

"Spare my life?" asked the slave.

"Why should I?" asked Fardad.

"I was merely following orders. I can help you escape," said the slave.

"Why do you think I would trust you?" Fardad

questioned. He was asking the slave's motives in his head.

"I want to escape from here, too. I desire freedom, and this place is a prison for me," the slave said with a sigh.

Fardad found honesty in his statement. He thought about what the slave had just said and inspected him.

"Answer me," said Fardad thoughtfully. "How has the Satrap accumulated so much wealth?"

The slave looked into Fardad's eyes as he answered, "Friend, beware of lust; it corrupts both the body and the mind. Appearances can deceive, and I would advise you never to trust someone you don't know. This world is a cruel place and will never let you live if you trust it."

Fardad found his whole body shaking. At that moment, he knew he could trust the slave, but he hadn't gotten his answer yet, so he pressed on.

"Go on," said Fardad.

"Darazdast was not that bad alas the lust; it corrupts both the body and the mind, Holy Zoroaster has rightfully said," said the slave, his full stature shaking. "He killed your father, too. I know you knew this, and there you go. Now that you know the man who took his life, do you trust me now?" The slave screamed out loud with utmost sincerity because he had no reason to live with the guilt.

He was doing himself a favor for buying his freedom by sparing Fardad's life. Fardad's jaw dropped, and he froze after he heard the revelation from the slave's mouth. He was sleeping in the enemy's villa all along, and this was why he was asked to stay behind and be a guest at the villa. Those dreams were all making sense now and why he was repeating die' to the Satrap in them. He wanted to know the reasons, and the slave might just have all the answers. Ukund would be so upset to find out and would not even waste a minute going after the Satrap.

Tears welled up in Fardad's eyes. "Do you know why he killed my father?" Fardad asked earnestly.

"Your father had discovered a treasure near the ancient ruins, and he had informed Darazdast about it and had asked him to send the information to Shah Kai Kobad. But Darazdast wanted to keep the treasure for himself, and so he murdered your father," answered the slave.

Fardad said nothing. The truth had deeply pained him, and it was apparent on his face. The slave was right. Lust and greed corrupt men of greatness, and no one can escape their temptation.

The slave continued speaking, "My friend...I'm sorry. I couldn't stop him from killing your father, but I don't want to kill you. I have killed no one before. I came here just because I was following orders, but I refuse to be deceived. I realized today that I should have escaped a long time ago. This is my chance to earn freedom. Let's get out of here, and you can decide later what you want to do."

"I swear to Ahura Mazda that I will not let Darazdast live longer," said Fardad in a subdued voice.

CHAPTER 2.   THE DESTINY

Fardad then took out his father's ring from between his clothes on the open shelf in one corner and showed it to the slave. "Do you recognize this ring?" asked Fardad.

"This belongs to Darazdast, and he got it as a present from the Shah Kai Kobad," stated the slave.

Fardad undid the rope on the slave's hands. The slave, however, did not move.

The slave continued, "I can help you escape. You can go to the king and show him the ring. The king will help you. Trust me, for I am on your side, please!"

"I trust you," said Fardad. He then asked, "What's your name?"

"I'm Gyasi. I'm Ethiopian," said the slave.

"I'm from a small village by the Kamrod Sea," said Fardad. "You know my name already."

"I know a lot more than your name," said Gyasi. "But we need to escape quickly. I should have killed and presented your head by now, and they'll come looking for me soon."

"Let's go then," said Fardad.

He handed Gyasi's dagger back to him. Gyasi picked up the rope of sheets from the floor, tied one end to one of the desk's legs, and flung the other from the window. "This way, my friend," said Gyasi. The two made their move, not knowing what dangers lay ahead.

Chapter 3

The Premonition

FARDAD jumped out the window. Gyasi followed him soon afterward. Gyasi had locked the door of Fardads room from the inside before jumping off the window. Both had also placed their daggers in their cases and put them in their kamarband (waistband). Fardad had also slung his bag, only carrying the necessities, on his shoulder.

They both had their feet placed firmly on the walls and had twisted the rope around their arms to hold it tighter. While holding the rope for their lives, the two men tried to look far in the distance in the dark night. They were trying to see the guards at the various towers.

They saw none of the guards had noticed them, and the guards sent by Darazdast hadnt sounded the alarm yet. It was their only chance of escape, if any. Fardad rolled over like a ball. He came upon a tree, and Fardad jumped down and landed on one of its branches. From there, he climbed down from one branch to another until he finally jumped on the ground.

Gyasi was observing his friends strategy through both his eyes and his ears. Gyasi was a little scared for a moment that someone might come to see why the branches on the tree were rustling so much, but then he remembered many cats roaming around the gardens at night.

In the villa of Darazdast, many Persian cats and peacocks were present. Apparently, they had learned how to live together, unlike Darazdast. As the cats refused to sleep at night, the humans in need of some rest left out their cats in the gardens. The cats came back to their owners on their own every morning to get some food. Fardad hid between the small space between the wall and the tree as he waited for Gyasi to climb down. When Gyasi finally dropped to the floor, Fardad pulled him by his hand.

"You took forever! The morning light will soon be coloring the sky; the time is running out. Come on, we better move before were spotted." Fardad complained. "I was being cautious! You made so much noise!" Gyasi whispered.

"Stay hidden; let me go first. If they get me, then you have to run," Gyasi told Fardad.

"No!" said Fardad. "Well escape together."

Gyasi knew it was no time to argue, so he gave in, and he and Fardad began walking as silently as they could through the shadows of various structures cast on the ground by the moon.

As they looked around to find a way, they could

see in the light of the small lamp in one tower that the guard–who was supposed to monitor anything moving in and out of the walls of the villa–was fast asleep. Fardad and Gyasi quietly walked inside and then on top of the tower. They were careful not to make any sound, for they couldnt risk waking up the guard. They had to make every move carefully until they were out of the villa and to safety.

Once they were on the top of the tower, they jumped from it. This was a risk they had to take. It turned out to be the back wall of the villa, the one toward the mountains. The two young men fell on their sides onto the bed of fine sand.

They werent hurt, and so they thanked God and walked toward the mountains. They couldnt risk going into the nearby town, as Darazdasts men were active over there. Besides, they knew that nobody was going to listen to them in front of the beloved Satrap. That evil man appeared too innocent and kind in front of everyone. Power and lust had blinded him so much that taking life gave him no remorse.

***

Darazdast was waiting for Fardads head. He was pacing the floor of the hall in his private chambers. This hall was used for secret meetings and evil plots, and only those dedicated to him were allowed inside Darazdasts private chambers. He had no clue that his guest-turned-captive had escaped with the man who had been sent to kill Fardad.

CHAPTER 3.   THE PREMONITION

As Darazdast walked back and forth, one of his most influential men, the one who sat on his left everywhere, Bahman, tried to assure him. Bahman was a sleek and tall young man with an evil smile. He was previously a criminal involved in human trafficking on Silk Road. When he was caught, he was brought to Satrap Darazdast. Darazdast liked the ruffians, and he spared Bahman, acquitting him from all charges. Since then, Bahman was present in most of the secret acts of Satrap.

"Gyasi must have done it already. You shouldnt worry, Satrap," said Bahman.

"If he has done it already, why isnt he here? Whats taking him so long! This is very disturbing as this matter would have been solved swiftly," blurted Darazdast with impatience and irritation.

"Gyasi must have been cleaning the blood, getting rid of the body. Its a messy business after all...." Bahman trailed off.

Darazdast nodded his head from side to side.

"The boy is too smart. Something doesnt seem right. I dont trust anyone, not that slave, at least. Hes a deplorable person; not good enough to take a life," he said.

"The boy is dead now! Im very certain, my master," said Bahman.

Before Darazdast could say anything, the door was knocked thrice.

One knock was reserved for Darazdasts wife and children, two for his close men, and three for his trusted

guards and slaves who did his dirty work. Darazdast nodded his head slightly in affirmation. Bahman
went and opened the door and saw the two guards
that Darazdast had sent after Fardad. "Is Gyasi back
here?" asked one guard before Bahman could ask anything.

"No," replied Bahman.

A wave of fear went down his spine.

"We couldnt find him anywhere, and we checked
everywhere, and he is not in the villa," said the other
guard.

"Wha-what about the boy from the village?" asked
Bahman, his voice small from fear.

"Not him, either. They seem to have escaped, perhaps," said the first guard.

The second guard shrugged his shoulders as Bahman looked at him.

"Go look for them! Bring them here! Ungrateful
slave! That imbecile will get what he deserves! How
dare he cross the Satrap!" whispered Bahman.

The guards nodded. They were about to leave
when Darazdast spoke.

"Come inside, at once!" He ordered.

Bahman moved from the door to Darazdasts private chambers to let the guards in. The guards bowed
silently in front of their Satrap.

"Where is the slave?" asked Darazdast.

"We havent found him," the guards replied together.

They had both replied in a small voice, but their

voices being synced had also become audible.

Darazdast looked from one guard to another. He then turned toward Bahman.

"Come here, Bahman," Darazdast said.

Bahman walked with silent steps and took his place beside the two guards.

"Tell me something, Bahman," began the Satrap.

Bahmans nervous gulp was audible to all.

"Who did I say was going to be good for the job?"

"Babak...my nakh–" replied Bahman, his voice shaking.

"Who persuaded me to send Gyasi instead?" asked Darazdast, interrupting Bahman.

"It was I...Bahman," replied Bahman. His voice became even more anxious.

"Ill ask this only once, Bahman," said Darazdast as he walked toward Bahman. He stopped only a foot away and yelled at Bahman. "Were you involved in this or not? Speak the truth, and I will spare your life; otherwise, you will join that wretched boys father buried six feet under, and no one will find you ever!" Bahman, shaking, fell to the ground on his knees.

"I didnt know. Im sorry. I didnt know," said Bahman. He was holding Darazdasts legs, and his entire body was shaking terribly. Darazdast jerked his legs one by one to get rid of Bahmans hands around them. He walked straight to the door of his private chambers, opened the door, and turned around to look at the three men.

"If I dont get Gyasi and Fardads heads by tomorrows moon, it will be your head instead. I am a man of my word. Bring them to me, or youre ancient history!" said the Satrap, his eyes boring into Bahmans back.

Bahman knew Darazdast had addressed him. He was trembling and wondered why the Ethiopian slave would betray them all and make him look bad. Still shaking, he stood up, turned around, and with a lowered gaze, walked toward the gate. He exited Darazdasts private chambers.

"You two, Ashkan and Afshin," said Darazdast to the guards.

The guards turned around.

Darazdast continued to say, "Keep an eye on Bahman and help him find those two men. I dont trust that man because he could be in on all of this." The guards bowed to their Satrap and left his private chambers. Darazdast closed the door as they left. He then went into his bedroom and poured himself some wine.

***

Bahman had gone to his chambers. He had planned to escape. He was too scared not to find Gyasi and Fardad and knew that his death was inevitable. He didnt intend to inform his wife and kids of his decision, and he had planned to leave them all behind. His life was at stake, and he was hoping to get these two fugitives back so his life could be spared. He worried about his family and did not want to let them be without his protection, not like this, at least. Bahman packed a small bundle of things in the dark, slowly and quietly. Just as he stepped outside his chamber, he dropped it on the floor. He crouched down and started collecting the things and bundling them up again when a pair of hands reached out for help. Bahman was scared and shocked to see the hands. He turned in the direction where the hands had entered from and backed off out of shock. It was Ashkan and Afshin. "Where do you think youre going?" asked Ashkan.

Afshin laughed.

"I...I thought they might have left the villa, so Im going out to search for them. I packed the necessities so I can survive as I look for them," said Bahman. "Right. You cant fool us; were one step ahead of you. Why do you have sympathies with that astrologers son?" said Ashkan.

"Yes, Bahman. I see how youll need jewels, gold coins, and extra clothes, but not any food or water as you roam around the wilderness," said Afshin. "I-I-I...I will buy the neccessi–" said Bahman, trying to clarify his choices.

"Lets just cut it short, yeah?" said Afshin.

"Youre coming with us!" Ashkan announced.

Afshin stepped forward and snatched the little bundle from Bahmans hands.

"Put this back inside and grab your sword. Were waiting outside. Do not dare to run. We have our eyes on you!" said Afshin. "H-he will kill me," said Bahman in a small voice.

"He wont kill you if you find Gyasi and Fardad,

even if it takes more than one moon. But he will kill you if you try to escape. You know how he killed that astrologer, and you could be very well next," said Ashkin.

Bahman sighed.

"Ill be back," Bahman said, standing up and taking the bundle from Afshin.

"You better be," said Ashkan.

Bahman went inside, and the two guards waited for him outside his chambers. Bahman was back shortly. This time, he was dressed in the proper attire with swords and daggers placed in his kamarband (waistband).

Ashkan and Afshin looked at Bahman, then at each other, and nodded.

***

"He threatened me he would pluck my eyes if I didnt kill you," Gyasi told Fardad.

The two men had walked deeper and higher into the mountains and had come upon a small cave. They were both scared to go inside it, but they had no other choice. They sat at the outer edge of the cave, talking. The sun was going to come up soon, and they had to continue their escape. Fardad was getting worried about his mother because she had no idea what was going on. He could not go back to her now because that would put her life in danger.

Gyasi knew a little of the paths through the rocks. He had never walked on one before, but he had learned of them through other slaves, through the ones who had tried escaping time and time again.

"Why did he assign you this job when he has other men?" asked Fardad.

"Its their way of training us, dehumanizing us," answered Gyasi.

"Im sorry," said Fardad.

"No," said Gyasi. "I probably deserved that, and I did a lot of things for both Bahman and Darazdast that Im not proud of. I wanted redemption and an escape from this life. This isnt for me, my friend. I cant live my life in guilt any longer!" Fardad listened quietly.

Gyasi began again. "Theyd send me to villages and make me snatch whatever valuables the poor had. I would beat up any horse owner who wouldnt gift their healthy horse to Darazdast. Im not a good man, my friend, and I know this. . . ."

Gyasi looked at Fardad. There were tears in his eyes.

". . .but Im not a murderer," added Gyasi.

He started sobbing quietly.

Fardad silently embraced his new friend.

"Youre a good man, Gyasi," he said. "A bad man never realizes his deeds are bad. At least, you admit your wrongs and want to turn your life around. I admire such men."

"I always knew my deeds were bad," Gyasi admitted. "I always knew it. I did it just so theyd trust me enough to send me on my own for once, and then Id escape. I wanted out badly."

"Isnt that exactly what you did?" asked Fardad.

"Once we have truly escaped, you can start a new life," said Fardad. "You can do good in the world, do good to others, even to people you once snatched things from. You can make up for them someday."

Gyasi wiped his cheeks. "Youre right," he said.

Fardad smiled and patted Gyasis back.

"Thanks for being my friend. I owe you my life and am forever indebted to you," said Gyasi.

"Thanks for not killing me," said Fardad.

The two young men laughed.

"I didnt mean to kill you...honestly," said Gyasi.

"I know, I know," said Fardad. "You gave up within a moment and blurted out all truth as if you were waiting for it. It means a lot to me, dear friend." Gyasi smiled and nodded his head. He said after a slight pause, "I swear I will put an end to the Satrap and his cronies evilness. I am sick of that evil man, and he has done nothing but harm since being overcome by lust and greed."

"I swear Ill avenge my father. I will make this man pay for this if its the last thing I do!" said Fardad.

Chapter 4

The Goodness of Ruins

F ARDAD and Gyasi went toward the north in panic, and they lost a sense of direction. After moving over the rocks, they realized they were heading toward the ruins. But it was probably better for them, as no one would expect them to be there.

Fardad and Gyasi waited for fates return in their favor as they reached the ancient ruins. As they both stayed inside their hideout, Fardad was tired and nervous because of the cold weather and running, which resulted in him dozing off to sleep.

Lost deep in his sleep, Fardad woke up to very similar voices calling him again; he looked around but saw no one. Thats when he saw the light at the end of the cave. As he got closer, the voice became louder. Thats when he saw a lighted person shining so brightly that he couldnt see correctly. "Who are you?" Fardad shouted to the light.

"You know that when its the right time... remember, Fardad, your dreams are no ordinary dreams but guidance to Persias destiny. You want answers, and I bring you answers," the voice replied.

"Huh! Huh! Huh!" Fardad woke up panting; the sound of his breath was so loud that even Gyasi woke up. Fardad narrated his entire dream to Gyasi. As they were lost in the discussion, Fardad heard steps entering the cave. They made a move for it. They didnt want to risk their lives and return home to plan their next step. They figured theyd need to tell someone important and respected, someone who they could trust. Fardad saw King Kai Kobad and told him the entire account of Grand Vizier and his corruption. They were still near the ruins and were planning to head back to their village.

By midday, Fardad and Gyasi went out. "Humans are not treading there, but stray dogs and wolves could come. So, we cannot stay inside the ruins for long," Gyasi said. "Okay! Lets make a move then. We need to go toward the mountains. In a panic, we lost the way. Time is running out. Lets get there before the Satrap and his men do!" said Fardad.

***

After covering a distance of a parasang (5 km) along the shores of the Kamrod sea, Fardad and Gyasi found a rock with a cave. They entered the cave and found it to be a monastery. Fardad saw men dressed as monks and praying in silence to their deity, Gautama Buddha.

A monk welcomed them inside. Finally, both men were in a safe place and out of danger. They needed this rest and some peace of mind. Both were starving and far from the feast of the villa.

"Thank you! Can we get something to eat?" Fardad asked humbly.

To Fardads reply, the head monk turned toward one of the fellow monks and nodded his head. Within a few minutes, bowls of soup and bread were presented to Fardad and Gyasi for dinner.

"Thank you for the food, sir; it was delicious," Gyasi said. The head monk said nothing, and he smiled.

The head monk then took Fardad and Gyasi to an empty wooden cottage. The cottage was very basic as it had two wooden beds, which seemed like they had been handcrafted by the monks themselves, and one old mat.

The head monk finally asked Fardad and Gyasi in Persian who they were.

"I am a slave, and he is my master. He was going toward Ateshkadah Nobahar that the bandits looted us and took our horses and money. We were stranded and had no option but to walk," Gyasi replied before Fardad could say anything. Fardad had now trusted him enough to cover for them, as they both couldnt trust anyone else at this point. Anyone they meet could be their enemy. They had to tread carefully and not reveal too much.

The head monk showed them three fingers as if he

were trying to tell them something by actions. Gyasi understood what he meant.

"Fardad, they are offering us to stay here for three days and that we can pay them back on our next visit," Gyasi told Fardad.

"Okay! I accept their offer," Fardad replied in a soft tone as he was trying to comprehend the situation; he did not know why the monk wouldnt say a word and how was Gyasi talking to them with such ease.

The head monk wished them goodnight as he left the room. Fardad accepted the deal and thanked God for this relief.

"What is happening here? Why isnt anyone talking?" Fardad asked as he turned over to Gyasi.

"These monks probably have vowed silence, and thats part of their belief system. These are safe men and mean no harm to us. Dont worry about getting killed here," Gyasi told Fardad.

"Oh! Now I understand," Fardad said, "But how do you know all this Gyasi?" he added.

"I have traveled a lot under Darazdust; with time and exposure, you learn a lot," Gyasi replied.

"You have impressed me once again, dear friend. Now, I am indebted to you for my freedom and getting us to safety and food!" Fardad said as they both planned to sleep.

***

The next day, the monk woke them up in the morning and offered them breakfast. Fardad and Gyasi enjoyed the breakfast, which was nothing but dry fruits and goat cheese. This was not a meal of grandeur like the one at the villa dinner but good enough to satisfy their hunger.

After breakfast, the head monk offered the two of his horses for a total cost of ten gold coins, to be paid later as a promise.

"We accept your offer, thank you so very much," Fardad said as he thought they had no other option than this to reach the king as fast as they could. Also, this offer could help them get far away from this place as soon as possible. Time was running out, and they had to move fast. They had taken a break, but they couldnt stay there too long. Fardad wanted justice, and he would do anything to get that.

Chapter 5

Takht-e-Shah

Sometimes, when the authorities were bent on finding a runaway civilian or slave, they would look in the ancient ruins and dark forest. But mostly, the pasbaans (police) wandered on the outside, waiting for the runaway to show up.

As the morning sun appeared in the sky, the two friends and fugitives had set out for their journey along the Kamrod Sea. They were walking toward the East, in the suns direction. They planned to cross the Alburz Mountain to reach Takht-e-Shah, on the other side of the mountain range. They were far enough removed from the villa and were moving steadily to get to their destination–the palace of the Shah, which was what the name Takth-e-Shah referred to.

***

None of them had been to the Takht-e-Shah before. They didnt even know if their decision was the correct one to make. They just knew that Darazdasts region of governance was no longer safe for them. They still had a chance of being heard; they could still tell their side of the story. They had to take a chance with the Shah, who might listen to reason.

After a long journey of three days, Fardad and Gyasi finally saw the tall towers of the city, Takht-e-Shah, and the massive mounds sculpted into human faces. It must be the legendary capital in the Alburz Mountains base, they thought.

This city, which Manuchehrs had chosen for their residence, had earned the new local name Takht-e-Shah, meaning the crown seat. Because of the royals, the citys trade had boomed too, and it had become a trade and cultural hub. It also would become a haven for the two friends, or so they hoped, as they made their way toward it. Fardad and Gyasi looked at the city from above the mountains. It seemed tiny, and they could make out the entire irregularly shaped boundary, too.

There were three gates to the city, and each gate had a different pair of stone sculptures guarding it. Each gate opened onto a path that curved on its right. The three pathways then merged into one another, where each started. This made the course the shape of the irregular boundary as it laid alongside it.

Fardad and Gyasi were careful to look in all the directions before descending the mountain. However, as they began to climb down the steep slope, they got ambushed by three men dressed in black robes with their faces covered by a white cloth. The three men retrieved their respective swords that seemed to gleam under the rays of the sun.

"Are these Dardzaasts men?" Fardad inquired anxiously.

"Perhaps," Gyasi mouthed.

Before they could attack, Fardad and Gyasi galloped their horses briskly and tried to go past them. Unfortunately, the three men were quick enough and slashed the horses with their swords which caused them to tumble, while Fardad and Gyasi went rolling across the slope.

The two heroes managed to halt and get onto their feet with their elbows bleeding profusely.

"Thats it! Fardad exclaimed and darted towards the swordsmen like a roaring lion. One of the swordsmen swished his sword, but Fardad swerved to avoid the attack and kicked his arm, and the sword fell off the rocks. Immediately, he delivered a tremendous blow to his face and knocked him off the mountain. The man screamed horrendously and met his end.

In the interim, the two swordsmen ran towards Gyasi, who grabbed a tiny rock from the side and struck one of them squarely on the forehead. The man howled in pain and went rolling across the slope. And before the last swordsman could make a move, Fardad grabbed him from behind, twisted his neck, and threw him below. "Gyasi, are you alright?"

"I am fine, my friend. Lets get to the city quickly before any other foe shows up." Fardad nodded briskly, and they walked in the citys direction. They were nearly there and could soon seek justice for the crimes of the evil Satrap. Finally, they approached one gate after some time.

***

"Where are you from?" asked the guard at the gate, looking from Fardad to Gyasi.

The guard sat in a cubicle that was built inside the city wall, right beside the gate. A window opened from the cubicle to the outside, while an open arch led the way from the cubicle to inside the city. The two friends were prepared to answer them. They had no fear, as they had done no wrong, and they were only here for justice. "Im Fardad, and Im from a small village by the eastern shore of the Kamrod Sea," said Fardad.

"Im Gyasi, and I work with Satrap Darazdast," replied Gyasi.

"What business do you have in the city?" the guard asked.

Before Fardad could say anything, Gyasi spoke. He always had the best answers, and Fardad knew he could now depend on him for those. Fardad stayed silent, knowing that Gyasi could get them through the gates.

"Were here to interpret the mighty Shahs dream," he said.

Fardad looked at Gyasi, his eyes wide in horror. He wanted to interpret the Shahs dream, but he didnt want to do without his friend Ukund. Ukund was too far now to call on for, and it seemed like they had to go at this dream interpretation alone. A slight nervousness took over Fardad, but he kept calm until they were allowed past the gates. Gyasi knew his way around and learned how to get past the gates and straight to the Shah.

"Parviz," called the guard to another man sitting on the other side of the arch. "Take these boys to the kings palace, and theyre here to interpret Shahs dream." The other man, stout and serious looking, came to see the two men outside, and he looked at them from head to toe.

"Okay, send them in," he said.

This man was named Ariom. He was one of the many guards responsible for taking visitors directly to where they were supposed to go. It was one of the many ways the Shah maintained security in his home city. He was dressed in royal garb, wearing the seal of the Shah and covered with full-body armor. He had a sword in one hand and a shield in the other. Along with the guards, he was trained in combat and rose through the ranks to become one of the citys gatekeepers. He proudly played his role and vowed to protect the city and the Shah with his life.

***

Fardad and Gyasi were told by the palace guard that the palace had no more room for visitors and that they should check back after a few days. Fardad was terrified. He didnt think they could stay hidden from Darazdasts pasbaans.

"What do we do now?" Fardad asked Gyasi.

"Decide soon. I dont have all day for you guys," said Ariom.

Gyasi looked at Ariom displeasingly. He turned toward Fardad and asked, "Where do you think we should go?"

"I dont think we can go anywhere. Shah Kai Kobads palace is the safest place for us at this moment," answered Fardad.

Gyasi thought for a bit. He then turned toward Ariom.

"Can you find us a place to stay which wont cost too much? We are two poor men, and we came to see if we could interpret the kings dream and earn our reward," he said to Ariom.

Fardad was shocked at his friends response.

Ariom rolled his eyes. "Let me see," he said.

Ariom went close to the palace guard and talked to him for a bit. The guard let him inside while Fardad and Gyasi were standing at a distance from the palace gate, and they kept standing there, waiting for Ariom.

Ariom came back after a while. The boys looked expectantly at him.

"So, the court will be in three days. There, some visitors who are staying in the palace will try to interpret the dream. You can be a part of the court. If the matter is resolved, then there will be no more visitors for a while. If not, then there may be room for you," said Ariom. "Thank you," said Fardad.

"So youre helping us to find a place to stay, right?" Gyasi asked Ariom.

Ariom rolled his eyes at him.

"Im not a tour guide, and Im just a guard, following the Shahs orders," he said. "Please?" asked Gyasi.

Ariom sighed.

"Roam around the city. Check back with me at the gate at sunset. Ill see what I can do," said Ariom.

"Thank you, thank you, thank you, Ariom! Youre a great host!" said Gyasi excitedly. "Im not your host," said Ariom and left.

"According to rule, we allow the dream interpreters to stay until the court day starts, and the Shah sees the visitors. I hope you know the consequences in case you fail–we have explicit orders about it." Ariom spoke and then closed the door.

Fardad was looking at Giyasi with bewilderment and showed him the fingers crossed sign.

***

Fardad and Gyasi found many food vendors in an open plaza. It was at the center of the city and was surrounded by a garden on all sides. There were benches and chairs and tables carved out of pieces of big rocks. Locals sat there, eating food they had bought from the food vendors, drinking wine and smoking tobacco, and laughing and talking and playing. As they made their way across the bedazzling city, a slim young woman with floor-length ebony hair wearing a niqaab (head cover) walked briskly towards them and brushed past Fardads shoulder.

Fardad turned a blind eye to the trivial incident and continued to walk. A few moments later, he felt his pocket lighter than before. Placing his free hand inside the pocket, he became stunned as the gold ring which he got from his fathers dead body fist had vanished. In a state of utmost frenzy, he began to inspect himself thoroughly and then began to search insanely on the ground.

"Whats the matter?" Gyasi inquired anxiously, but Fardad turned a deaf ear to him. Instantly, the realization hit him, and he turned around quickly and noticed the woman twenty yards away and continuing to rush from them.

"Hey, You!" Fardad shouted, causing the people nearby to turn their attention towards him. Immediately, the woman stopped in her tracks for a moment and then began to run away. Without wasting a single moment, Fardad sprinted towards her at lightning speed.

"Fardad, wait!" Gyasi yelled on top of his lungs, but there was no stopping him as he began to chase her like a furious bull shown a red cloth. The woman was surprisingly very fast and quite sturdy for a slim figure as she bolted past a group of muscular black men and pushed them aside as she ran. Suddenly, the woman tripped and fell with a gut-wrenching thud on the ground.

Fardad grabbed her arm and lifted her onto her feet.

"Leave my hand, you filthy foreigner, I said leave!" she shouted at him, struggling to break free from his tight clutch.

"Miss! Crimes like theft do not suit a woman."

"Go flog your wisdom somewhere else! Leave my hand!"

"Miss, I can hand you over to the King Kai Kabad. But I am giving you a chance, return my gold ring, and I will pretend that we never met."

Fardad gazed deeply into the young womans eyes which were a dazzling light green, and caused him to get attracted to her slightly.

Eventually, the young woman concluded her struggle and handed over the gold ring that she had skillfully stolen from his pockets.

Immediately, Fardad released her arm, and she ran away.

"Who in the name of the Lord was that?" panted Gyasi as he approached him.

"Just a beautiful thief," remarked Fardad with a half-smile.

***

The woman in the black face cover turned left and entered a tiny dark alley in the marketplace. A deep voice called her name from the darkness.

"Whats the news, Meher?"

89

CHAPTER 5.   TAKHT-E-SHAH

"Master Soroush!" the slave girl addressed the man in the darkness with a low bow. "The man has entered the Takht-e-Shah along with a black man." "Very good!" echoed the deep voice across the darkened valley.

***

A while before the sun was about to set, caretakers of the city arrived and lit up the small fire pits made along the paths. They crushed rocks together with wooden sticks between them. They then added more dried wood and leaves until they were happy with the fire. The whole place lighted up. The warm glow of the fire and the cool light of the moon merged.

Fardad and Gyasi were mesmerized by the view. Gyasi had seen many luxuries at Darazdasts villa, but he had never seen such activity and buzz of people. "They said it right," said Fardad. "Life is different in cities."

"It really is. Ive seen nothing like this before," added Gyasi.

"We have such activities in our village, but theres no food, and its only on special religious rituals," said Fardad. "Ive never seen this done so...casually." "Its beautiful," said Gyasi. "I can sit here all night."

"Hey!" exclaimed Fardad. "We have to go see Ariom so he can find us a cheap motel or place to stay."

Gyasi sighed. "Of course," he said.

***

"All right, lets find you a place," said Ariom as the two friends approached him.

He began walking toward the closest residential area. The city was divided into many residential buildings with plazas, markets, and temples between them. Fardad and Gyasi followed Ariom.

"This old woman Im taking you to is my aunt," said Ariom. "She wont charge you much, but you have to be respectful towards her and act like youre not there." Confusion appeared on Fardads and Gyasis faces.

"I mean, sleep in the corner she tells you to sleep in. Do not make a noise. Wake up quietly and eat the food she gives you. Clean your bowls and do your business at the designated place in the public plaza. Do not ask her questions and do not complain," added Ariom.

Fardad and Gyasi did not reply, but they kept following in Arioms footsteps.

Ariom stopped, turned around, and asked, "Understood?"

Fardad and Gyasi did not reply but nodded their heads in the affirmative. Ariom acknowledged their nod and began leading them again.

***

Arioms aunt was older than Fardad had expected. Despite her old age, she reminded Fardad of his mother, and she wasnt as much senior but was as alone as his mother. She charged Fardad and Gyasi only a minimal amount. Fardad knew Gyasi had nothing to his name, so he paid for both himself and his friend. Gyasi had betrayed his master for Fardad and helped him escape where he was bound to lose his life; Fardad didnt think he could ever repay Gyasi for this.

Both Fardad and Gyasi followed all the instructions Ariom had given them and behaved their best with his old aunt. However, they found Ariom had a softer heart than he let on, and his aunt was a very sweet old woman who let travelers stay with her so that she could have a filled house for a while. Her only son had died a premature death, and since he didnt have a wife or children when he died, the older woman was left all alone. Ariom, however, often visited his aunt and took care of her as much as he could.

***

After three days of resting at Arioms aunt and roaming around the city, it was time for Fardad to join the kings court. A night before, he had requested Gyasi not to join him.

"We cant be found together, my friend," Fardad had said. "What if there are some men who are Darazdasts spies, and they kill us both? At least one of us has to stay alive to expose the truth about Darazdast."

Gyasi hadnt argued. He knew that Fardads reason was valid.

Fardad had borrowed a piece of headcloth from Arioms aunt. He placed it on his head and wrapped it around his neck, hiding his face a little. He then made his way toward the palace.

A few people were waiting in line to go inside. It was a public court, and anyone could join as long as they showed up on time.

Fardad patiently waited for his turn. Many came after him and waited for their turn, too.

***

Once Fardad entered the palace, he was surprised to see it was not even half as glamourous as Darazdasts villa. The palace was tastefully decorated, too, but it was very simple compared to where Fardad had experienced a murder attempt.

Fardad followed the instructions of the many guards standing every few feet and reached the enormous hall or the public diwan-khane (court). The Shahs throne was empty, and the guests and visitors all sat on the velvety floor cushions placed in rows on the thick, beautiful carpet.

Fardad took his place on one of the velvety cushions. He looked around, especially at the guards, and nobody seemed to observe him. Fardad let out a sigh of relief.

***

Suddenly, the sounds of mace striking the floor could be heard rhythmically. It was a sign for people that the king was approaching the court. Then an announcer entered the hall and said: "Lo-and-behold, the king of East and West, the king of northern and southern seas, mighty Shahanshah Kai Kobad, is entering the hall. Everyone rise to honor his arrival. "

People stood up with their heads down. The king with a fist-size beard arrived and sat on the throne. He was wearing a jeweled crown and had long white hairs till shoulders. His embroidered azure dress was exquisite. Fardad was breathless for a while as the man sitting beside him pat his calf to sit down. Fardad came out of his awe moment and saw that people were already sitting in their places. He quickly sat.

The announcer said again: "Mighty King Kai Kobad is all ears to public queries and complaints."

People started giving their requests written on small pieces to the slaves, giving them to the announcer. One by one, the announcer read out the requests while the requesters were diligently listening to the kings order.

It took some time to finish up all the requests.

All were looking at the king for the next course of action. Fardad was waiting, and finally, the moment arrived.

The announcer said, "Anyone here who would like to dare his life to interpret the puzzling dream of our beloved king?"

Few were there to interpret the kings dream bowed and accepted failure. Once a man or a woman received their disappointment, they left the palace hall.

Shah sat on his throne. He looked bored and sad, and he was clearly much anxious about his dream, and the failure of so many people only added to his frustration. Once those who were there to interpret the dreams left, the royal announcer asked anyone who thought they could interpret the kings dream to step forward. There was a murmur in the crowd. Fardad stood up and walked toward the Shahs throne. As soon as he had stood up, he had felt the eyes of everyone in the room at him. And to think that I was trying to keep my identity hidden, he thought.

He stopped the right distance away from the throne and kneeled to the Shahanshah Kai Kobad.

Fardad could hear his heartbeat at that moment. He was terrified of interpreting the kings dream and feared failure. But solving the kings dream correctly and gaining his trust was the only way that could help him expose Darazdasts reality, and Fardad knew he had no other choice.

"May the Lord, the Ahura Mazda, be happy with Shahanshah, the ruler of the east and the west of Persia," said Fardad.

The king was impressed by the sweet words coming from the courageous young man in front of him.

"Whats your name, oh brave and loyal one?" asked the king.

Shah Kai Kobad looked at Fardad from head to toe. There was an indistinct murmur in the crowd, and the people were fascinated by the conversation between a stranger and their king.

"Im Fardad, son of Aardburzin the slain," Fardad answered.

"Fardad," said the king, "If you interpret my dream correctly, Ill make you my vizier."

The crowd gasped. Fardad felt the pressure of interpreting the dream correctly, even more so than before.

Suddenly one of the Kings ministers who appeared cunning cut him in with a loud snort that turned everyones attention towards him. The minister was donned in a jet black shalwar and jameh with a wide belt called Kamarband. In addition to that, he wore a white headdress called Sarband. The minister was quite a towering figure with shoulder-length hair and a lengthy black beard. His complexion was pale with rosy cheeks, a big nose, and thick eyebrows that made him look more or less similar to a lion. He stroked his huge beard and spoke in a mocking manner.

"Yeah, right! Look, the man from the north! We have seen many big mouths like you in this palace before who have claimed to be highly sagacious and capable of advising the King, but all of them turned out to be nothing but frauds. So you just cannot trick us into believing your nonsense!" "Silence Mahali!" howled King Kai Kobad as he stared at him distastefully. At that point, another one of the Kings ministers with a red headdress moved forward and bowed, who was a short and a plump figure with tiny hands and a thin beard along with an aquiline nose.

"My King! Forgive me for interrupting you! But I

am forced to agree with Mahali. This man from the north is no different from the deceitful men that have come before him who made huge claims but, in reality, were nothing but frauds! Trusting this man from the north would be repeating our past mistakes, which would result in nothing but mere disappointment! Our intuition cannot be wrong, my king,"

King Kai Kobad looked at him as though he had something bitter in his mouth.

"Do you want me to dismiss both of you from this court right now?" the King asserted in a calm yet, intimidating tone. The ministers looked at each other fearfully and shook their heads slowly. "Then wag your tongues only when it is necessary!"

The two cunning ministers threw Fardad a series of dirty looks and whispering amongst each other, they retreated. The wise king turned his attention back towards Fardad and gestured him to continue, and the smile replaced the frown that his ministers had brought onto his face.

"Your highness, if I lie, I curse myself that may the Lord, Ahura Mazda, burn my tongue right here and now," Fardad said confidently.

"Very well then," interrupted the king. "If your tongue didnt burn, Ill cut it out and throw it to the stray dogs of the city, along with other parts of your body."

The crowd gasped once again. Nobody had expected the conversation to become this intense.

"Whatever the mighty Shah Kai Kobad decides for

me, I do not complain," said Fardad.

The Shah smiled. He was amused by the young mans words, who didnt seem to fear anything.

"Your loyal servant is waiting to hear your dream," said Fardad when the king didnt speak for a few moments.

"Youre brave and impatient," the king commented. "Now, lets see how loyal you are. This is what I dreamed...."

Chapter 6

The Revenge

"I was sitting at this large banquet and waiting to try on this amazing dessert prepared by the royal bakers. I excitedly took a spoonful, and as soon as I put it in my mouth, something extraordinary happened. I couldnt believe my eyes, and what I saw just made my jaw drop. A black dog had jumped in and took the spoon right out of my hand. Then, I just woke up and wondered if it meant something or it was just a silly nightmare. I hope you have an answer; so many had failed to interpret it rightfully before you were given a chance. Dont make any interpretation to gain my favor, but do it to help me. I know I have offered an incentive to you, but I want to know what this enigmatic dream is about. It has brought me many sleepless nights," the king said.

Fardad listened to it keenly and took a few minutes to think about it. The Kings dream was not something that could be interpreted by listening to it, and

CHAPTER 6. THE REVENGE

it needed more time for studying and thinking.

He then replied to his Royal Majesty, "Beloved Shah, I would require more time to study your dream and give you an answer, but rest assured, I will have one. I would humbly request His Royal Highness to allow me to stay here for three days and His Majesty to let my friend enter the palace and enable him to dwell with me here for a maximum of three days. I hope that is not too much to ask."

The king looked straight into Fardads eyes and saw the truth that this man could have the answer he had been seeking for. He spoke two words loud and clear for all to hear, "Request granted. "

That was enough for Fardad as he could now have Gyasi stay with him, too.

The king continued, "I award you and your friend the royal dress of honor as long as you two stay in the palace. You and your friend may stay at the palace and enjoy it however you wish. You are to stay in my court for three days, and I must warn you, you will be thrown in front of the hungry dogs in my dungeon if you fail in this quest."

Fardad breathed a sigh of relief, almost ignoring the possibility that he and Gyasi could be eaten up by the palace dogs and turned into mincemeat. He knew that because he had an idea regarding how to interpret the dream. Hence, he was not afraid of the consequences of any failure.

He took a few deep breaths and replied to the mighty king. "I will do as you wish, your Majesty, and accept the terms of the punishment if I fail in my quest." Fardad didnt mince words or make a long speech as this one sentence was enough to let the king know he knew what he was doing.

Fardad was then roaming around the palace as the king had given him full authority. He was playing detective and searching for anyone and everyone, behaving a bit differently and mysteriously. These included concubines, princes, princesses, courtiers, and others. There were several such people, including ten concubines for each male royalty. It was quite a daunting task to see which one behaved strangely, as you cant pinpoint the wrong person. He roamed around the entire palace area and then decided to talk to the guards, hoping they would cooperate and not give him any trouble. He was also afraid that some of the guards could be in on it and may not divulge any information when asked.

Fardad looked around and saw royalty and realized how intense things had become. From one royal villa to another regal palace, he lived in luxury and was getting bored. To survey the entire palace and to observe the different people there was getting too monotonous. Suddenly his mind switched to home, as he was becoming very homesick. He hadnt seen his mother or best friend Ukund for some days now and was severely missing them. The royalty and luxury werent attracting him as he was living a very simple life. He was so used to living that way that it all was becoming way too much for him. He feared for his mother but was happy that Ukund was with her and cared for her needs. Ukund was like his brother and always looked up at him. He was his best friend and confidante and would always be there for him. Thankfully, there was another new friend who was becoming another Ukund. His unlikely new best friend was Gyasi, who was tasked to kill but decided to set him free. Gyasi was an intelligent and wise slave who knew his way around people and guards and asked the right questions. He had been helping him the same way Ukund was. Gyasi and Fardad were butting heads trying to figure out what the dream meant because they wanted to help the king and get to the bottom of Fardads fathers murder. Both these young men spent two days constantly surveying the area and connecting any dots but were utterly clueless. They knew that theyd find the answer and not be sent to the dungeon. The king seemed quite serious because he had wanted his dream to be correctly interpreted. They tried making connections to the people they came across with the dream but could not conclude. Perhaps the answer lay in Farhads dreams as he had seen so many in the recent past.

Fardad didnt intentionally wish to dream, but sometimes it just came to him unexpectedly. This time, he dreamt again and saw quite vivid images of the mighty king. He saw him being engaged in a banquet with sumptuous dishes all around. He was in the presence of his concubines, who were dancing and playing the lyre. Some were even offering the king fruits. Suddenly, the moment of truth emerged as a black concubine approached the king with evil intentions.

She had a dagger she was holding behind her back and coming very near, and it was pretty evident that she was going to take out the king. The king was completely unaware of this as he was enjoying his feast and company.

It was pretty surprising that he saw similar images that the king saw, which made him think there must be some connection between their dreams. However, he soon woke up with a suspicion that the kings life was in danger. Usually, his dreams foretold the future, and that was a sign. He decided to tell Gyasi about the dream and explained that the kings life is in peril, and the chances are that their dreams are connected to his fathers murder.

Gyasi said, "My friend, the King, needs to know. Today is the third day, and he will summon you. Make sure to be very honest with him and tell him everything you know. If you want to get revenge for your fathers murder, this is the man who can help you. You earn his trust, and he will offer you the best protection." Fardad then replied, "You are right, Gyasi. I will tell him everything, and I dont care if he makes me the vizier or not; I just want no more innocent lives to be taken. Weve lost enough already, and my father was an asset to this land. This king is a great man, and I dont want him to be taken out by some concubine." Both men embraced each other and wished each other luck as they prepared to be summoned by

CHAPTER 6.   THE REVENGE

the king.

The next day, Fardad was summoned by the king via a message from one of the guards. Gyasi was asked to stay behind until he returned from the meeting. The guard told Fardad, "His Majesty has requested your presence in his private room. Please follow me." Fardad followed him to the kings private library. The library was full of ancient books and scrolls, and it seemed that the king was very knowledgeable.

The guard told him on the way, "The king sits in this library in his spare time and reads the ancient books to figure out the meaning behind his dream. I hope you have an answer for him."

Fardad smiled at him and didnt say a word. Once he was inside the library, he was left alone to speak with the king. It was a massive room with two levels, and there were books all around. The king was on the second level, and he asked Fardad to take a seat. There was no throne or royal seat. The King was walking around the room aimlessly. There were piles of open scrolls all around the tables, and it seemed like he had exhausted all his options to interpret his dream. It was known that the king would spend a lot of time alone to figure out what was going on with his dream. The guard had mentioned that the king rarely comes out of the room until he is needed. He was not wholly alone as his queen was there in the room comforting him.

They had been talking before Fardad had entered the room and been asked to take a seat. Both the royal couple were talking to each other.

The king said, "My Love, I am worried for my life as I fear my life may be in danger. It would be best if you left the palace and headed to safety in one of our safe houses. I will send my most trusted guards to be with you, and I cant risk you getting hurt. If I go, I need you to carry on my work."

The queen was in tears and said, "My King, please dont worry yourself. That young man may have answers. At least, hear him out. He may have clues to who is going to take you out. I know that this man has the answers, and I can just sense it."

By the time the queen finished her sentence, Fardad was in their presence. He respectfully bowed toward them and saw that the queen was dressed in her royal robes and looking magnificent. She was looking stunning from head to toe with her crown placed firmly on her head. She was a beautiful lady, and Fardad was standing there completely breathless.

The King looked at him and said, "That young man is here, and I hope he has answers. He knows very well that if he is wrong, he could be breathing his last right now."

"Have you found what youre looking for? This could be the last day of your life if you dont figure out the interpretation of the dream."

Fardad spoke with utmost confidence and respect, despite being nervous, "My Lord, I have spent the last two days doing exactly that, so I dont disappoint you. You dont have to spare my life, as it means nothing.

CHAPTER 6.   THE REVENGE

Your life is more valuable than mine, and we are your people who hold you in very high esteem. I am just a common man, and my worthless life may as well be over. I do have an answer, but I will show that to you in person. I cant simply just interpret it in words. You have to see it to believe it. I would humbly request you to hold a banquet feast tonight and invite all the fair maidens and concubines in this palace to serve us food and wine." "I will let you show it to me, but beware of the consequences. I understand you feel your life is worthless, but I know that you have a still-alive mother. If anything, your life is valuable to her more than anyone else. Therefore, your wish is granted!" the king said.

***

Fardad took his leave to inform Gyasi about the feast, and both would later return in his presence by the tram before the feast began. Gyasi was very excited to learn that Fardad was given a chance to prove his skills by virtue of the feast. The King ordered his guards to make preparations for the grand banquet and send out the invites. The preparations started instantly, and the hands approached with their spoons and knives. The concubines and eunuchs appeared with the guards and started pouring the wines in the chalices. Everyone was in the courtyard for the feast and getting ready to enjoy the grand dinner. There were kings, queens, consorts, princes, and other guests. Fardad and Gyasi were the guests of honor and sat right in front of the king across his table. It was a delicious dinner. Fardad didnt enjoy it because his throat was parched.

In the middle of all the guests, one person stood out like a star that came down from the sky. She was a breath of fresh hair, someone that Fardad had never seen. She caught his attention the instant he set his eyes on her. She had this fantastic heavenly glow surrounding her, and Fardad couldnt resist. He continued to look at her and thought that this was not an ordinary human being but an angel. She was stunningly beautiful, like a fair maiden with soft red lips. Her hair was long, black, and covered her entire back. She was simply magnificent from head to toe. She was wearing an eclectic blue dress and was just standing, holding a cup of wine in her hand. Fardad knew that this might not be the time for an introduction, but he took his chances.

Before he could say hello to her, the king approached her and asked her, "Lovely daughter, Parinaaz. You look stunning today. I am sorry I had to pull you away from your hunting trip on short notice. You can go some other time this week."

Parinaaz replied, "I would never refuse your invitation, and its quite a beautiful party, but I must know what is the occasion that you called me on such short notice?"

The king smiled and said, "Parinaaz, youre always the curious kind. Youll know the reason soon, just like the rest of us. Enjoy the food and wine, and have a good time!"

Once the king moved away, Fardad approached Parinaaz and made a slight bow in respect to her.

He said, "Princess, I couldnt resist but had to speak to you. I am sorry to catch you off guard, my fair lady. My name is Fardad, and I am staying at the palace as a guest of His Majesty. I hope you dont mind me approaching you...."

Parinaaz cut Fardad off and said, "Youre one fine young man too, and I like bold men. You can win my fathers trust for courage and taking a chance, and this is such a boring affair. I only came because my father and the king are old friends and soldiers. I must thank you for alleviating my boredom. Fardad is a nice name, but it cant be better than Parinaaz. Thats my name, and you can stop referring to me as princess! I am just joking, and I hope you dont mind my sense of humor. Yes, its nice to meet you as well, and we can be friends. Besides being the guest of the king, what brings you here, my friend?"

Fardad couldnt believe his eyes and ears that Parinaaz was giving him attention. He had to pinch himself several times to ensure he wasnt seeing one of his dreams that started nice but ended up scary. He secretly wished she didnt turn out to be some evil witch, but she turned out to be lovely and approachable. They seemed to get along well, and he knew he couldnt reveal the purpose of his visit yet, but will do so in due course.

He says, "You see. Curiosity killed the cat, and

youre so divine that I cant see you die of curiosity, so Ill tell you. I am here to help the king with something, and I am not at liberty to divulge the rest of the information yet. Its my pleasure to be your friend, and I would love to get to know you more, my fair lady. Your name is wonderful, and I am not competing with names yet because Fardad is just an ordinary name. Yours is as magnificent as you look. I must say youre gorgeous. I cant keep my eyes off of you!"

Parinaaz was blushing and let out a sweet smile.

She said, "Fardad, youre so amazing with words, and youre not so bad-looking yourself. Youre quite the handsome young man, and rare few men even come close. So, I could say that were made for each other. And I know I am beautiful, but I have yet to find a man who appreciates not just my outer beauty but inner beauty too." Fardad instantly replied, "Parinaaz, you are as beautiful inside as you are outside. I am honored you think so highly of me. I am truly and honestly very flattered. I like you very much because everything about you is just incredible...."

Parinaaz interrupts him and says, "I get it, Fardad. May I call you Fari if thats okay? And Im very bored with standing and drinking. Lets do the waltz. You can dance, can you?"

Fardad smiled and said, "You can call me whatever you like, my darling. May I call you Pari, and yes, lets dance, shall we!" Fardad signals the royal musicians to play a slow number, and the two of them break into a dance, in each other arms, with the entire halls eyes on them. Both of them look at each other with lovelorn eyes. This was such a magical moment for both of them, and Fardad couldnt believe he was dancing with the most beautiful person he had ever seen in his life. Both these lovebirds stared into each others eyes the entire time as the music was playing.

The royal musicians ended their song, and both stopped their dance. They were met with applause from all the guests. Fardad kept wishing this moment would last forever. Both of them bowed toward each other and then went back to walking around the hall before they drifted apart.

Fardad asked Parinaaz, "I hope I can see you again, Pari. Im at the palace for a day or two and will be heading back."

Parinaaz smiled after giving a peck on the cheek and said, "Dont worry, Fari. I will know how to find you. And yes, we shall meet again! It was my pleasure to enjoy your company."

Fardad couldnt stop blushing, either.

He said, "The feeling is mutual, Pari."

As he moved away from Parinaaz, he noticed something strange. All of a sudden, he saw a black eunuch approaching the king. The uncanny similarity between his dream and the site generated an internal urge in Farhad to be ready. Farhad pushed Gyasi to be vigilant. The black eunuch approached the king and took out the dagger, and he was about to attack the king. Farhad quickly jumped and held his hand in the air. Gyasi had the eunuch by his throat. The guards moved quickly and arrested the eunuch. Everyone inside the banquet hall was shocked.

"My Lord, this is the interpretation of your dream. The black dog you saw in your dream is this eunuch, and your enemies have sent him to kill you. I had seen a similar dream, so I figured you should see this in actuality," Fardad said.

A minister of king moved forward and came in the middle of the hall. He was moving his hand on his goatee beard. "Soroush, question him!" ordered the king.

"Who is he?" Fardad asked.

"The interior affairs minister," Gyasi informed. "My lord, our enemies who hate Persia knew that if they can remove your generous tutelage from us, then they can attack us easily. I am sure that this eunuch is also up to something."

"Say it filth, who sent you," minister Soroush said as he moved around the eunuch, who was now on his knees, and his hands were tied on his back. He was shaking his shoulders aggressively. Two guards were behind him.

Soroush, through the movement of his eyes, asked the guards to move aside. The royalties, minister, Fardad, and Gyasi watched from a distance. Soroush kicked the eunuch in his belly, and he fell to the ground. Soroush then moved forward and sat on the eunuch. He became aware of something which the rest of the people present in the hall didnt notice.

The eunuch started speaking, "I seek refuge of the

mighty king. I have been cursed and was under the possession of a demon. Thanks to the honorable minister, the demon left my body, and I am surprised to see myself here."

"Liar!" Fardad said and moved forward.

Gyasi held his hand and pushed him back. All looked at Fardad and then to the eunuch.

"My Lord, the eunuch is telling the truth. I felt a power come out of him," minister Soroush said.

"My Lord, you do whatever you think is true," Soroush exclaimed further.

The king said, "Put him in prison and interrogate him!" "As you have saved my life and interpreted the perplexing dream which I have seen and fulfilled your promise, I want you to stay in this palace and be one of the ministers," the king said.

Fardad and Gyasi were delighted to hear that. Fardad wished that his mother would know so she could be proud of him, too. Fardad said, "Long live the King. I would like to place my wish in front of you, my Lord. It is about Satrap, Grand vizier Darazdast. He killed my father, Aardburzin, and I found Satraps Signet in my dead fathers hand. My friend Gyasi is the slave of Darazdast, and he is well aware of all the misdeeds hes committing in the name of our mighty king. I want justice to be fulfilled."

The king became furious and then ordered General Suhraab: "Bring Darazdast in front of me!"

General Suhraab was a sturdy middle-aged man with stubble. He was the commander in chief of the

Persian army.

"Very well, my King!" General Suhraab said with a deep voice that was enough to incite fear in his enemies.

At this time, Fardad looked for Parinaaz, but it seemed she had left after the commotion. He felt something in his coat pocket and saw a napkin that smelt of her perfume. Fardad decided to guard it with his life.

After a few hours, Darazdast was in front of the king, and all the bureaucrats and courtiers were present. The princes and princesses were also present. Fardad was sitting right beside the king, and he had noticed that Darazdast had realized that something was seriously wrong.

"Why did you kill my father, Aardburzin? I want answers, and I want them now!" Fardad asked.

Darazdast said, "By the ancients, I swear I didnt kill him. I dont know what youre talking about."

"Liar! You left your signet in the grave of my father. Besides that, you even sent your Ethiopian slave to kill me in your villa. This man, Gyasi, is that slave, and he will confess to everything. There is no turning back now," Fardad said.

Darazdast became nervous and started biting his fingers. His eyes were wide open, and he was looking here and there. Fardad took out the ring from his pocket, presented it to the king, and informed him that this is the signet he found clenched in the fist of his slain father. The king immediately recognized the ring, as the king himself gifted it to Darazdast.

Gyasis presence was enough to convince the king that he had been sent as an assassin to take out Fardad and explained that he decided to help him, and they both escaped the villa together to make the journey here.

"Poor Aardburzin was a famous astrologer. Through his knowledge, he found a calamity that would befall this kingdom, which we have not seen since the times of Mighty King Manuchehr unless we do something to prevent it. While coming toward me, he wandered through the ancient ruins, and he found a heap of treasures, sevenfold to what our might our king has now, hidden inside the ancient ruins. Aardburzin told me about this, and alas, Aharman deceived me and made my avarice. I did not want anyone to know that, so I killed the great Aardburzin. Now that the matter has been revealed, there is no point in hiding from anyone. I will receive my fate as it has been destined. I request the mercy of our beloved king and grant me pardon! I am very ashamed about what I did, and Fardad, you didnt deserve this, but please forgive me!"

Listening to this, the mighty King Kai Kobad became furious and ordered the treasurer to go to the villa of Grand Vizier Darazdast and estimate his wealth. The king then said to the murderous Darazdast, "You committed murder and concealed the treasures from the state. All such crimes make you worthy of capital punishment, and I now order that Darazdast be crucified in the center of the city. The people of our land need to see an example made out of you. What you did was horrendous, and there is no forgiveness for such grave sins. I can, in no greater conscience, forgive you, so you must accept your fate. These evil needs to be made an example of and eliminated from our lands."

Darazdast pleaded to the mighty king once again, saying, "My dear King, I have done wrong, but please do not execute me in front of your people. I would rather have your guards slice my head and take it to the public because I would not be able to face them. If you can forgive me, I will forever remain indebted to you and make sure to get back your enemies with the same vengeance you possess. I will make sure that this young man, Fardad, gets the justice he deserves. I plead with you to give me a chance to rectify my mistakes and redeem myself, so I can become a better human being."

The king had heard enough and said, "Silence, you Traitor. Fool me once; shame on you. Fool me twice; shame on me. I can never trust you again for what you did. You deserve to be slain in front of these people as you committed a horrendous sin. You will get your punishment, and there will be no pardon for you. Guards, take him away. Get this wretched scoundrel, murderer, and traitor out of my face!"

The guards took Darazdast and the eunuch away from the king and placed them in the dungeons. On the morning of the next day, Darazdast was executed in the city center while the Soroush, the interior minis-

CHAPTER 6.   THE REVENGE

ter, informed that the eunuch had committed suicide.

The king appointed Fardad as his special adviser and announced to the guards, "This young man, Fardad, is now my special advisor, and you need to pay him the same respect you have paid to me. Fardad, you have done me a huge favor, and I can never repay you, and I will be honored to have you as my advisor." Fardad nodded gracefully and bowed to the king. His mother was constantly on his mind, but he knew his work was still not done. Gyasi stood next to him, proud and happy that he helped save two lives. Both men still had unfinished business, but for now, it was time to rejoice.

***

The dense prison was extremely gloomy and suffocating, especially since there was no window for ventilation. In addition to that, there were no guards as it was midnight. The black eunuch named Banoo was lying pathetically inside his cell. The wretched humans eyes were lowered, and his head was placed on the freezing prison floor. There was fear and shame in his eyes. The black eunuch was about to close his eyes when all the lamps inside the prison extinguished, and there was pitch-black darkness. Abruptly, a deep voice boomed from outside the bars of the cell.

"Banoo, my faithful slave!"

The figure was not visible in the darkness.

"Master!" Banoo exclaimed as he got up and grabbed the bars of the cell. "Master, I apologize from the depth of my heart for failing to kill King Kai Kobad."

"It is alright, Banoo. You have been a very precious slave who has always been obedient,"

"Thank you, Master!" he expressed with tears in his eyes.

The figure marched forward and lit a small torch on the side of Banoos cell. Most shockingly, the figure of Soroush emerged, and he beamed at Banoo with affection. "Banoo, I suppose you are hungry,"

"Yes, Master. Those bloody guards of that ruthless king havent given me anything to eat. I am starving," the black eunuch sobbed loudly.

The minister advanced towards his cell, and placing his hands forward, he offered him an apple.

"Here, I nicked it from the kings dining area, just for you!" Soroush claimed with a sort of dangerous relish in his voice.

"Oh, Master! You are the most wonderful person in the entire kingdom!"

Immediately, Banoo grabbed the apple and began to munch on it ravenously. However, after a few bites, Banoo felt something strange. He seemed to be choking, and his mind began to ache horribly.

Soroush smiled viciously and stared at his faithful servant, whose eyes were widened in extreme shock.

"Master...what did you do?" he choked.

"Banoo...I am sorry, but your presence here can turn out to be a noose around my neck. So, I must say regretfully that you need to depart from this world. I hope that the almighty Lord of the worlds grants you a place in Baheesht (heaven)....goodbye."

After saying that, Soroush blew the torch and marched away, leaving Banoo to vomit blood and perish instantly on the prison floor. Soroush marched towards his royal chamber and threw a goblet down in frustration.

"Every plan and every action of mine is backfiring! Curse that damned Fardad! Oh, how I despise him so!"

One of his girl spies caressed his shoulder as he sat on his couch.

"Relax, master Soroush. Do not stress yourself so much. Here, have some grapes,"

The girl offered to feed him some black grapes, which he rejected with a wave of his hand.

"How can I not stress! That bloody Fardad is thwarting all my plans! Even those stupid men that I had sent to have him and his slave companion, Gyasi, killed at the mountainside couldnt do anything! And he killed them all single-handedly!"

Suddenly, he got onto his feet and moved forward with intense fear on his face as droplets of sweat appeared on his large forehead.

"If...if King Marduk gets to know that I have failed in my attempts to have King Kai Kobad and Fardad killed. He wont spare me....he will cut out my flesh and feed it to the eagles!"

Soroush shuddered horribly at that gruesome thought.

"I must quickly do something! Fardad! I wont let you thwart my plans anymore! I will have you killed soon!"

The girl began to massage Soroushs shoulder and giggled loudly.

"What are you smiling about?"

"Nothing, Master. Its just that Fardad is a very charming and interesting man. I have been spying on him since the day he arrived at this palace. He is quite a charmer,"

"Well, I am not really interested in what you are saying! Just keep doing your work and keep an eye on that accursed man and his scornful black friend, Gyasi!" "As you say, Master Soroush!"

The spy girl in veil bowed graciously and left his chamber.

Chapter 7

The Rocks

After a long and eventful day, Fardad went to sleep, thinking about what had happened. He had a lot on his mind from his mother, his best friend Ukund, and his new lady loved Parinaaz. The beautiful enchantress had captured his heart, and he dreamt of her the entire night, and the two were passionately kissing each other in his dream. They had locked lips, and Fardad wished this dream would never end. He felt he was in heaven, and life was beautiful. After so much stress, this was what the doctor had ordered.

He was smiling the entire time in his dream and could hear Parinaaz say, "Fari, my love, stay with me forever, and be mine. I will always love you!" Fardad then said, while dreaming, "Youre my Pari, mine, always and forever, my beautiful fairy. I want to hold you in my arms and never let you go." Parinaaz replied, "My dear Fari, I will always be yours. Never forget. Our destinies are aligned together. You will see that because your dreams tell the truth. If

CHAPTER 7.   THE ROCKS

youre seeing me now, know that I will be yours forever. Now, open your eyes, my love."

"Open your eyes, Fardad, open your eyes. Time to get up, my friend," said Gyasi.

Fardad suddenly woke up and looked around, and Parinaaz was gone, and Gyasi was sitting next to him, looking straight into his eyes. Fardad was in a complete daze, as he had been dreaming about Parinaaz for so long.

Gyasi said, "My friend, youve been talking so much nonsense the entire night, and I couldnt sleep. You were even kissing someone in your sleep, and I wont be surprised if it was that fair maiden, Parinaaz."

Fardad smiled and said, "Youre right. It was her. We were together and kissing each other passionately, and I swear she has left me so mesmerized. Last night, we danced together, and it was unbelievable."

Gyasi let out a laugh and said, "Fardad, you are deeply in love. She is someone special, and you are a lucky man. But, do you have any idea who she is?" Fardad replied, "Gyasi, she told me her father and the king are friends. She was asked on short notice to attend and was bored."

Gyasi laughed out loud and said, "My friend, you have no idea. She fooled you, and she is not what she says she is!"

Fardad became shellshocked and said, "What do you mean? If she isnt His Majestys daughters friend, then who is she!"

Gyasi laughed hysterically and said, "My dear Friend.

She lives here in the palace. She is Princess Parinaaz, heir to the throne, and the daughter of King
Kai Kobad and Queen Anahita. She was just messing
with you."

Fardad quickly asked, "And...how do you know all
this?"

Gyasi continued laughing and said, "I know a lot
more than you, my dear friend. Now get ready. The
king and queen have summoned us, and you are now
their special advisor, dont forget that."

Fardad had a lot on his mind and several questions
to ask Gyasi. He knew he had to get ready, so he decided to ask one ultimate question to his new assistant,
"And...you, Gyasi, are my assistant. So, I need to ask
you...what else do you know about the princess! This
is important to me. No wonder she said she would
know where to find me! Maybe she knew I had the
answers!"

Gyasi took one deep breath because he was getting
tired of playing with 20 questions in his head. He
replied, "Fardad, I told you whatever I know. You
can ask the rest of her later yourself. Lets get ready.
The king and queen are waiting."

At the same time, one of the guards knocked on
their door. Gyasi said, "We need to make a move now.
They already sent one of the guards to fetch us!" Fardad changed into his daytime clothes and got ready
while Gyasi asked the guard to wait for a few minutes.
Fardad got ready quickly and joined the guard with
Gyasi to be escorted to the royal chamber. The royal

CHAPTER 7.   THE ROCKS

chamber, like the library, was a private room where both the king and queen met guests and advisors for meetings. The room had been crafted with the best wood in the land and had the most exquisite oil paintings on the wall, all handpainted by the best artists of the land. The king was a huge connoisseur of art, and it showed in his choice. He had delicate taste in women, too, as his wife was one of the most refined ladies of the kingdom. The beauty had been passed on to Princess Parinaaz.

King Kai Kobad and Queen Aanahita were both alone in their chamber when they called upon Fardad to appear before them. Both of them seemed pretty worried and concerned about what had happened the night before. Once they were in the presence of the king and queen, they bowed, showing respect. The queen then asked both of them to take a seat across the table from them. The table was a square meeting table with chairs on all four sides designed for personal meetings. The two young men obliged and took their seats.

"Our beloved king is worried about the premonition that your father Aardburzin knew and wanted to reveal to Darazdast. He highly appreciates your help and is indebted to you for saving his life, and mine too, because I cant live without him. He is the love of my life, and Id rather give my life for his. You must understand that if someone can infiltrate the royal palace and attempt to take his life, others will dare to do the same. We need to get to the bottom of this. The situation is dire. I understand youve done enough for us already, but we would appreciate it if you could do more for us. It will help you come to peace once and for all because it concerns your slain father, too. It is your choice completely, and we will understand if you choose not to do as asked. We are requesting you to help us, and you arent obligated to accept it. If you want to take some time to think about it, then do so. Otherwise, if you can even guide us on what to do and how to move forward, we will appreciate that as well. The choice is all yours, dear Fardad. Rest assured, we will be okay with whatever decision you make. Thank you once again for helping us out; it means so much to us." Queen Aanahita spoke.

Fardad quietly heard the queens request and quickly glanced toward Gyasi after she finished speaking. Gyasi nodded, "Yes," toward him. Fardad knew he had to accept the request of the queen as justice had been served for his fathers murder. The king did help him, and it was his generosity that he had been protected for the past few days at the palace. However, there was a significant concern for the young man.

He had been missing his mother and best friend Ukund, which was bothering him for a long time. He had feared their safety. This was perhaps the right time to reunite with them, and maybe the king and queen could accept his request in exchange for him accepting theirs. Fardad then politely and humbly said, "Im more than willing to help you out in any way I can. This means that you allowed me to stay here and have appointed me as your special advisor. I would just require a small favor from you both if its not too much to ask."

Queen Anahita felt delighted and replied, "We are so glad that you have accepted our request. What is it you need? How can we help you? Do you require any monetary assistance?"

Fardad smiled and said, "My Queen, please dont embarrass me. You have already done so much, and your gestures are more than enough. I have a very small request for you. I have a friend called Ukund, who was also an apprentice of my father when he was alive. These days, he is looking after my mother Kanisha in the town of Mehrdad. May the mighty King permit me to call upon my best and dearest friend Ukund and my mother in the capital. I will be highly grateful if you reunite us because I have not seen them since I left my village. Ukund is well-versed and knowledgeable and can help us out a lot, and he can prove to be an asset to us." The queen looked at the king, and he nodded back to her, saying, "Yes." She then said, "Fardad, we would be more than happy to bring them both here. We understand they are your family and you wish to see them again. We will make arrangements for them to return and will make available our guest rooms for their stay. The palace guards will be escorting them from Mehrdad to the capital at once. We will send a team right away to bring them here. We will handle everything, so you dont have to worry about anything."

Fardad then said, "My Queen, please thank the king for his kind gesture. I am delighted to learn that you are arranging to bring my mother and best friend here, and I will be highly indebted to you for everything."

The king then broke his silence and spoke, "You are like a son to me, Fardad. Do not worry about repaying any debts. I think we can call it even. You are now my special advisor, and your friend Gyasi is your righthand man. You two are critical to us, and we will help you in every way. Your mother and friend will be brought here soon. Until then, relax. You and Gyasi can take it easy until their arrival. We will reconvene and plan our next move. Thank you both for everything." Fardad said, "The pleasure is all ours. You are also like a father to me, Your Majesty. We will help in any way we can. Thank you, my king and queen. We shall take our leave now."

With that, both Gyasi and Fardad bowed toward the king and queen and left their chamber. They were escorted back to their room by the palace guard. The guard informed them they would be notified once Fardads mother and a friend arrived at the palace and that he was at their service. They need to pull the lever next to the bed to summon them. After this, he bowed in respect and took his leave.

Fardad looked at Gyasi and said, "This is incredible. I can finally see my mother and dear friend Ukund. . ."

Gyasi interrupted him and said, "Why, Fardad, am

CHAPTER 7.   THE ROCKS

I not your dear friend? After all that I have done for you? I am very depressed you dont even feel that way for me." Gyasi was just teasing Fardad and was pretending to be sad. He tried his best to hide his smile and keep a straight and sad face. Fardad got a bit concerned and said, while patting Gyasis back, "Now, you are no less than a friend to me, Gyasi. Your loyalty and commitment will never go unappreciated. Please dont think that I dont care about our friendship. Its just that I havent met my mother and Ukund in a long time. ....ever since I left my village. I am worried about them both, and Ukund, like you, is a brother to me and. .."

Gyasi interrupted him again, this time smiling and saying, "Fardad. I get it, dont worry about it. I was just teasing you, dear friend. I know you think highly of me as much as I do of you. You allowed me a chance of freedom and me to be your righthand man. That is more than enough for me, my friend. I, like you, am very much looking forward to meeting the lady who brought you into this world. Such a mother would be an inspiration because I never saw my mother, and I would think of her as my own. Your friend Ukund is my friend because any friend of yours is a friend of mine. Lets go out for a walk in the courtyard and get some fresh air. Perhaps, we may just run into that fair maiden you so much admire and dream of!"

"Princess Parinaaz," Farzad said out loud, "How I long to see her again. Your guess is always spot on. Lets go and take our chance!"

Both friends laughed, and they headed to the courtyard in hopes of running into the princess. On the way to the courtyard, Fardad asked Gyasi, "By the way, Gyasi, why did you not speak in front of the king and queen?"

Gyasi listened carefully and explained, "My friend, I have to follow certain protocols as I have been taught in my time as a slave. I have to obey and respect people in the position of power and look down to show humility and respect in their presence. At the same time, I only speak when I am spoken to, and both the king and queen were addressing you and not speaking with me. I was standing there as your friend and righthand man. Therefore, I will continue the same protocols even if I am no longer a slave. I am still a servant of the king and queen and your assistant. Since we are friends, I speak while looking into your eyes, but that isnt part of my protocol. I hope you understand now why I have to maintain respect in front of people of power."

Fardad then said, "I understand completely, dear Gyasi. You are an honorable man, and I am very privileged and lucky to have you by my side."

"Dont mention it, my Friend. We are like brothers, and there should be no sorry and thank between us. We dont need to be this formal. I will forever stay in your service until you relieve me of it. Even then, I will forever remain your friend and ally," said Gyasi.

Fardad smiled and put his arm around Gyasi, and said, "Its my pleasure. Well always be friends, partners, and brothers!"

Both of them then shook each others hands firmly and embraced each other. By this time, they had reached the courtyard and were just enjoying the scenery. Princess Parinaaz was nowhere to be found, but they still walked around the courtyard breathing the fresh air. The weather was sunny, while the skies were clear. There was an air of positivity all around, and Fardad felt quite relaxed. The garden in the courtyard was well-maintained, and there were beautiful flowers and greenery all around. The birds were chirping, and there was a pleasant feeling all around. It looked like one of those heavenly gardens, and there were lovely scents all over the place. One would feel right at home sitting there.

As they walked around, Gyasis eyes caught someone familiar. A fair maiden was sitting in the courtyard gardens near the flowers. He nudged Fardad to look at the maiden. She seemed familiar, and Fardad guessed who that was. His dream had almost turned into reality. He whispered to Gyasi and asked whether they should approach her. Gyasi held his hand and took him straight to the lady who was....

"Princess Parinaaz, Fardad here is to meet you!"

Fardad was red in the face as he had been taken by surprise by Gyasi. The princess looked up at them and then said, "Oh my! What a pleasant surprise! Nice to see you, two gentlemen!"

Gyasi nudged Fardad, and then Fardad replied, "Your Majesty, very nice to see you here, too. We were just enjoying some fresh air and saw you, so we came to say hello."

The princess laughed and said, "Thats very cute. Stop calling me Your Majesty, please. Youre Fardad, right, and you are a guest of the King Kai Kobad. I remember we met at the banquet last night, and we shared a wonderful dance together. You also saved the king. I decided to stay for a few days as my father had gone on a trading trip and would fetch me on his return to the capital. I enjoy staying at the palace, and by the way, you were supposed to call me Pari, and I was supposed to call you Fari, as we had decided. How can you forget!? I understand being a hero was too overwhelming for you. But dont worry, youre forgiven. Why dont you both have a seat right here in the courtyard garden!"

Gyasi didnt want to be the third wheel, so he excused himself. "Miss Pari, I just remembered that I have some urgent business to take care of back in our room. Your father...I mean...the king...had requested me to look at something for him."

Gyasi had slipped out "Your Father" because he was unaware that Parinaaz knew what they knew about her.

Parinaaz smiled and said, while pretending to ignore Gyasis slip of the tongue, "You are excused, and by the way, what is your name?"

Gyasi smiled and said, "Its Gyasi, Miss Pari, and now I shall take my leave. It was a pleasure bumping into you, and I will see you back in the room later,

Fardad." Fardad was even thinking how Pari missed out on a slip of the tongue or was she playing along! He decided to keep a straight face and let her reveal herself as the conversation left. Gyasi had left for the room, and both Fardad and Parinaaz were sitting together with each other.

Parinaaz said, "Fari, so how does it feel to be the special advisor of the king?"

Fardad replied, "Pari, it feels incredible. The king is an honorable man, and his gesture completely humbles me."

Parinaaz then said, "Well, you deserve it for saving his life. Id love for my father to meet you too when he returns to the palace."

Fardad said, "I would be honored to meet him and would love you to meet my mother too, Kanisha, and my best friend, Ukund. Theyre arriving at the palace in a few days. She would be very excited to see you. However, were not royalty like you all. We live in the village of Mehrdad, and Ive always lived this way. You know about my father, right?"

Parinaaz smiled and said, "Fari, I know about your father, who was a famous astrologer. I may be born in royalty, but I have always been taught to respect our people and be humble. We are here to serve you and keep the kingdom safe. Now, you are the special adviser and are part of our palace. This is your home and will be your mother and friends home, too. They can stay as long as they want."

Fardad was so tempted to tell her she knew her

real identity but decided to play along, hoping shed say it herself.

"Thank you so very much. Thats very nice of you, Pari. Ukund is going to help me with some work your...I mean, the king...had me to do."

Fardad continued, "I wanted to tell you I have been thinking about you a lot and even saw you in my dreams!"

Parinaaz said, "Yes, I heard about your dreams. You seem to see the future. So what did you see about us? Honestly, Ive been thinking of you all this time too." Fardad said, "Well, we were together with our lips locked...and...I...."

Parinaaz then put her finger on his mouth, pulled him close to her, and said, "Like this?"

She then kissed him passionately, and instantly, Fardad was in heaven. It was his dream come true. Parinaaz had fallen for him, and they had their lips locked for a good 10 to 15 minutes until she slowly pulled back.

Parinaaz then got up and offered him her hand. Both had now gotten up, and then she said, "Fari, my love, your presence in my life is everything. I told you I would find you, and we would be together forever. This is my promise to you!"

Fardad said, "My dear Pari, I am yours now and forever. Just call my name, and I will be there!"

Parinaaz then smiled and said, "Yes, I know where to find you now. I have to attend to some matters for the king now, but you can see me here every day around this time in this garden. Take care, my love, and we shall meet tomorrow- same time, same place!"

She blew him a kiss and then walked away, leaving him completely spellbound! Fardad headed back to his room to catch up with Gyasi. He would have so much to tell him, but he decided he wouldnt say too much to his friend now. Let it all happen naturally, he thought.

Back in the room, he was all smiles and blushing all over. Gyasi figured out something was up. He then asked, "So what happened after I left. I figured you two had some quality time together. Your face says everything, my friend. Now, I wont ask you if you dont tell me, but I am happy you enjoyed yourself with that lovely maiden, the princess. By the way, did she figure out we know about her yet?"

Fardad snapped out of his love trance and said, "Yes. I did indeed have a lovely time with our lovely friend. I would leave the rest to your imagination, but I can just tell you that dreams come true. This is the most I can tell you at this time. And about her true identity? No, she has no idea that we know, despite your slip of the tongue. Either its that, or shes pretending to ignore what you said. I am sure shell let us know soon enough. She lives here because she is the princess of the palace. She is the heir to the throne. But for me, she is the love of my life. She has touched my heart as no one has ever touched it before. She has captured it and made it her own. She is just so, so beautiful. . .I am in love with her. . .she. . .she. . .she. . .."

Gyasi then interrupted and said, "My, my, without intending to say much, you have told me everything. So, whats next between you and your lady love...I mean...the princess!" Fardad laughed and said, "She has asked me to meet her tomorrow at the same place and at the same time. Thats all. And I will go tomorrow to spend time with her. She is too irresistible, and she makes me feel so complete. Every time I am in front of her, I am completely mesmerized. I dont know what comes over me."

Gyasi cut in and said, "Youre in love, my brother. Thats what love feels like. I may be a slave, but I know a thing or two about love, even though I have never been in love. A person is simply lost in love like you are right now. You love her, and she loves you. Now, I am sure your mother and friend would want to meet her too, and they will, as she is the princess. Your mother will be proud of you as you have found your bride!"

Fardad said, "My Friend, youre getting way over your head. Bride! Where did that come from! We just know were in love and havent thought much after that. As far as making her my bride, thats something she and her parents: the king and queen, have to decide. I am not of a noble family, even though my father was a famous astrologer. I am no prince, just an ordinary man. I am not sure if the king and queen would want her to marry a commoner."

Gyasi stopped him and said, "Say no more, my Friend. You are no longer a commoner, and neither am I. I was once a slave, but you have freed me from that bond. If I am of servitude to anyone, I am your righthand man, and you are now the special advisor to the king and queen. You are now royalty, so never forget that. That itself will make your mother proud of you. I never want you to call yourself a commoner because you have earned a position at the palace. This is your time to shine and live the life you always wanted to. You were destined for this moment. Your father will be proud of you up there. I understand youve been through a lot lately, but things will get okay once your mother and friend come here."

Fardad then said, "Youre very right. Weve had quite an adventure. Who knows what lies ahead! Lets take some rest now, my friend." The two of them then embraced each other and then got some rest.

The next day, the two of them woke up, and Fardad got excited to see the princess in the garden later in the day. Gyasi told him, "My Friend, I will go take a stroll around the capital today while you go romance your lady friend. I think your mother and friend should be here tomorrow or the day after." Fardad then said, "Have a good time, Brother. Yes, I will join Parinaaz in the garden later. I cant wait."

As members of the royal palace, they had attendants looking after them throughout the day, bringing them three meals a day and taking care of other needs. This was the first time either of these young men had been treated like royalty and waited on. Gyasi was more used to serving others but now was being served, which was why he kept pinching himself to ensure this wasnt a dream. Fardad was used to doing things himself and taking care of chores with his mother in the village but now had others taking care of him. Soon, his mother and best friend would also receive the same royal treatment.

Late afternoon, he headed down to the courtyard garden to see Princess Parinaaz waiting for him. The beautiful princess was sitting on the lush, green grass. She was wearing a lovely light green dress with matching shoes and was looking stunning as ever. She knew how to carry herself so well. She had the grace and charm of her mother and the sincerity of both the parents. She would be a great queen as she seemed like a wonderful human being. Princess Parinaaz was checking out some flowers when Fardad arrived. He then said, "These flowers are as beautiful as you, my dear Pari. May you bloom as they do forever."

Parinaaz smiled, pulled him closer for a small peck on the lips, and asked him to sit down next to her. She said, "I am so glad you came. I have been looking forward to seeing you since I left here yesterday evening. You look great as ever, my love. So, the news is that your mother and friend are expected to arrive tomorrow. You must be very excited!"

Fardad said, "Yes! I am very much excited about their arrival and cant wait to see them. Theyre the only family I have left, besides Gyasi and...well...you, my love. I cant see myself without you at all."

Parinaaz said, "The feeling is very much mutual. I

137

want to be with you forever, and I promise you I am with you. My heart, soul, and body are all yours!" Fardad went into a state of trance. He was simply captivated by her beauty so much that he just wanted to hold her, kiss her, and just be by her side. After staring into each others lovelorn eyes, they both locked lips once again passionately. Fardad wished this moment would never end, so he cherished every minute of it. After spending some time together in the garden, they wished each other a good evening. Fardad said to Parinaaz, "Till we meet again, my love."

Just like the previous day, she departed from the garden after blowing him a kiss. Fardad then went back to his room and lay down on the bed, thinking of the entire afternoon/evening sojourn with the princess. Gyasi was still out enjoying the sights and sounds of the capital and would return soon. He had left a note saying, "Out in town. Have one of the palace guards with me." Fardad figured he wouldnt be allowed to leave the palace without protection as a guest of the king. He is also part of the kings special advisory team along with him. As he thought about Parinaaz, Fardad drifted off into slumber.

He kept thinking about the princess in his sleep, seeing both of them in each others arms and saying romantic things to each other.

Suddenly, the door opened, and Fardad woke up, seeing Gyasi in front of him. He said, "Oops, my Friend. I got some very nice kobideh from the market. Lets eat. Im hungry!"

Both friends dug into the kobideh and bread and enjoyed the meal. Gyasi talked about his time out in the town, and Fardad told him he desired the princesss company. The other guards said that the guard accompanying Gyasi had arrived at the palace, in which two guests were expected to arrive in the morning. The caravan that went to fetch them was on its way back to the palace. Gyasi informed Fardad about this, so they both planned to call it an early night. This way, theyd be up bright and early to receive Kanisha and Ukund.

The following day, Ukund and Fardads mother, Kanisha, had arrived in the capital. The attendant guard had gone to fetch Fardad and Gyasi. Both men had woken up early and gotten ready to meet their two guests. Fardad was very excited and couldnt wait to meet them. The guard was asked to escort them to the king and queens private chamber, where Kanisha and Ukund were waiting for them.

Both men followed the guard to the chamber and saw that the king and queen were not there, but two very familiar faces waited with bated breaths. There were smiles and joy all around as Fardad was finally reunited with his mother and best friend, Ukund.

After embracing Ukund, Fardad embraced his mother and held her tightly with tears in his eyes. His mother had become very emotional because they hadnt seen each other in a while. After their embrace, Fardad introduced his mother and Ukund to Gyasi, "Mother, Ukund...this is my friend Gyasi. He used to be a slave for Darazdast- the man who had taken out his father. He freed me from captivity and helped me reach the honorable King Kai Kobad. So much has happened, Mother, but I must tell you that justice has been delivered. Darazdast was sentenced to death for murder and has been executed. He has paid for his crime and injustice to our family and this amazing kingdom of ours. Now, nothing will keep us apart!"

Kanisha said, "My Dear Son, you bring me amazing news. I am so glad justice has been delivered. You look in great spirits, and thank you so much, Gyasi. We are indebted to you for saving his life."

Gyasi then said, "Fardad is my brother, and he rescued me before I rescued him. He freed me from the bond of slavery, so that makes us even. I must thank you for giving birth to such an exemplary human being–no need to thank me. I was doing what was right. You must be very proud of your son as he is now the special advisor to the honorable King Kai Kobad."

Kanisha then said, "Oh my, that is amazing. Id love to hear the entire story.....your father must be so proud wherever he is." The guards interrupted the reunion, saying, "Excuse me, please. I am very sorry to disturb you, but I have been ordered to inform you all that you have been invited tonight to have dinner with the king and the queen. It would be best if the guests get some rest as they have arrived from a long journey. We shall escort them to their rooms."

Fardad said, "Go on, Mother. We shall speak tonight at dinner, where I will tell you everything."

Kanisha embraced her son once again and then left with the guards. Ukund followed the other guard to his room while Gyasi and Fardad went back to their room. After reaching their room, Fardad told Gyasi, "Didnt you see how happy she was. I am so glad Ukund was with her all this time. The king and queen are very glad to have them over. Finally, well get a chance to tell the entire story over dinner. I would love for the princess to be there too, so she can meet my mother." Gyasi said, "I am delighted that youre happy, my friend. Your mother loves you very much, and I think you should take it easy. Let things happen naturally. The princess will meet your mother in due time."

Fardad nodded in agreement, and then both of them went for a walk around the palace.

Later that evening, Fardad and Gyasi joined Kanisha, Ukund, the king, and the queen for dinner in the banquet hall. The chefs had cooked up excellent kebabs and spicy dishes for the guests.

King Kai Kobad spoke, "Lady Kanisha, your son is a hero. His friend Gyasi worked tirelessly to decipher my dream and saved my life from one of Darazdasts eunuchs. Then we delivered justice by hanging that scoundrel in public, so he deserved the ultimate humiliation in death. I have made him my special advisor and his friend Gyasi, his righthand man. They are working together to aid me in a major concern I have regarding your husbands murder. He knew something about Darazdast, and we need to get to the bottom of it. Rest assured, you all remain under my protection, and no soul will harm you. You have my word on it! May the blessings of Yazdan be on all of us present here!"

Kanisha then spoke, "Your Majesty, I am very thankful to you for taking care of my son and his friend. Gyasi, thank you as well for helping Fardad out. I am very grateful to you, dear king, for delivering justice to Darazdast, and now my husband can finally rest in peace!" Surprisingly, the princess wasnt seen at the dinner table. It seemed that the king and queen had arranged the dinner to have Fardad, his friends, and mother together to discuss the matter at hand.

The queen then spoke, "Dear Fardad, you mentioned your friend Ukund could help us, so if its okay with you, can we discuss our concerns so we can finally get to the bottom of this. There is the impending danger that is lurking, and we need to put a stop to it. Your father knew it, so we need to use his knowledge, and the only one close to him is your friend. I hope you can help us, and well be indebted to you."

Fardad responded, "You are right. Ukund has worked closely with my father, Aardburzin, and can help us. Well help you in every way possible. After dinner, I will sit with Ukund and Gyasi, and we will get to the bottom of this and find out what my father was trying to protect or warn us." After dinner was over, the three young men convened in the Kings private chamber to discuss their next plan.

Fardad told Ukund: "My father Aardburzin had noticed something imminent danger for Persia using his astrological charts. Can you please guide us and help us out with this knowledge?"

Ukund then said, "Thank you so much for bringing your mother and me here. I will gladly help you because your father and I were very close, and if he knew something, I know more than anyone else who he spoke to. There is a book I brought with me that could help us, and let me go through it, and then I can guide you." Ukund gladly agreed and took the book of esoteric knowledge from his bag, which his master Aardburzin has kept in the niche of his house. Fardad immediately recognized the book and said, "Is it not the same book, which my father has kept hidden? I havent seen it for so long!" Ukund said, "Yes, brother Farhad, it is the same book. It has a lot of details on your fathers work but also has the information you are not aware of. We need more knowledgeable people and experts in the field to help us out, and I may not know how to decipher it properly without help. Perhaps, our hosts, the king and queen would know of experts that can help us."

Fardad asked the guards at the door, "Please set up a meeting with His Royal Highness so we can move on with this matter." The guards nodded, "Yes," and then passed on the message to the king. He then returned after a few minutes, saying that they would reconvene in the same room to discuss the matter. The next day, Fardad, Ukund, and Gyasi showed up in the

CHAPTER 7.   THE ROCKS

kings chamber and showed the book of esoteric knowledge to the king and queen. After going through the book, the king said, "My friends, this matter is tied with the survival of our kingdom. You are all now tasked with going on a critical mission. Should you choose to accept, you need to go to the Temple of Fire near Lake Urmia and meet the high priest Kartir. Give him my Farmah (orders) that you have been appointed to decipher the book as quickly as possible. He has the answers, and you have to seek him out. It will not be an effortless task, certainly not one for the fainthearted. However, I trust you three brave men have what it takes to get this done. After all, this is a matter of our survival. Your success in this mission depends on it, so you have my blessings and my backing. Whatever you need for this, I will give it to you to make your mission comfortable."

"Having said that, you will not go alone. I am from the descendants of mighty Arash, the legendary archer, and I taught my daughter Princess Parinaaz the same archery skills. She will accompany you on this journey. Parinaaz hasnt seen that part of the kingdom, and it would be good for her to have a visit and see the lives of common people closely. Rukhsaar will go with my daughter as her assistant. She is our trusted spy and trained in the arts of deception. I have already informed both of them about this mission, and they shall meet you this afternoon to plan the mission. May the blessings of Yazdan be with you!" Queen Aanahita added. After hearing this, Fardad got very excited to know that the princess and his lady love would join them on the mission. She must have known that they will never be apart, and their destinies are locked together.

While King Kai Kobad was busy assigning Fardad the mission, a pair of veiled eyes was eavesdropping from the chamber door. As Fardad and his two friends moved out of the chamber, the figure concealed herself behind the massive door of the chamber to prevent herself from being caught.

Immediately, the spy girl rushed to Soroushs chamber. Soroush, who was lying on his royal bed with his arms behind his neck and contemplating on the best possible way to kill the two thorns in his skin, Fardad, and Kai Kobad, rose up instantly as she arrived. "Yes, Roxana! What news have you got for me?"

Roxana bowed graciously and said, "The news will blow your mind, Master! Fardad, his friend Ukund, Gyasi, and Princess Parinaaz are leaving tomorrow to visit the temple of Fire near Lake Urmia and meet the high priest Kartir and give him King Kai Kobads Farmah,"

The color rushed back into Soroushs face, and he rose up in exhilaration. "Brilliant news, Roxana! You are indeed an excellent concubine!" he remarked in excitement, planting a kiss on her cheek as she blushed anxiously.

"Well, now its time to end the chapter of Fardad and his friends forever!" Soroush declared and let out shrieks of cold, vicious laughter that echoed across his chamber. In the afternoon, Fardad, Gyasi, and Ukund were ready outside the palace, waiting for princess Parinaaz and her assistant Rukhsaar.

Parinaaz looked very beautiful, as always. Her long shiny hair big eyelashes were latching on the heart of Fardad. He once again got starstruck when he saw her again. Fardad had never been in love with anyone before, as much as he had been with her. She was the first, and perhaps the last. Gyasi and Ukund were intrigued to see Rukhsaar and found her to be a naughty-looking girl. Both Rukhsaar and Parinaaz were of the same age in their early twenties. Parinaaz explained the plan to them and said that they just needed to follow her cues, and they would get to the Temple of Fire to meet the high priest Kartir. Theyll have to be on guard the entire time. The horse caravan was ready for the whole team to hop on to, leaving that very instant.

Parinaaz was a very confident girl. She climbed the horses and asked Rukhsaar to do the same. Their caravan was ready to move. The team hopped onto the caravan, and they were on their way.

It was getting dark, and it was almost six hours since the small caravan had traveled. They approached a dense forest, and it began to get dark. Abruptly, he heard some noise in a large bush nearby. They turned a blind eye to the noise, thinking that it would be some small animal. However, the moment they started to pass from that area, they got ambushed by a group of assassins wearing black cloaks with white veils on their faces, similar to the men that had attacked Fardad and Gyasi at the mountainside when they were near the Takht-e-Shah.

Two of the assassins were equipped with bows and arrows, while the others had swords. One of the archers shot Fardads horse with an arrow which caused the horse to tumble, and Fardad was thrown forward and went rolling across the forest floor. The other archer aimed an arrow at Ukunds horse, but he missed. And before he could take out another arrow, Fardad rose on his feet and sprinted towards him and delivered a flying kick on his shoulder, which sent him flying backward, and he collided against the trunk of a tree while his arrows fell off the quiver. The other archer tried to aim an arrow at Ukund, but Gyasi galloped his brown stallion towards him and pounced over him, and they fell with a gut-wrenching thud on the ground.

In the interim, the three swordsmen surrounded Rukhsar and Parinaaz. Rukhsar seemed petrified at the sight of the huge swords and began to shiver. Parinaaz, on the other hand, didnt leave her cool and shot an arrow at one of the veiled mens eyes. The arrow pierced through his socket, and he let out a horrendous scream of agony and collapsed on the ground. The rest of them howled in fury and attacked the two maidens.

But before they could cause any harm, Ukund came galloping from behind, and unsheathing his sword, he made a tremendous swish and beheaded one of the assassins. The assassin's head zoomed through the air and landed on the branch of a tree while the torso lay motionlessly on the forest floor. Rukhsar placed her arm across her face to avoid the blood-curdling sight and flinched horribly.

Meanwhile, Gyasi continued to wrestle with the archer as they continued to roll across the ground. Suddenly, the archer lay on his chest and began to punch him mercilessly. Gyasis nose began to bleed, and he was feeling helpless when he discovered one of the arrows lying on his side. Instantaneously, he picked up the arrow and thrust it in squarely the veiled mans chest. The man spat a mouthful of blood and fell onto the side. Fardad came running towards his friend and lifted him onto his feet.

"Gyasi, are you alright?"

"Yeah, my friend, I am okay, just a small nose bleed,"

Suddenly, Fardads eyes were directed towards Ukund, who was battling the two swordsmen who had injured his horse.

He was in a sword fight with them and was about to get stabbed when Fardad ran at lightning speed and clutched the back of their heads; he jumped in between them and smashed their faces on the ground. The men perished instantly. In the interim, the archer who had collided with the tree regained consciousness and ran away as quickly as he could.

"Is everyone alright?" Fardad demanded, eyeing Parinaaz, particularly who nodded with a gloriously flirtatious smile which made Fardads heart melt even more.

***

Soroush let out a howl of fury that echoed across his chamber. The archer stood with his head hung down in shame. Suddenly, Soroush regained his calm and walked over to his man and asked, "So you failed to kill them?"

"Yes, master. They are extremely skilled and brave," he muttered while shivering profusely. Soroush nodded sarcastically with an evil smile.

"And your comrades died fighting them?"

"Yes, Master."

"Then why in the bloody kingdom are you alive, you cowardly rat!" saying that Soroush retrieved his sword and beheaded the archer in an instant while the blood splashed across the ministers face. He wiped the blood off his face and ordered his guards to take dispose of the torso and the head.

"Fardad!" he roared loudly and punched the side of his royal bed. Parinaaz and Rukhsaar were tired and wanted to rest. Fardad, Gyasi, and Ukund were behind the ladies and the princess. They quietly obeyed all orders, and the team decided to camp there, and all of them slept.

Later Fardad was in a deep sleep. He saw he was walking alone barefoot; his dress was torn, his feet had blisters, there were scratches on his face, and it was dusty; he was looking at the red lake, but the Fire Temple was not there, and it was burned!

Fardad woke up. Was that a premonition, clairvoyance, or just a fear! He was wondering and sweating,

CHAPTER 7.   THE ROCKS

and he had several intuitions before. The danger was nearly at their doorstep, and he had to warn the team.

Chapter 8

The Encounter

WHEN Fardad woke up the following day, he saw Rukhsaar was already up and ready. She spread a map where she had marked the places with stones.

Rukhsaar said, "The temple is at a distance of five days, but we have Blackstone Mountains ahead. I suggest we take a detour; we could reach there in two days." Fardad said, "No, its better to follow the same route."

"Do as Rukhsaar is saying." The voice from behind ordered. Fardad looked back and saw the gorgeous Princess Parinaaz behind him. The princess smelled of lilies and rose petals and dust; her skin and hair seemed like the finest silk, a scent that men would kill for.

"My princess, this is the way which is good for travelers. We could run into problems if we end up following the deserted path," Fardad said.

"I know this area well. These mountains are mysterious, as it is difficult to perceive the bandits hiding in them. Darazdast had sent the pasbans here many times, but they failed to capture anyone," Gyasi added.

"At the moment, time is important. And as far as the safety of the princess is concerned, I am responsible," Rukhsaar assured the men while Parinaaz smiled. Both Parinaaz and Ruskhsaar were adamant about going for the adventurous path, and men had to agree on their plans.

"But I suppose we have to be cautious as no supporting army is near us," Ukund said in a serious tone.

Parinaaz replied, "We are just planning our route. I understand you may play it safe, but I am a highly-skilled archer, along with being a princess. I can take care of all of us as long as you stay behind me and be on guard at all times. I hope thats clear to everyone!"

Ukund didnt seem too amused but went ahead. He also wasnt sure of the princesss abilities and looked toward Gyasi. Both exchanged giggles, but perhaps they were just underestimating her abilities.

Fardad then stated, "I understand that some of us want to play it safe, but the princess knows what shes doing. The honorable King Kai Kobad has asked us to trust her, so we shall."

Parinaaz then said, "Lets move ahead now. Follow mine and Rukhsaars lead. Lets head out!"

Fardad then looked toward his two friends and said, "My friends, I understand that danger may lie ahead, so we should be prepared for everything. Lets stick together until we get to our destination."

The team of heroes headed out, following Princess Parinaaz and Rukhsaar. While traveling, Fardad said, "The path we are now going is well-known for the den of bandits and ruffians. So be aware of any attacks. Sharpen your swords, guys."

Princess Parinaaz and her assistant Rukhsaar started galloping the horses, and Fardad, Gyasi, and Ukund also caught up with them. It was a long journey, and during that time, Fardad was in deep thought.

It had been quite an adventure since he discovered his father was no more. From being almost murdered to saving the king and romancing his daughter, he had done everything. He had been through hell and back and survived through it all. At the moment, he and his group of merry men and women were facing the calm before the storm.

***

In the interim, Soroush paced left and right across his chamber as he was fuming with intense rage and frustration.

"What on earth is happening?!" he bawled like a raging beast. "All my attacks and plans to thwart that bloody wart, Fardad, is backfiring!"

Suddenly, his voice lowered and turned more fearful and anxious.

"If this continues, Master Marduk will have me slaughtered and fed to the eagles!"

Huge droplets of sweat spread across his forehead, and he placed his hand across his head with his eyes widened in agony.

"Fear not, my beloved master," came a soothing voice from behind him. He turned to look and found Roxana gently plucking the petals of a fresh red rose. "How can I not be fearful, Roxana?! That darned Fardad keeps thwarting my plans without breaking a sweat! I just dont know what to do!"

"Shall I suggest something, master?" she piped in calmly as she continued to pluck the petals.

"What, Roxana?" Soroush asked with a deep sigh.

"Just send a group of masked assassins to kill them, simple," she said peacefully. Because of her statement, Soroush burst into fits of cold laughter. "Oh, my Dear Girl! It seems you have lost your mind!" he mocked spitefully. "Three groups of assassins on different occasions couldnt harm a hair on Fardads and his black friends hair! You must be joking!"

"Send the assassins, master," Soroush gawked at her as though she had truly lost her sanity.

"Roxana...I have sent dozens of highly skilled assassins to kill Fardad before. They met their deaths. How would the outcome be any different this time? Can you explain, please?"

"The outcome would be in your favor because..." Roxana paused as she plucked the last petal from the rose. "I would be leading them this time, my Dear Master..."

***

After a while, the horses were exhausted, and the

terrain had also changed. It was no longer green but stony and semi-mountainous. The horses were sweating, breathing hard, and covered in the dust and the thud of their hooves against the ground made a hollow sound.

The bags under their bellies were filled with food, but their hunger was starting to build after hours on the road. Their nostrils were filled with the smell of sweat and the earth. It was midday, and they were all passing through a narrow valley.

"Hey guys, we need to feed these horses, or else our journey would be doubled," Gyasi said.

They all started feeding their horses with the husk, straws, and hay. Suddenly, they heard the commotion and realized they werent alone. Around thirty men were seen wearing black face masks, and they were uttering strange chants. These men were descending from the rocks and had probably watched them from afar. They were waiting for the perfect moment to strike while hiding in the nooks and crevices. Apparently, the attackers were not throwing any arrows, which was unusual. And Roxana was leading them with a black veil across her face such that only her gorgeously sharp light green eyes were visible. As she descended the rocks along with those masked assassins of the evil minister Soroush, she commanded them to unsheathe their sword and get ready to attack.

Fardad shouted, "Swords! We are under attack, and we need to back each other!"

Parinaaz then said, "You all take cover. I will show

that they cant mess with a princess!"

She took her arch and bow and aimed toward their enemies. She had an excellent aim and took their enemies out with swift precision. She was joined by Rukhsaar, who then took out some small balls from her bags and threw them around the entourage. These werent ordinary balls but explosives, detonating upon impact, forming dust clouds. It blinded the enemies and Fardad, Ukund, and Gyasi. All they could hear was shouting and the hissing sound of arrows and screams. Fardad located Parinaaz and saw that she pulled his attire, asking him to prepare for an escape.

She said, "Fardad. Get your friends together and make a run for it. Follow Rukhsaar; shell get us to safety."

Fardad then told the others, "Gyasi, Ukund, follow Rukhsaar. She will guide us to safety."

They left their enemies in the dust clouds, following Rukhsaar. She kept throwing the bombs toward them so she and her friends could escape safely. Farhad, Gyasi, and Ukund were marveled by the arts in which Rukhsaar was trained. After running around a half parasang (5 km), the galloping horses started feeling extremely thirsty.

The surrounding rocks were changing colors, giving them the impression that these rocks were talking about them. Luckily, they found a small rivulet. The water's gushing sound was more like a gurgling of a small brook than a roaring waterfall. The sound was very relaxing, as it gave them time to listen to the rocks and relax.

Gyasi was the first who jumped from his horse and rushed toward the water. The heroes finally had time to rest and lay down their arms. It was a long trip, and the horses needed rest too.

"Darn it! We have lost all the food and husk! What, in the name of the Lord, are we going to feed these poor horses?" Gyasi exclaimed, patting his brown stallion. "They are getting weaker with every moment. We cannot travel much with these poor creatures suffering. We need to think of something quick!" "We have some gold coins which are good enough for us, but for horses ...," Parinaaz said and started thinking.

Fardad did some self-contemplation and stated, "With these horses, we can travel around five parasangs a day."

It seemed like he was speaking to himself and saw that Parinaaz nodded in the affirmative. Rukhsaar spread her map on the ground, and she explained the plan. "Now the holy fire temple is twenty parasangs away from us, and that means we have two more days to travel. Rest up, everyone, as we have another long and tiring journey awaiting us soon."

***

In the meantime, Soroush began to pace hither and thither again across his chamber. His head was filled with a mixture of fear, rage, and anxiety. Despite being well aware that he had sent men to lead by Roxana, who was way more skilled and strong than his average assassin, he felt extremely fearful due to Fardad. Nearly half the day had passed since Roxana had left the palace along with the assassins, and Soroush hadnt heard from her at all.

"What is taking Roxana so long!" he murmured irritatingly. "She hasnt even sent any messenger to me either! Oh, that girl can be so frustrating! Would it kill her to send someone to inform me about the situation!" he shouted in annoyance.

Abruptly, he stopped moving, and a horrendous thought struck his mind. Has she been killed? No! That cant be! She is the only most faithful and skilled spy that I have left! I cannot let her die. I must do something immediately!

Instantaneously, a brilliant idea flashed in his mind, and a maleficent smile began to spread across his sharp jawline.

In the meantime, King Kai Kobad and his wife Queen Anahita were seated on their thrones. Queen Anahita appeared quite anxious and said, "My king, I am getting worried about our daughter."

"My dear queen, please do not overthink; our daughter is an extremely brave and courageous girl who has been competently trained in archery and fighting. She can take very good care of herself."

"Umm, I know, but still, was it really a good idea to send her on this critical mission?"

"Of course, my Queen! Please do not underestimate her capabilities. And besides, she is accompanied by Fardad and his friends. . ."

"And thats the thing to worry about, mighty King," Soroush cut him in instantly as he marched towards them. He greeted them and bowed graciously. "My King, I beg your forgiveness for interrupting you. However, this matter is of high importance. I strongly agree with Queen Anahita about sending Princess Parinaaz on this mission."

"Soroush, please not now–"

"My King, just tell me one thing. How much do you know about this man Fardad? We have no information on his background or the place where he comes from except for whatever rubbish he has fed us with!"

"Soroush, let me remind you, his mother is staying here with us."

"My King, please forgive me but, how can we be so sure that the lady is his mother? She could be someone whom Fardad paid for playing the role of his mother to deceive you," he exclaimed, trying his best to break down the strong wall of trust that Kai Kobad had built around Fardad.

"I beg you, my King, think about this entire matter with a cool head. We cannot trust that man, Fardad. Who knows, he might try to trap our innocent Parinaaz in order to get your throne? And to be perfectly honest, my King, I have seen them mingling very closely in the first few meetings. Trust me, my King, the man is up to something hostile."

"Soroush, do not forget, the man interpreted my dream and saved my life."

CHAPTER 8.   THE ENCOUNTER

"Forgive me, my King, but please think about it. The black eunuch could have easily been summoned and bribed by Fardad to attack you through which he could pretend to interpret your dream and gain your trust. In addition to that, the black eunuch was murdered the same night in prison. I can bet my life and say that Fardad killed him to erase every bit of evidence that could be dangerous to him!"

These words had a profound effect on the king. His thoughts began filling with doubt and worry for the safety of his daughter, and for the first time ever, a seed of doubt was sown inside his mind against Fardad.

He took a deep breath and asked, "Soroush, what do you suggest I do now?"

"My King, I strongly suggest we think of a clever way to summon Princess Parinaaz back."

King Kai Kobad contemplated for a few moments and then got up from his thrown.

"I have a better idea...."

***

The team spent a few hours catching up on some sleep, and both Fardad and Parinaaz seemed to relax. Fardad saw the princess had found a tree to rest her back on and take a nap. She seemed content, and that was enough for Fardad. He could find a nice patch of grass to lie down on and close his eyes. He went into dreamland and once again saw him and Parinaaz in each others arms with locked lips. They were smiling at each other while enveloped in an embrace, constantly repeating the three words: "I love you!"

Fardad was smiling the entire time he was dreaming. It was a beautiful feeling, all warm and fuzzy until he heard a voice in his sleep.

"Wake up, Sweet Prince," Fardad heard this voice, thinking it was coming from Princess Parinaaz.

He heard it coming several times, and he thought he was already a prince. After a few cries of "Wake up, Sweet Prince," Fardad finally opened his eyes and saw two familiar faces staring down at him. They were none other than Ukund and Gyasi, who were smiling and laughing at him.

Gyasi was aware of Fardads feelings for the princess, but Ukund knew little about it. Ukund hadnt spoken with Fardad about the princess, so he was pretty confused about their relationship.

Fardad, dazed and confused, stared into the wilderness and saw others getting ready to move ahead. Gyasi gave Fardad a hand and lifted him.

Fardad told his friend, "Thank you, my Brother. I would like to know what was so funny."

Gyasi took Fardad aside, smiled, and said, "My friend, youre in love, and you get into a trance when youre asleep thinking about our princess. I figured you were dreaming of her in your arms, as you always do. I think your friend Ukund has no clue. You have some explaining to do to your friend as he was asking questions, but I had no liberty to answer. This is your personal life, and I dont want to speak on your behalf.

CHAPTER 8.   THE ENCOUNTER

It would be better you let him know because he may get more confused about your relationship with the princess."

Fardad then replied, "I understand your concerns, and thank you for letting me know. This isnt the time to explain my love life, as I dont know what the future holds for the princess and me. We like each other and want to be together, but nothing is certain until this mission is complete. This is our priority, so lets get this taken care of soon. If I have time to speak to Ukund about it, I will. My mother is back at the palace but does not know about our relationship. Therefore, we should worry about these matters later. Theres more work to be done, and the king has asked us to go along with his daughter, and she being royalty, we must listen to her. She is an exceptional archer and can help us immensely, and Rukhsaar is very helpful. Lets follow their cues and assist them the best we can."

Gyasi then said, "My Friend, you are also royal. Dont forget that you now have a place in the palace as the special advisor to the honorable King Kai Kobad, and I am your assistant. Youre part of this royal entourage on a mission for the king. Youve earned this, and you should be proud of yourself. Now, lets get back to the others as theyre waiting to move ahead. Well hopefully stop on the way somewhere so that you can dream about the princess some more!"

Both friends laughed and embraced each other. They then met up with Ukund, Rukhsaar, and Princess Parinaaz. They got on the horses and rode off toward their destination. It was another long journey until they came to the point of giving the horses some rest.

***

They had already covered the distance of three parasangs, and they went through many towns buying food but not revealing their identity. They couldnt risk it because their enemies could be on to them. They also couldnt reveal they were royalty because it would only create problems for King Kai Kobad and Queen Anahita. They were now passing through a small town called Bukan and stopped at a guest house to recuperate for the rest of their trip. This could be their ultimate break before they reach their destination.

They rented two rooms for three gold coins. Parinaaz and Rukhsaar stayed in one room, and Ukund, Gyasi, and Fardad stayed in the other. The guest house or motel was known as Saraie, and that place had arranged for their dinner. After a long and tiring journey with very little to eat and getting involved in a skirmish, they needed a more civilized place to sleep in and eat. Rukhsaar and Parinaaz ate as much as they needed, but the men were super hungry. They just ate and drank their heart out and were quite full by the time they were done. The ladies wished the men goodnight and mentioned that they would knock on the door in the morning to continue their journey.

None of them had talked to each other, as they were too busy eating and drinking earlier. Fardad and company went to sleep after they reached their rooms.

CHAPTER 8.   THE ENCOUNTER

He went to sleep as he had a bit too much to drink. Once he had gotten into bed, he drifted off to sleep and was out cold.

Before he hit the bed, Gyasi had told him, "Pleasant dreams, Sweet Prince! May you see what you wish for!"

He then winked at Farhad, and then Farhad smiled back at him. Once Fardad was asleep, he hoped to see the princess, but he saw nothing this time. He thought, Be careful what you wish for. However, he perhaps only wanted to see the princess as he usually did in his dreams. This time around, all he could see was just darkness. It was like a void or some empty space, and he could hear something strange from a distance.

Fardad started hearing voices as if someone was calling from a deep cavern. "Come to me; come here!" The voice was quite authoritative and mystical and was creating a resounding echo in his body. For a while, Fardad thought that this was his imagination inventing things. He thought perhaps it was the effect of the wine. But the voices grew deeper and deeper. Fardad found no other option but to get up from bed and follow the voice; he came out of the motel.

Ukund and Gyasi woke up too and called him from his back, but their voices were diminishing as if the surroundings had changed. He seemed very disturbed by what was going on. He wondered if he was dreaming or if this was some alternate dimension. He also wondered if this was something he would see becoming a reality in the future, as he could see such things previously, too, to figure out the kings dream and his fathers murder.

Fardad was now on the street. It was already sunset, and very few people were walking on the road like gray and black silhouettes. Fardad was losing his sense of color, and his head was feeling heavy. He was walking on the street, then on some marshy ground, and then on rocks that looked like the pillar of salt. Suddenly, he found himself in front of the cave.

Fardad felt no hesitation entering the cave as if he were entering his den. The calls became more assertive and deeper, and he knew that the wind was calling him inside. The cave was dark, and there was no light, but Fardad still knew where to put his feet. He neither fell nor tumbled and descended gracefully down. He found a dimly lit area and saw someone sitting there, and it was a lady wearing a cloak with her head and face covered. Fardad came back to his senses and said, "Who are you! Why are you calling me?"

The person sitting in front of him said, "You were summoned here by me."

Fardad shouted, "I am in no mood to listen to any nonsense tonight."

The person removed its cloak, and Fardad could see the face of an older woman with a rustic look and mud.

The woman stated, "I want to give you a premonition, son."

She had a lovely and comforting voice but that

of warning. She meant business and sounded serious every time she spoke, despite having an amicable demeanor. Fardad said, "What is the danger that you are seeing? Why have you asked me to help? I am just a mortal man."

The old woman said, "Marduk from the Kingdom of Babylon will unleash a disease. This disease will cause amnesia to everyone it infects. All the inhabitants of the Kingdom of Persia will forget their past and their present. They will forget the art of war, manner of living, glorious history, and every survival skill. Only you can save them. You had saved the honorable King Kai Kobad from near-death. You should know now that you are the chosen one. You can save Persia from destruction because you hold the key. You are the one, Fardad. You can do it along with your future queen, Princess Parinaazd!"

Fardad was quite concerned about her premonition. He didnt know he carried special powers or would be a king himself. That could hold true if he ended up marrying the princess he had dreamed of since he met her. If this oracle was correct, he must be the one. He never knew that an ordinary man, a mere mortal, could change the destiny of their kingdom. He picked the womans brain a little more. He also wanted to know why she predicted he would be the future king.

Fardad first asked, "I understand what you mean, and I have seen the future in my dreams, but to be the chosen one is a little too much for me to swallow. I am overwhelmed by this premonition, and I want to ask you first how you know all of this. Of course, you say youre the oracle, but I am sure theres more to this than meets the eye. And one more thing. Whats the meaning behind this future king prediction? How do you know Ill be the king and the princess will be my queen? I assume you think I will marry her because we love each other. However, all of this is very confusing for me. Please help me understand!"

Fardad then said, "That would be great. So, what do I need to do?"

The oracle stated, "Okay now, please listen closely. We have little time. Take a journey toward Abzu. There, you will find in the deep, the waters of life. But remember no human from the surface of the earth can survive if he descends deep into Abzu."

Fardad said, "Then, how do I survive if no human can. You mentioned I am the chosen one, and is that why we will survive?"

Oracle said, "You are the chosen one, but you are still a mortal human being from earths surface. Listen closely. This is very important. Once you reach the pit of Abzu, you can track the holy spring of life and drink from it. You will become a being who diseases cannot kill, and poisons of any kind will be useless on your body. This is how you will survive. However, the holy waters cannot protect you from the betrayal and treachery of humans. You cant trust everyone, but you will know who to and who not to. Time will tell you that, so you dont need to worry so much. Dont consider yourself to be an eternal being. You will remain a mortal, and you will die like a mortal just like your father died like one."

Fardad said, "I never desired to be a god; I am fine, being a mortal. Who wants to live forever, anyway! However, I am very interested in knowing how I can save Persia?"

Oracle said, "You will save them, but for that, you need to take the sands of spring of life from Abzu...."

"Fardad...Fardad," Fardad heard someone calling him from behind. He turned, but there was no one.

He turned back and started listening to the old lady.

The old woman said many things to him, and he remembered some, and some went into his unconscious mind, and then the old woman said, "...Go, my Son. The fate of Persia is in your hands!! May the blessings of the Yazdan be with you!" The oracle explained, and her voice faded as she finished her sentence.

Suddenly, there was silence all around Fardad as his head was shaking, and his vision started blurring. The woman was no longer there. He was in a state of confusion and disbelief simultaneously. He didnt know what had happened, but he started walking and realized he was no longer in the cave. He found himself back in front of the motel where he and his friends stayed. He was standing on the street and saw that his two best friends, Gyasi and Ukund, had dozed off on the side walls. He thought they had probably drunk too much. Suddenly, everything around him turned dark, and he could see his eyes closing, and then there was nothing but complete and utter silence.

**

When Fardads eyes opened again, he saw he was back in his motel room on his bed. He was hoping to hear Gyasi say his favorite line, "Wake up, Sweet Prince," but all he could see was Gyasi and Ukund staring straight at him. It was late morning, and those deafening stares were right in his eyes. His friends werent in the mood for jokes, and it seemed like they wanted answers.

Ukund asked, "What happened to you last night?"

Fardad looked at him straight in the eyes and said, "I dont know what youre talking about!"

Ukund then said, "You must have some bad dream or an intuition. Well know soon enough as you were constantly mumbling the entire night, something about being the chosen one. What was that all about?"

"I must have seen some nightmare. You know that happens to me a lot, and I must have drunk a little too much." "We all took a little more than we can handle. The good thing is that you lived through it all. Do you even remember what you saw? Something that can help us?" Gyasi asked.

Fardad said, "Theres a lot that you need to know. Let me get ready, and I will brief you two. And I wish it was just the wine that had me talking so much. One of these days, I will lose it."

Ukund asked, "Take it easy, brother. Were here with you. And what are you going to lose?"

CHAPTER 8.   THE ENCOUNTER

Fardad replied, "Brother, I meant I am going to lose my mind, and thanks to you and Gyasi for keeping me sane. I dont know how much more of this I can take. Its taking a huge toll on me mentally. I could just go crazy one of these days had it not been for you all. Thankfully, our lady friends have not done bad themselves!" Ukund then said, "Freshen up and get ready. Well talk then. Next time, stay off the wine!"

Fardad then laughed it off, changed into his day clothes, and put on his gear. As he was changing, he thought about what had happened last night. An encounter with a strange being appeared in his dream as he went to some cave. He was still not sure. Maybe I hadnt slept well, and then my imagination went wild. But what if the meeting with Oracle was a genuine encounter?

"She called me chosen one," Fardad uttered while holding his head. His eyes were closed, and he was on the husk-filled leather bed.

"Who called you to choose one–the princess? " Ukund laughed, and Gyasi followed as both were giggling and looking at Fardad.

"Come on, guys. Be serious!" Fardad shouted.

"You were dreaming, man?" Ukund said.

"You will not understand," Fardad said and stood up.

"You wont believe me even if I tell you," he said further.

Gyasi and Ukund winked eyes and said, "Yeah, we know!"

Fardad smiled and jumped towards them to hit them, but they moved, and all burst into laughter.

"Come on; I am hungry!" Gyasi said.

"I need to look for someone who calls himself chosen one," Ukund said smilingly. "Lets see what princess and Rukhsaar are doing." I met with an older woman in my dream who advised me to go to Abzu, but why?

Fardad was struggling to recall what he saw in the dream. The conversation with the woman was so vividly recalled that he felt like he had met her in real life. Fardad was very confused, as he didnt know whether to trust his dream. She could just be the Ahrman in disguise, playing tricks on me and my mind. Anything was possible. Fardad was even worried if it was normal to see such visions in his dream or not.

He had not heard many having such profound visions and conversations with other strangers. The oracle seemed wise and safe, but could she be leading him and his friends into a trap? He wasnt so sure and was clueless about recalling the complete dream. He was hoping to make it back in one piece. It seemed like his journey was far from over, considering the latest revelation.

Once he got ready and geared up, he told his friends, "Gyasi and Ukund, we need to talk."

Ukund said, "Whats on your mind?"

Gyasi said, "Yes! I figure this is about that nightmare? You mentioned you will talk to us after youre ready."

CHAPTER 8.   THE ENCOUNTER

Fardad said, "Yes, I did, and its about that nightmare, or whatever you want to call it. I spoke to some lady known as the oracle, and she–"

Ukund cut in and said, "Hold on a minute there...are you sure you saw a beautiful maiden, and she called you the chosen one?" Ukund giggled.

"Yes, the old lady said so. I had a long conversation with her, but I recall only part of it? How do I know if this was real or a trick of Ahrman? " Fardad thought Ukund would explain, as he knew some things better than him.

Gyasi then chimed in, "My friend Fardad, we shouldnt waste any time. Lets talk to them so you can explain your dream, and we can decide our next course of action." Fardad went silent. He was a little confused.

Fardad then said, "I agree with Gyasi; lets speak with the girls."

At that very moment, there was a knock on the door. Gyasi went and opened the door. Rukhsaar entered the room, and she said, "The princess wishes to see you all downstairs. The motel has arranged some breakfast for us before we move forward. She also wants to discuss our next plan with you all. Please come downstairs so we can get moving."

The men promptly took their belongings and followed Rukhsaar down to the meal chamber. The chamber was reserved for them as it needed to be booked with the innkeeper ahead of time. Parinaaz and Rukhsaar had made the arrangements, so they all assembled there. It was posh because it seemed to cater to royal

172

guests from time to time, although the girls didnt reveal their identities to the motels management.

Parinaaz was waiting for everyone as they followed Rukhsaar down to the chamber. Parinaaz was all ready and geared up, and she had the table set with the food prepared to eat. It seemed like the breakfast of champions. A variety of meat and vegetable dishes all fit the Persian palette.

She said, "Thank you for joining us, gentlemen. I feel we should plan our next course of action right now. We are to move north. There may not be any danger lying ahead, but I urge you to stay on guard."

Gyasi then said, "With all due respect, we will follow your course, but theres something Fardad would like to tell you. He had an interesting dream in his sleep and discussed it with us, and I think you should give him a listen and decide what to do afterward."

Parinaaz kept a straight face as she loved hearing Fardad talk, but she had to maintain the impression that they were only friends and not lovers. She said, "Fardad, please tell us what you saw, and then we can decide what to do."

All eyes were now on Fardad as Parinaaz said, "Fardad, please tell us what you saw. Please speak."

"Fardad saw a lady in his dream," Gyasi cut in.

Parinaaz then quickly asked as if she was a little insecure too, "What lady? Who spoke to you?"

Interestingly, Gyasi mentioned the lady was old, so Parinaazs curiosity increased tenfold. There was worry all over her face, and it was as visible as day. However, she let Fardad finally speak, and no one would dare to cut in then.

"Let me explain what happened. There was an event that happened last night in my dreams. I saw an old lady in a nearby cave. I am not sure whether I was dreaming or sleepwalking. But I had a vivid dream of meeting a woman in a cave, and I went to her as she called me. She said to me that the Persia is in danger, and I need to go to Zagros Mountain to reach the pit of Abzu."

"Abzu," the princess said, looking quite surprised. She thought no one knew about the place, as it was now a legend. Very few people in Persia knew of its existence, and she remembered the stories told about that place by her father, King Kai Kobad. Just the fact that the lady mentioned this place made her grow suspicious of the oracles intentions. She had never thought that she would go there herself one day, but it seemed she would have to with the rest of her team. She continued, "Abzu is a long-lost legendary place. I heard from my father that it was utterly destroyed, and it doesnt even exist anymore, as per my knowledge. Are you sure shes speaking the truth and not fooling us? She could lead us into a trap, or it could be Ahrman doing this."

Fardad then replied, "Honestly, I am baffled about this dream and where to go. The honorable King Kai Kobad commanded me to go to the Temple of Fire at Lake Urmia in the north, whereas the Zagros Mountains are in the west."

"Please tell us exactly what you saw in the dream. I think if you take your dream seriously as earlier, you could get clues to solve the kings dream, " Ukund then cut in.

Fardad then said, "I remember some things she said, but then I forgot the later part of it. The rest I will leave up to you, Parinaaz."

Parinaaz then stated, "You have permission to speak. I want to know everything that this lady told you."

Fardad then explained the part of the dream conversation that he remembered to his friends.

The rest of them listened to every word of Fardad attentively as he recalled everything that was said between him and the woman. After a few minutes, Fardad had explained everything to his team.

"Now that you all have heard the story, please suggest what we do next. The older woman from the dream gave me the instructions that I go towards Zagros mountains, but Ill follow our Kings order and will go to the temple first."

Ukund did not believe the woman to be evil, as she seemed knowledgeable. She had her unique way of reaching out to the chosen ones, and Fardad was one of them. Gyasi seemed indifferent, as he had never heard of such dreams before, not even from his former masters. Similarly, Rukhsaar said a bit too loyal to the princess. She would follow her orders and guide her on the best route to their destinations. Ukund hoped the princess understood Fardad was speaking the truth.

"Its on the 5th of Espand, and we still have some

days before we reach back to the capital; I mean, the noble Zoroasters birthday is coming soon. I guess we can go to the temple and then Abzu, and by the festival day, we will be back in the capital," Ukund said.

Rukhsaar, the ever-quiet, then chimed in: "Yes, we have a mission at hand, and the honorable King Kai Kobad has commanded us to visit the High Priest Katir at the Urmia Temple first. I would suggest that we stay on course for that. He could guide us if we explain to him the quest given to Fardad in his dream. We all could benefit from the answers from someone who knows more than we do. Katir may have the answers we seek, so it could help us decide what to do. Also, maybe this dream thing is just a whimsical play of the night."

Ukund then said, "With all due respect, I am not stating at all that we change course. We must complete this mission, as the fate of the Persia hangs in the balance and is very much in our hands."

Fardad said, " Lets talk to the High Priest and see what he thinks about this matter."

After listening to everyone, the princess finally spoke, "Fardad, if we want to go to Abzu later, then we must make a move right away, so we can reach the Urmia Temple as fast as possible. If the world requires saving, then we will do the right thing. I would suggest that we all get our gear and horses ready. Rukhsaar, as usual, will guide us to the fastest route to the High Priests Temple. Lets get going, everyone. Time is running out, and we have to race against it." Everyone else nodded in the affirmative and went back to the rooms to gather all the gear and get ready to move. Fardad hoped they were doing the right thing. He didnt want to betray or leave his friends because he wanted to confirm everything in his revelation with someone equally knowledgeable as the oracle. The team started packing, and 30 minutes later, they had assembled outside the motel. Rukhsaar signaled everyone to follow her, and they were on the move. Fardad wanted to have a word with Parinaaz alone, but there was no time to waste, and he was hoping the two of them could speak later.

There was a lot on Fardads mind, as his dream conversation with the oracle had been enlightening. So much had happened, and perhaps he was prepared for this ultimate quest to save the world. There was one thing that Fardad didnt mention to his friends or Parinaaz. It was about the fact that he would be a future king with her being his queen. This was what he wanted to tell her, but he figured time would tell if this happened or not. If the oracle said it would, he would live through it all and eventually become the king with Princess Parinaaz as his queen.

For now, he just had to focus on following Parinaazs orders to get to the Urmia Temple and then Abzu. His work was just about to get started. He would take this opportunity to save the world because thats what his father would have wanted him to do so as well. He would not disappoint him; he kept telling himself as he rode along with his friends toward the

CHAPTER 8.   THE ENCOUNTER

Urmia Temple.

When they were about to leave, they noticed a man riding a horse approach him. The man looked familiar, and he had worn the attire of King Kai Kobads soldier. He stooped his horse near the heroes and bowing before Princess Parinaaz and Fardad, and he introduced himself. "Princess Parinaaz and Fardad, I am Shamsheer, one of the soldiers of King Kai Kobad. I have been ordered by His Highness to deliver this letter to you." After saying that, he handed a yellow piece of parchment to Fardad, who unrolled and read it aloud.

"Dear Fardad,

It is with great regret that I am informing you that your honorable mother, Kanisha, has fallen terribly sick and is under medical attention. She has been calling out your name since then. Therefore, you are ordered to return to Takht-e-Shah immediately.

Your King, Kai Kobad."

Chapter 9

The Temple

THE letter from King Kai Kobad had a profound effect on Fardad as he got overcome with anxiety and sadness. He was squeezing the scroll as a tear emerged across the side of his eye. He began to heave heavily and was about to jump on his horse to go back to the palace when the soft hand of Princess Parinaaz grabbed him quickly.

"Parinaaz, leave me! I need to rush; please leave my hand!"

He tried to break free, but the princess held onto it unceasingly.

"Fardad, listen to me! I understand that your mother is badly under the weather, but you must know one thing—"

"What, Princess!?"

"You forget that she is at the Takht-e-Shah. I can bet my life and say that Father would have placed her under the best care possible! Trust me on this!"

Fardad continued to break free from her grip, and

she eventually let go of it.

"Fine, go! If you do not trust me, then go!" she exclaimed. She turned her back towards him and folded her arms in annoyance. Fardad overcame his feelings of anxiety and began to think with a cool head. He placed his palm on Parinaazs shoulder and turned her towards him."

"Fardad, Princess Parinaaz is absolutely right. Your mother will be under the best care at the kings palace,"

Fardad overcame his uncontrollable feelings and was brought back to his senses. He moved towards Princess Parinaaz out of guilt.

"I trust you, Princess Parinaaz. Whatever you have said is bound to be true no matter what," he asserted, and she smiled widely. "I am sure my mother is taken care of at the palace of your noble father and my honorable king, Kai Kobad!"

Parinaaz nodded her head approvingly and turned to face the messenger named Shamsheer.

"Shamsheer!" she called, looking at him straight in the eyes, and the man bowed deeply.

"Yes, Princess Parinaaz."

"Kindly inform King Kai Kobad that we are all in fine and on top of our health, and we will be returning next week."

"Your order is my command, Princess Parinaaz," saying that he gave her another deep bow and climbing his horse, he galloped away.

In the interim, a slim figure donning azure robes with a veil stared at them from behind a tall tree;

her light green eyes narrowed in intense fury as she clutched her fists.

"You all got away from me then, but trust me on this... I will get to all of your throats, and very soon, you all will be begging me for mercy!" breathed Roxana with an evil glow in her eyes that had appeared in her eyes for the very first time.

Suddenly her eyes turned grim and saddened.

Its nothing personal, Fardad and Princess Parinaaz. I am merely trying to free myself from that bloody ruthless minister, Soroush. He has promised to set me free if I accomplish this task for him, she thought. My freedom matters the most to me. So even if I have to splatter my hands with someones blood in order to attain it, I wouldnt mind.

The fearsome five had resumed their journey and were on their way to the temple and had been traveling for good three days. They took some rest as their horses were tired; it was time to make one more stop before reaching their destination. It had been a long journey, even with breaks. The last stop was an interesting one in which Fardad went into a trance during his sleep, conversing with an old lady known as the oracle.

She stated he was the chosen one and had to go on a quest to save Persia and the world by throwing the sands of Abzu into the holy fire. All of this was overwhelming for him as he kept thinking about it. He just wanted to get over all of this and then enjoy a peaceful life with the love of his life, Princess Parinaaz, and his mother, Kanisha.

He leaned his back against a tree and closed his eyes, and soon, he slipped into a daydream. This time, there was no oracle or nightmare but the beautiful princess in his arms. Both of them were looking into each others lovelorn eyes. They then locked lips, investing their sensuality. One thing led to another, but then a voice woke Fardad up.

"Wake up, lover boy, its time to regroup and plan for our mission!"

The voice was of Gyasi, who had been tasked with getting everyone together for a quick meeting.

Fardad woke up with a groan and spent some minutes oscillating between reality and his dream. I wish that were true, Fardad thought while preparing to join others for a team meeting.

When all assembled, Princess Parinaaz addressed, "Were all going to rest here for some time and then plan to move ahead. The horses need to rest to be useful to us for the upcoming journey. You all can explore the area if you wish, but please dont venture too far off from here. Alright, I leave you all to whatever you want to do, and we shall meet here later in the evening."

The rest of the team nodded in agreement and then left the area in different directions to explore. The group split into smaller teams to explore, with Rukhsaar, Gyasi, and Ukund going hunting.

Ukund asked, "Fardad, would you like to go hunting with us?"

Fardad replied, "I have my prey to hunt if you know what I mean. You guys can carry on!"

Ukund then laughed and said, "I understand. Good luck with the hunt!"

Fardad walked up to Princess Parinaaz, who was slouching behind a tree. She looked up at him and smiled.

"My love, sit beside me. Finally, we have some time for ourselves. You do not know how hard it is to keep a straight face in front of all of them," said the princess. Fardad sat beside her and held her hand. He rubbed his hands against hers and felt the soft sensation of her skin. Both of them then looked into each others eyes and made sure no one was around. A few minutes later, they had their lips twined, kissing each other passionately. The adrenaline rush surged as they had covertly wanted this for the longest of time yet had pretended not to know each other in front of the others. Rukhsaar was unaware of Parinaazs feelings for Fardad, but his two friends knew the blazing passion. These two lovers knew nothing mattered more to them than each other. They had chosen each other and would do anything to protect their love.

Soon they heard voices and realized that their friends were returning to their camp. Fardad and Parinaaz got up and walked toward their friends and saw that they had hunted a deer and were getting ready to cook it.

Fardad asked Parinaaz, "Do you need anything, my love?"

She replied, "Yes, I do!"

CHAPTER 9.   THE TEMPLE

"Oh! What can I get for you?"

"All I want is you…and yes, I could do with a bath!" Parinaaz expressed, and Fardad couldnt help but notice a twinkle in her eyes.

"Where would you bathe, my princess?" came the response in a husky voice.

"I would like to take a bath in Lake Urmia before we enter the temple, but I will only take a dip in the lake until its made fragrant with roses." "This must be the secret of your beauty." Fardad tried to be candid and lighthearted with the princess.

Both of them had given their hearts to each other and knew that their happiness belonged in each others presence. For the sake of the mission, they had to keep their relationship a secret because their enemies could use that to harm them. They would tell everyone after the mission ended and make it all official. It would be a shock and surprise for everyone, but they knew they couldnt keep this a secret for too long.

The princess turned toward him and said, "Fardad, I must tell you Ive been sought after by so many princes, but my heart only beats for you! These were some of the finest men in Persia, but you just stood out from the rest."

Fardad then looked straight into her eyes and said, "Why is that so, dearest princess?"

She matched her gaze with his and said, "Why? Do you want to know? Its because I like men of taste, and youve got it in spades!"

Fardad then asked her lady love, "So, my dearest

princess, do you like flowers? I ask you because you are the flower of my life!"

Parinaaz smiled and said, "I love them. Therefore, I spend time in the palace gardens every evening, surrounding myself with them. I love the aroma, and theyre the most beautiful thing Ive ever seen in my life."

Fardad then said, "Nothing can ever be as beautiful as you. You are the most beautiful flower in the world."

"So, why dont you do something for me?"

"What is it you ask of me, my love!"

"I would like you to find a flower in the jungle that is as beautiful as I am. Can you do that?"

Fardad grew startled as that would be quite a challenge but replied, "Your wish is my command, dearest princess!"

With that, he bade farewell by sending her a quick flying kiss and left for the jungle to look for flowers. He would do whatever it took to make her happy, so he took on this challenge. He did not want to tell Gyasi and Ukund about it because they were too busy cooking the deer with Rukhsaar. He loved the princess so much that he would go to the ends of the jungle to find the flowers.

Ukund, Gyasi, and Rukhsaar were cooking, and it was evening time. The birds were singing, and the winds were blowing. It was supposed to be a cold season, but apparently, the weather in that region was pleasant.

CHAPTER 9.   THE TEMPLE

Searching throughout the jungle, Fardad went deep into the forest, and apparently, he reached the spot where multicolored flowers were present all around. The fragrance was simply mesmerizing. Roses, jasmines, lilies, and lavenders were all growing there. It was a delightful engagement for the sight and senses. He didnt want to spend too much time in the jungle, as the rest of them were waiting for him for dinner.

After gathering many flowers, Fardad returned to the camp. He couldnt wait to give these flowers to the princess and kept thinking about her the entire way back. He imagined her smiling when she saw them and giving him a warm embrace and a peck on the cheek.

In a matter of time, he arrived back at the camp but was shocked and surprised to see the campsite completely barren. He thought his friends were playing some joke on him and that this wasnt the time for such pranks. He was also starving and wanted to have a bite of that deer. However, all of that vanished when he saw that none of his team were there, including the princess, Rukhsaar, Gyasi, and Ukund.

Interestingly, the food was still cooking in the pot. He called out their names but could hear no response. He went all over the campsite and shouted their names in different directions, but nothing came of that exercise. He then observed the ground and saw that there were plenty of footsteps. This showed an ambush, and the enemies had attacked his friends. He kept wondering what went wrong, as this was supposed to be a safe campsite.

"Oh! It looks like something happened here," Fardad uttered.

Fardad also noticed that the horses were also missing. Have they gone somewhere? he thought.

Maybe they went looking for him and had not been captured. But it could also be an ambush. He waited for some time to see if any of his friends showed up. After a couple of hours, he realized something was seriously wrong. He concluded the situation was not as simple. They had gone nowhere but had been captured. Learning all of this, he started feeling lightheaded. He again called upon the names, but the sound echoed back to him. There was no one around but just the sound of the leaves moving in the wind. The food had been cooked, and he was famished. He took a few bites because he needed the energy. He had to look for his friends, and it could take some time before he found them. He ate as much as he could of the deer until his stomach felt full. He then kept some food with him in his bag to keep him energized on the way.

Fardad started walking and analyzing the ground. After spending some time, he figured that some horses had gone up north toward Lake Urmia. He decided that this was the direction he was supposed to go anyway and headed there. Hopefully, hed find out what happened to his friends. The journey was long, so Fardad would run and sometimes walk. He drew his sword out as if he was expecting an attack. This was after he heard some noises. He felt he was being watched, but he shouted some names. But couldnt see or hear anything. He had come a long way from where he had initially camped with his friends.

After walking for some hours, he realized he had taken the food with him but had forgotten to take the water. He started cursing himself for why he went to find the flowers so soon. He could have stayed back and located those flowers with his team on the journey to Lake Urmia. He was way too much in love with the princess and had focused on that over the mission at hand. He had grown exhausted and wanted to rest, but the mystery of his friends disappearances was troubling him. He was sweating like a dog, and it was already very dark when he saw a dimly lit house. He asked himself whether he should see who was inside. Perhaps he could ask to rest for some time before moving further. He saw who was inside because he had nothing to lose. His friends were gone, and he was super thirsty. At least he could ask for some water and hydrate himself before. Fardad knocked at the door and waited patiently to see who lived there.

After a few minutes, an old man opened the door and asked, "I dont get many visitors around here, traveler. I like my solitude and dont like to be disturbed. What is it you want?"

The older man looked up and down at Fardad and saw that he was wearing royal gear and had a sword in his hand. He then became nervous, panicked, and ran inside. "Dont kill me, please. I am a harmless hermit living in the jungle, and come in peace!" the old man shouted.

"I will not kill you; I need your help. Please let me stay with you for some time. My friends have disappeared, and I am looking for them. I will keep my sword in its sheath, so you know I wont hurt you," Fardad said.

There was a sign of relief on the face of an older man. He was thinking it was some bandit wanting to steal from him. He rarely had visitors, and it had been a long time since he dealt with a bandit. He lived humbly and was fine with limited resources, and he had nothing to look forward to in life but peace.

"What you want? How can I help at this hour? I am very poor, and I have nothing to share with you, soldier. I can see that you belong to the royal guard with your sword and gear. I dont get a lot of visitors at all, and this is an anomaly for me, especially right now," the old man said.

"I apologize, but I come in peace. I dont mean any harm, but I just have a simple request for you if you would help this weary soldier in front of you." "Speak, Soldier. What do you want me to do for you? I really cant do much, honestly, as you can see. I will try to help the best I can," the old man answered. "I just need water and a place to sleep tonight. I have traveled for hours without rest, looking for my friends. Its late, and I require food, rest, and water to gain enough energy to move ahead with my mission. I will highly appreciate it if you can help me," Fardad said.

CHAPTER 9.   THE TEMPLE

"You may come in. Youve made your argument, and I wouldnt want to turn you away. It would be great if you could sleep on the floor down there. I will get you some water. This is the best I could do for you. You look really tired, so best if you should rest."

Fardad nodded in agreement and went inside. He unloaded his gear and lay down at the place where the older man had pointed him to. By that time, the older man had come with a cup of water and gave it to Fardad. Fardad took the cup and thanked him. The older man went off to sleep, and a few minutes later, Fardad slept. He didnt see any dreams this time around, but only a lot of haze. He would see images of his mother a few times, but nothing else. He didnt see his friends or Princess Parinaaz. He was too tired, so perhaps his subconscious couldnt think of anything.

Fardad woke up bright and early and saw that there was still time in the sunrise. He was feeling anxious and worried about his friends and the princess. He saw that the older man was up and praying. He went to the older man and greeted him.

"I hope you rested well, Stranger. You seemed exhausted, so I just wanted you to sleep. Heck, I dont even know your name. You mentioned looking for some friends. I wanted to ask you whether you were also heading toward the Urmia temple. So many pilgrims go there, but no one ever stops by here. I dont bother anyone, as I dont want any trouble. I like my solitude and prefer to stay that way," the old man stated.

Fardad then said, "My names Fardad, and I was on my way to the Temple of Fire, the one you call the Urmia Temple. If you can guide me there, that will help. I have a strong feeling that my friends are there. I also dont know your name, my friend. I am not sure if we will ever cross paths, but Id like to thank you by your name for helping me."

The older man had figured that Fardad was heading to the temple and was lost.

The old man said, "You may be a soldier, but I consider you a pilgrim, Fardad. I always assist those who are searching for our temple. These are the only ones who come here knocking on my door, but I rarely get them anymore. I shall guide you when youre ready to head out. By the way, my name is Farishta."

"Farishta, thank you so much for hosting me. Your hospitality is highly appreciated, and I shall let the honorable King Kai Kobad know you helped one of his men. I wanted to know if you noticed anything unusual yesterday? If you remember, I mentioned I was looking for my friends." "Yes, I remember you mentioned something about looking for your friends and being lost. That being said, you were the most unusual thing I saw yesterday, hahaha," Farishta laughed.

"However, before you arrived, I heard many horses galloping to the north toward the direction of the temple. When I came out of my house to see who they were, I could only see their backs. I suppose there were around 25 men, and I figured they were just pilgrims, and I am not sure if that included your friends,"

CHAPTER 9.   THE TEMPLE

Farishta continued.

After hearing this, his worst fears were confirmed. This could only be his friends, but they werent alone. They were captives of bandits or had been ambushed by some hostile people. Whoever these were, Fardad was now more sure than ever that his friends had been kidnapped. He knew now what he had to do to save them. He had to head in the same direction because who knew what these captors would do with his friends.

Fardad asked Farishta, "My friend Farishta, youre a very kind man. Your name means angel, and you surely are one for me. I was wondering if I can borrow a horse, and I dont see any, but if you do, that will help me travel the long distance toward the temple."

Farishta sighed and replied, "I am very sorry. I dont get out that much, and for that, a horse would be useless to me. I just have a donkey, and I cant let it wander off beyond this house. He will be too slow for you to use, so there is no point in letting you take it. It will only slow you down. I can do this much for you. I can escort you further until you get the clear direction to the temple. You would have to travel on foot, and I would go on my trusty steed. I am not a miser, but I cant risk going too far off. He may panic and run off elsewhere. I hope you understand. I am no angel, but I just try to be a good man. My father gave me this name, and hes long gone now. Its just a name and nothing else. I wish I were an angel who could help you more, but as you know, I am a mere mortal and can only do so much. We have little time to waste. If you want to catch up with your friends and captors, we need to move now. Get your gear ready, and well head out now." Fardad nodded in agreement as he understood why this man known as Farishta had no horse and he had only one donkey, which he did not want to give to Fardad. Fardad realized Farishta was not a miser but as helpful as he could. He knew that the very skinny donkey would be unsuitable for the rest of the journey and too slow. Therefore, it would just be better to walk on foot.

Farishta sat on the donkey, and Fardad followed him by walking to the side. Farishta gave many marks and signs for the travel and then advised Fardad to go further on foot.

"Fardad, may you find your friends and whatever else youre looking for at the temple. I hope they are safe and sound. I wish I could join you, but I will be of no help to you. Please follow the path ahead as I have guided you, and you should get to the temple. I am not sure if we will ever cross paths again, but know that you and your friends are always welcome to stay at my house if you ever come by this way again. I must take my leave, and you need to get moving. Farewell, soldier, and may the blessings of the Yazdan be with you," Farishta said.

"Thank you so much, once again, for your hospitality, and I will indeed look you up when I come around here again. If you ever find yourself by the capital, you know youre always welcome to stay at the

CHAPTER 9.   THE TEMPLE

palace. I will make my way, and may the blessings of the Yazdan be with you too," Fardad said. After they bid farewell, Fardad moved on foot toward the temple. After walking a few minutes, the terrain became uphill and turned into rock and stones. Fardad was expecting a mountain to come, but he found an immense lake when he reached the top of the rock.

The color of the lake was red. Fardads eyes were searching for the temple, and he then said to himself, "Ive been here before...nay, its just dj vu! Oh, I saw it in my dream. I just hope it doesnt turn into a nightmare. I wonder where everyone is."

The Urmia Fire Temple stood in front of Fardad in all its glory. It was a grand and majestic temple that mesmerized Fardad, and he thanked Yazdan that his dream did come true and ran toward the temple, hoping to find his friends, their captors.

He saw the huge fire in the middle burning and the surrounding priests as he approached the temple. Their mantras and chants were loud but unclear. Fardad tried to locate his friends but could not see them among the priests. He wanted to show respect to the prayer ritual and only speak once it was over. Fardad then said, "My Dear Priests, please lend me a year. I am the royal minister, Fardad, the son of Aardburzin. The honorable King Kai Kobad sent me here to speak with the high priest, Katir. Here are the orders of King..."

"I am Katir," an old man, wearing a white robe, cut in, speaking with a soft voice. He looked very much like a priest. Katir was an old, religious, and knowledgeable priest who lived at the Temple of Fire near Lake Urmia. Tales of his wisdom were well known throughout the lands of Persia. He sported a long beard and wore white clerical clothing. He was a truthful man who believed that people could change for good.

Fardad, as per the orders of the king, took out the Farman in the metal case which was in his belt. Katir then read it loudly, and all priests bowed to the royal minister, Fardad. The king ordered, "We are in imminent danger. Aardburzin, the astrologer, had found something unusual. We need to help this man, Fardad, look for the answers in the book of Aardburzin. Your cooperation will be highly appreciated, as the future of our kingdom and the world is at stake. Please help us in this hour of need, and we will forever be grateful."

High Priest Katir then asked, "Where is the book of Aardburzin? I would like to see it."

Fardad realized he didnt have the book with him, but they were with Ukund and the others, so he said, "Its with my friends, and I have lost them. I do not know where they are, but I know they came this way with or without their captors. A man known as Farishta told me he saw 25 men come this way. I assume my friends were among them. Princess Parinaaz, the daughter of the honorable King Kai Kobad, was among them, along with Rukhsaar, her assistant. The other two were my friends Gyasi and Ukund."

CHAPTER 9.   THE TEMPLE

Fardad narrated to the priest how he lost the princess and his friends. Katir responded, "Brother Farhad, our temple is open to everyone. We do not stop the wicked, as they could be here for repentance. Yesterday, the general Nabuzardan had come in here. You had mentioned 25 men. People come here all the time, and our doors are always open."

Fardad had never heard this name before, so he asked, "Who is this man, Nabuzardan? I have never heard of him. Did he come with some captives or soldiers?" "He is the general of King Marduk. He told us he was on a peaceful mission and passed through. He said nothing more than this, so I cant help you with any other information," Katir said.

"Was it peaceful or kidnapping? His men may have my friends as captives! I must find them!" Fardad said with utmost urgency. "I dont understand what benefit they will get in kidnapping the princess and my friends? I came all this way to find them and see your advice in saving our kingdom and the world!"

"I am sorry that I have little else to tell you. Once we find your fathers book, I can guide you further. I am are not aware of Nabuzardans intentions, so I cant speak ill of him. I believe that the most wicked can seek repentance and change, and I help them get there. I would suggest you get some rest. My fellow priests will get you some food and drink, and meanwhile, I will find out whatever I can about the whereabouts of your friends. I have high respect for your honorable King Kai Kobad, and if he has intended me to help you, so I will," Katir answered.

With that, Katir left, and Fardad stood there even more confused. He kept praying for the safety of his friends. His mission was far from over.

Chapter 10

The Dark Forest

FARDAD sat down and figured out how to move ahead. He started wondering whether all that oracle said was true. He was the chosen one, and the prophecy seemed to come true. He had been left behind while his friends were captured and taken away somewhere, and the priests had done all they could to help him. He was deeply worried about his dearest Princess Parinaaz and constantly prayed to the Yazdan for her safe return. Tears fell from his eyes, and he knows not when he drifted into sleep as visions came in front of him.

Suddenly, a vision depicting the princesss face called out to him. "Fardad, Fardad, I am calling you. . .."

Fardad thought the princess reached out to him via telepathy, but he saw a familiar face as he moved closer.

"Its me, the oracle. Fardad, listen to me."

"Huh, what! Where are you speaking from?"

"Only you can see me and talk to me through the

vision. I told you I would always be with you and call upon you when needed. You are not alone in this cause, and we will work together to save the world!"

"I think before saving the world, we should save my friends. Theyre in grave danger... I can sense it. Can you show me where you are?"

"I will not show you the way. You will know because youre the chosen one. All I can tell you is that youre in the right place and you will find the way to your friends. They are in peril, but they will be safe until you meet them. I would advise you to look for them and get them on your side and then continue with your mission."

"I have met the High Priest Katir, but we need the book of Aardburzin that my friend Ukund has. It will help us in our cause." "Fardad, dont forget that youre the chosen one, after all. You will find your friends and bring them to safety, and you know what to do because I have shown you the path to salvation."

"Oracle, I need to make sure my friends are safe, and then I will follow through with the mission. I understand that the mission is a priority, but my friends lives need to be protected, and theyre counting on me to save them."

"Fardad, my dear, dont you worry about your friends. They are safe and sound, and Yazdan will protect them. If you dont find them, they will find you. Just go on the path that you are going on, and you will reunite with your friends."

"I will take your word for it then, Oracle. Who are

their captors?"

"Fardad, the answers you seek will reveal themselves in due course. Till we meet again, just follow the path...follow the path...chosen one...."

"Oracle...wait, wait!"

Fardad called out to the oracle as she faded into oblivion, and he came out of his sleep. He kept wondering whether she would call him out again. This was quite unbelievable for Fardad, as he had never experienced such an out-of-body experience other than the last dream meeting with the oracle. He was glad to know that his friends were safe, at least.

Fardad talked to the priests to secure a horse to rescue his friends from their captors. Meanwhile, Fardads friends were all shackled and taken on foot by their captors. Princess Parinaaz, her assistant Rukhsaar, Gyasi, and Ukund were all wondering what was happening; they couldnt help but fidget with the thoughts that lingered in their heads.

Ukund was worried about his friend Fardad and that he was by himself and very vulnerable. Fardad might be in colossal danger because he had no backup, which concerned Ukund. Oh God, Fardad does not know where we are, so he could be lost. If there were a way to let him know, I would do so.

Gyasi was also anxious about Fardad. They were ambushed by their captors and taken by surprise. Overpowered and surrounded, they had to surrender. The soldiers had crept behind them with their swords on their necks. Gyasi and Ukund couldnt defend themselves or employ measures, as they had been trained earlier for a good reason. Princess Parinaaz and Rukhsaar had swords on their necks, and the soldiers warned they wouldnt hesitate to proceed if Gyasi and Ukund tried doing anything evasive. The captors general said, "One move, and you know whats next. Dont provoke me because I dont like to repeat myself!"

The saviors had no choice but to surrender and give up their freedom. Soon, they were all tied up and moving along with their captors.

They had all been gagged for some time until Princess Parinaaz tried to move her mouth outside the gag and scream, "Take these off, you Bastards! You cant treat us like this! Were from the Persian capital, and my father is honorable King Kai Kobad. Treat us with respect, and take this stupid thing (gag) off us! Let us breathe!" The general leading the soldiers ordered them to take the gags off, after which Princess Parinaaz spit at their faces. They got upset and attempted to hit the Princess, but the General warned. "Not her, men, not her; she is our special prize, so we need to make sure shes unharmed and in one piece." Princess Parinaaz saw if she could loosen the ropes, but they all were tightly tethered together.

"Let us go, you slimy bastards. Is this any way to treat a princess and her friends?" Rukhsaar was shouting at her captors.

"Friends? You call these donkeys your friends?" one of them remarked.

"Call them what you want. Theyre still more civilized than you!" the princess fired back!

"Hahahaha. We will use this black donkey for our fields, and for sure, he will come in handy! Once we get back, well put him to work right away!" One man pointed toward Gyasi and laughed.

Gyasi, Ukund, Princess Parinaaz, and Rukhsaars hands were tied on their back. There was nothing they could do, and they hoped Fardad could rescue them. However, as circumstances dictated, they knew he would be outnumbered. They had to get free to get even against the odds, so each of them was wondering how they could get free. They had to make sure they did it sooner than later.

Gyasi and Ukund were blowing air in anger through their nostrils. They didnt like being treated like slaves and being tied and forced to walk in a particular direction.

Gyasi was used to being treated like dirt when he was a slave before and didnt want to relive that life. He was dreading this the whole time in captivity. He kept trying to signal the others to see if there was a way to get free.

One man tried to kiss Rukhsaar, compelling her to spit on his face. Rukhsaar was a no-nonsense lady who would return a kick if given the slightest chance. She had no problems fighting men and took them out with ease. She had sworn to honorable King Kai Kobad to protect his daughter from all harm and give her life for the princess. "What do you want? Why have you kidnapped us? This is no way to treat royalty! If my father, honorable King Kai Kobad, found out, he will send an army after you and feed you to the dogs."

General Nabuzardan then laughingly said: "Princess Parinaaz, please be calm. King Marduk is waiting for your arrival. It will take us around seven days to cross these lands and enter ours. Until then, we have to tolerate each other. You should stay quiet; the journey will be very peaceful; otherwise, I will slice your friends heads one by one and will throw them to the wolves. I can do even worse, and youd better not tempt me. If you try anything else, I will make sure they face the worst torture ever. You see, when you refused the kings offer, he took you in by force because he doesnt like taking no for an answer."

"I dont marry wicked magicians, and you do not know what youre setting yourself up for. The general, my father, will make an example out of you by beheading you in front of the entire kingdom for harming his daughter and friends. These are my friends, my allies, and if you even lay a hand on them, I will make you pay dearly for this. Mark my words. My father knew Marduk very well, and he knew your king was a dishonorable man. There is no way he would ever let the union of the kingdoms take place. I already have a prince in mind, and he is better than your king can ever be. He is coming for you and will take you all out¡' The fire was eminent in the princesss eyes.

Gyasi murmured, "I hope Fardad finds us before we cross the border. We need to find an escape route quickly because the further we get away from here, the harder it will be for him to find us and fall back."

Ukund muttered, "Whats she talking about? Who is this prince? Is this prince our Fardad? And why dont I know about this?"

Gyasi replied in a faint voice, "My Friend, you do not know, and we have a lot of catching up to do. For now, figure out how we can get free so that we can reunite with Fardad."

Ukund whispered, "Watch out for this lady, Rukhsar. Shes quite aggressive and has a lot of tricks up her sleeves and in her bag. So, we can count on her to initiate a distraction."

Right there and then, the general asked for one of his men to check the bags of their captives.

One man promptly obliged and started the search. He then found something interesting and said, "Sire, look what I found here! It looks like they love to play with balls." He laughed with his yellow teeth.

Rukhsaars eyes lit up because she knew exactly what they were talking about. "These are the bombs that will light up your asses, assholes," Rukhsaar murmured. One man started jiggling with Rukhsaars weaponry, thinking they played balls, and he did not know that he was playing with fire.

Rukhsaar gesticulated to the princess, Ukund, and Gyasi that the bomb could explode any moment. Ukund then winked at Gyasi as he knew what would happen next: they were about to get free.

And then the same thing happened; a bomb exploded, which created commotion and nervousness among

CHAPTER 10.   THE DARK FOREST

General Nabuzardans men. The juggling man dropped all the bombs and was turned into flesh pieces. Everyones face turned bloody at that very instant, and there was panic and chaos everywhere.

The bombs created a cloud of dust, and nothing remained visible to the soldiers.

Luckily Gyasi, Ukund, Princess, Rukhsaar were safe, and they all ran together toward the dark forest. Rukhsaar led the way and shouted at them to get away from the soldiers as far as possible. They needed an escape and found it. They wanted to get away from the soldiers to figure out how to get hold of their friend Fardad. They ran for their lives because the soldiers could catch up once the smoke was clear. Therefore, the further they were, the better for them.

After running for a while, they found themselves in a deep jungle full of flora and fauna. Although it was noontime inside the jungle, it looked like sunset or sunrise. There was silence everywhere except for birds chirping and frogs croaking; finally, the air offered some peace.

Rukhsaar, Ukund, and Gyasi looked at each other with baffled faces. They finally had gotten away from danger.

Rukhsaar used a sharp bark of a tree and cut her hand ropes; then, she quickly untied everyone. Everyone relaxed; they were free but were still concerned about Fardad. Their friend was now on his own and did not know where to go. Still, they were hopeful.

"Thank God for the relief. I started wondering

what had happened. Those bombs sent shockwaves to our captors! What was his obsession with you, dear Princess? Why was he so hellbent on taking you and making mincemeat out of us!" said Gyasi.

"King Marduk of Babylon wanted to marry me, but my father and I didnt like the proposal, and thats why Marduk no longer likes us and wanted to destroy Persia. He has made it his lifes mission, so he must have gotten word that were in the jungle and sent his men to capture us. They were smart enough to take us by surprise. Thanks to my able and handy assistant Rukhsaar, were free. Now we need to locate Fardad because he is lost and has no clue where we are, and he could fall into the same trap we did," the princess said.

Rukhsaar then spoke. "Dont worry about those men. Theyre barely a few men now. I took care of most of those bastards. How dare they even place their hand on me and try to take the princess and me out! They had to pay, and they did with their lives. Were stronger, and theyre weaker. Next time, well surprise them. And dont you worry about Fardad. Hell figure out where we are through the horses hooves and our footsteps. We will catch up with him soon. I suggest we lie low for a while because those idiots and their general will come this way to look for us. We will set a trap so that Fardad is unharmed.

Lets find a place to hide within these bushes so we can keep a lookout. Everyone stay quiet! I will lay a trap for our guests; they will run straight into these mines and explode on contact. So, be careful. Stay out of sight!"

Gyasi said, "Well need to stick together. We cant split up. Lets hide in one place and keep our eyes open. If one of us is spotted, then our trap will be spoiled." Ukund added, "If those bastards lay a hand on Fardad, I will strike them all down one by one, and there will be hell to pay. Fardad, my friend, I hope youre safe." Princess Parinaaz then spoke, "Guys, relax. Rukhsaar is setting a very nice trap for our enemies. We need to calm down and take it easy for a bit. First, we will hide under those bushes there, and each of us will take turns looking out for our enemies. If any of you spots Fardad, secure him so we can be reunited and be on our way. He could come this way, and we need to wait for him."

"The princess is right. Lets get situated and keep our eyes and ears open. Fardad, my brother, may the Yazdan keep you safe!" Ukund responded with his eyes set on the sky.

All of them assembled and in the nearby bush. They kept watch every 15 minutes and awaited the surviving soldiers.

Meanwhile, the general was fuming at his men who were in terrible shape or wounded. The ones injured could still stay on their feet. The rest of them were in so much pain that they couldnt move their legs. They were on the ground and scathing in pain.

"Bloody rascals, you cannot work in the army...curse the day when I selected you for this mission. We had them, and thanks to you playing with those balls, theyve escaped our clutches! I have always warned you all about training. Never underestimate our captives or our enemies. They have many tricks up their sleeves. That ladys bag of tricks did painstaking work for all of us. Now we need to catch up to them, or were going to die at the hands of our leaders!" General Nabuzardan shouted.

One man then said, "General, we did not know...they looked like harmless balls. I thought they were food..."

"King Marduk will make you suffer, you assholes! Do you have any idea what you did? You let the princess escape, and we needed her alive to be transported to our king. Now, shes escaped with her friends, and you guys are in terrible shape. How can we even be a match for them? I must warn you. Knowing that lady who tricked us, she will do it again. We must tread carefully, moving ahead!" General Nabuzardan shouted some more.

He was walking here, and there was a frenzy, waiting for his men to gather. He looked at some of the fallen men and told them, "You weaklings will not join us, and I dont care what happens to you!"

One of the fallen men said, "Master, please have mercy on all of us. We have served you well, and you cant just leave us here...."

"All of you, listen to me. These men deserve to stay here. We dont need excess baggage. Leave the wounded for the wolves. You all may have served us well, but we dont need you anymore. How can you help us now? You got what you deserved. I would love to take all of you out right now, but you deserve a slow and painful death. I wont make it easy on you. You are of no good to us. Why should we even spare you? Now, you all better not screw up because I am more than enough to handle those people on my own! I will not spare either of you if you mess up just this much!" General Nabuzardan ordered mercilessly.

Those still alive but unable to stand or walk were crying for mercy, but General Nabuzardan took his surviving men and entered the deep forest to pursue the princess. "How do we trace them here? Seriously, they could be anywhere. So, we should split up to save time. How about we all meet back here after an hour?" one man asked. "Shut up, you skunk! I am the one giving orders around here. How dare you speak to me? You dont want to be with us; you can go off looking for them but dont even think of returning to us. When youre gone, youre gone! Whoever wants to come with me, come with me or never show your face again!" General Nabuzardan growled. "We must capture the princess and present her to the king. We cant take any chances. You soldier better are at your best, or youll be dead meat!" the general continued.

"Our pride and reputation are at stake. You all better scatter around and search for our lost captives. Listen to me once and for all. We need to get hold of that princess. You better take this seriously. She could be anywhere with her friends, so watch out for the traps!" the general was continuously barking orders.

One man asked, "Where could she be, General?"

The general barked further, "Now, youre making me angry with all these stupid questions. Just follow my lead, and well find her in the jungle. She couldnt be too far off now. Does anyone have anything to say, or do we move ahead? Speak now, or remain silent forever!" One man said, "Sire, please allow me to say something!"

The general gave a slight nod.

"She was talking about some prince, some man named Fardad. We can use him as bait to lure her in when we find him, and hes looking for them too." "Finally, one of you made sense. If we find that man, we will capture him and trap him. Lets hope we get to him before they do. Follow me!" the general appreciated the idea offered to him.

The general quickly entered the forest; it was so dense that horses could not gallop. Thanks to the bombs blasting in their faces, the soldiers were a bit shaken up and were all concerned about their fates. Adding to that, they were exhausted and wanted to go home. They didnt want to go into battle as the exploding bombs wounded them.

The general realized it would not be easy to move with the horses. So he asked all the men to leave the horses behind and walk through the jungle.

"Sire, they could be snakes and alligators. Are you sure we should go on foot? We will be eaten alive before we find them!" one man said.

"The choice is yours. You can either die here or

come with me! The horses stay here. We cant move with them, and well easily be spotted. Well have to search for them on foot. They will not know that we abandoned our horses, and they will not be expecting us on foot," the general said after drawing his sword.

He had only six men left, and he had asked them to search for four.

"The princesss assistant, the black guy, and that stupid looking guy, these three must die, and only the princess will be made captive for now. We cant take all of them with us. We need just the princess, or the king will have our heads! You better keep your eyes and ears open because they could still spot us on foot!" the general ordered.

***

In the meantime, the messenger named Shamsher returned to the Takht-e-Shah and rushed to the grand hall where the king was seated on his royal throne that was raised above the ground along with Queen Anahita while Soroush was lying on the couch below. At the sight of the messenger, King Kai Kobad got onto his feet instantly and demanded, "Shamsheer, what news have you got?"

"Your Highness!" he greeted with a deep bow. "Princess Parinaaz and her friends are all safe and sound and in good health. Princess Parinaaz has sent a message that they will finish the mission soon and return to the palace.

"And what about the letter that I handed to you?" King Kai Kobad demanded sharply as he eyed him.

The messenger paused out of nervousness and said, "My king, as you ordered, I handed the scroll to Minister Fardad, and he was ready to return, but..." he paused out of fear.

"But what, Shamsheer?" Soroush asked fearfully.

"But Princess Parinaaz intervened and dissuaded him from returning to the palace."

"What!" the king shouted angrily and banged his fist against the handle of his thrown.

There was a brief pause as the king and queen looked at each other and whispered, which Soroush couldnt hear.

"You can go, Shamsheer," he commanded, and the messenger left with another bow.

A massive bubble of fear crept into Soroushs heart. He began to shiver instantly, and his eyes widened. What will happen now? If they reach the temple, it will be catastrophic! And that darned stupid girl Roxana hasnt sent a message through one of her idiotic pigeons to me either! Could it be that she is dead? Just as these thoughts began to haunt him, he thought of turning this incident into an opportunity by adding fuel to the fire.

"See, my Dear King! I told you that man Fardad cannot be trusted. He has already placed our innocent Princess Parinaaz under his evil influence! Before its too late, we may face regret in any form in the near future. I strongly suggest that we take action!

Otherwise, that Fardad will harm our lovely princess!"
"Soroush!" King Kai Kobad called and raised his hand into the air to stop him from speaking.

"I have heard enough!"

"Didnt you hear the messenger say that the Princess is completely fine and in the best of health?"

"Yes, your highness, but–"

"Enough said!" King Kai Kobad cut him immediately. "I trust Fardad completely; he is a nobleman who will never betray someones trust. I have seen in his eyes, and my eyes cannot deceive me.

"So I strongly suggest you stop doubting him and filling my mind with preposterous doubts," Soroush nodded curtly, and with a quick bow, he left for his chamber.

***

While Fardads friends had made their escape as fugitives from the general and his men, Fardad wanted to catch up to them, unaware that they had escaped. Wasting no time, Fardad asked priests where King Marduks men went. Fardad then borrowed a horse, took some water and food with him, and went in the direction shown by the priests.

He was galloping his horse and then slowed down because of strategic reasons and jumped from his horse when he reached the bushes. He entered the bushes and tried to listen to any voices of people in the area. He thought it was his friends, as there were sounds of crying and agonizing. Fardad saw many people lying around, wounded and asking for water and mercy. Some were cursing each other, or some were cursing a man named Nabuzardan.

Fardad quickly went to them and started pouring water from his sack into the mouth of dying men.

He asked, "What happened to you? Who did that? Are my friends alive?"

"Its your curse," one man said. "We took your friends and girl with us to present to the king, and the unaware general left us here in the wilderness for dying. Please help us, and we will help you find your friends!"

"Which general? Where did they go?" Fardad asked.

"Nabuzardan, the general of King Marduk!" one man said.

"You rascals! You saw what Yazdan did with you? Now, youre paying the price! Where is Princess Parinaaz?" Fardad shouted.

"Where are my friends? What did you do with them? If theres even a scratch on them, I will slay you without mercy. You all deserve to die a cruel death!" Fardad continued.

One man said, "Were already dying...w-what more can you do to us? Do you...do you think we can move at all? We are...ugh...." The man attempted to suppress his squeals. "We are going to lie here until death...death it takes us all. They were four in all. One black man was among them, and there were two women. One of them was the princess...the girl we came to capture. The general and his five men have gone on foot to find your friends. Your friends could hide somewhere, and if I know better...I know better...setting up a trap for the general and his men. That lady Rukhsaar, the bombs lady, is one of her kind."

The man engaged in involuntary coughing, and when he was done, he continued, "We did not know she was hiding explosives! Our Master has left us here, and were no good to you too. You better find your friends before our master does...because...because he will not hesitate as he only needs to take back the princess. And are...are you that prince she talked about?"

"Rukhsar certainly is one of her kind. I wonder what she did to all of you; you ended up like this! This is incredible. I never knew she would have so many tricks in that bag of hers, and I am quite impressed. One womans bombs took out more than half of your entourage. This is hilarious!" Then, realizing that he was talking to the dying man, he became calm and started pouring water into their mouths.

"Men! you cannot survive here. Before you die, please do a favor for me and get your reward from the God Almighty. Tell me where are my friends and the princess! Do you have any idea which direction they went! I didnt mean to mock you, but you must realize that my friends and the princess are significant to me. If you have harmed them, then I will know!"

"We dont know...and we just told you that some balls...bombs...exploded and we saw dust scattered everywhere. There was complete chaos, and we dont remember what happened then. The general was very upset with us...and he...he left us here to die."

Fardad saw the dying soldier with anticipation. "I swear on the Yazdan...t-th-that none of them are hurt. They escaped, as we have told you, and theyre safe...until the general discovers them. We paid the price, but we hope you catch up with your friends too, dear prince!"

"Oh, Rukhsaars bombs! I hope none of your friends are my friends. And thanks for addressing me as a prince. The princess is very important to me, and I will give my life to her. As for my friends, theyre my brothers and sisters in arms. We will protect her at any cost!" Fardad told the wounded soldiers.

He searched the bodies to see if any of his friends were the victims, and he knew Rukhsaar would be smart enough not to hurt any of them. He quickly searched the bodies and thanked God that his friends were not among them. He counted all the wounded soldiers, and they were around 18.

It means there were seven more, including Nabuzardan, and he must have gone after his friends and the princess. He needed to find some hint or clue where they went because they could be anywhere right now.

Fardad looked at the markings of horse hooves on the ground and identified the generals direction, and Fardad followed them. "I am leaving. I am sorry to leave you all here, but you captured my friends. You deserve your fate! I feel sorry for you, but I despise you all, too. How could you be accomplices of such a bastard! He doesnt know how to treat ladies, and he doesnt even deserve to be called a man. Hes a pig, and I will challenge him and take him on in a duel. Lets see whose sword is stronger!"

But before he made another step to leave, he turned to the dying man and asked, "There is one thing I would like to know, though."

"What is it?" he demanded in a weak voice.

"How in the name of Yazdan did your General Nabuzardan know that we were in that place? Who is your informant?" Fardad demanded sharply as he pierced the dying mans eyes distastefully.

"It...it was Roxana; she is a spy," he managed weakly.

"Who is Roxana?" Fardad inquired instantly.

The weak man paused and stared into midair for a while. Filled with impatience and frustration, Fardad shook him lightly.

"Answer me! Who is Roxana?"

Yet still, the man continued to stare in mid-air and did not reply. Thinking that the man had died, Fardad let out a sigh of disappointment and started to walk away. Abruptly, the dying man began to speak, but surprisingly in a voice unlike his own.

The man said, "Go ahead, chosen one!"

Fardad then asked, "Chosen one...how do you know...."

Suddenly, the oracle appeared. "Dont worry. It

was I who was speaking through him. They are correct. You better make a move because your friends are waiting for you and the general has gone after them. I told you I am watching you, and you are not alone. For now, you need to reunite with your friends and then proceed with the mission. Time is of the essence. You will find them if you take this path I am showing you, chosen one!"

Suddenly, she disappeared, and then Fardad saw that there were just dead bodies lying around, quickly turning to dust, leaving just skeletons behind. He couldnt believe his eyes. These men were alive not long ago and were now just skulls and bones. They deserved their fate, and now it was his turn to head toward his friends. "I am coming for you, general!" Fardad thundered.

As Fardad was moving toward his friends, they were sitting comfortably in the bush, keeping a watch. Ukund had a few things on his mind. He asked the princess while whispering, "Princess, you mentioned your prince is coming, and you meant my friend Fardad?"

"Yes, I meant him. We are in love, and he is destined to be my prince. He is your friend and special advisor to honorable King Kai Kobad."

Ukund then whispered, "I knew of his royal position, but I didnt know of him being a prince. We never talked about it. I am happy for you both as he is like my brother, and his father, the legendary Aardburzin, is like my father. Not only that, his father was my guide and mentor. I just hope we make it out of this alive, so you two can start your new lives."

"Oh, we will. Well be out of here alive. Didnt you see the damage those men suffered, thanks to Rukhsaars bombs? Most of the army was wiped out clean. We will take care of them. I dont think well have to deal with a lot. As far as the General goes, he will pay once I get my hands on that rascal!"

Rukhsaar chimed in, saying, "You boys, dont worry. Just wait and watch. Those mines will kill them all, and the general and his men will not know what hit them! They could be here on foot or on horses. My bet is they wont take their horses because they would be spotted. They will be on foot, so we need to stay quiet and discuss the prince later when we find your friend. If I know better, your friend may be here before them as they will be on foot, and he will be on a horse. Anything is possible. You all better quiet and keep a watch. I have a feeling well be expecting visitors anytime now!"

Fardad rode fast toward his friends on his horse as they awaited their visitors. He wanted to meet them before the general, and his men got there. He kept thinking to himself that hed make it. If he encountered the general and his men before, he would take them on single-handedly because he couldnt let them go near his friends. Even though he thought a trap could be set up, the general was brilliant. He knew better. Chances were that Fardads friends were safe, but he had to be sure. With every gallop, he would get closer. He saw no sign of the general or his men, but they couldnt be too far. He had revenge on his mind. This was a race against time, and he had to find his friends.

In Fardads mind, only dwelled the princess and his friends. He kept repeating the Yazdans name and prayed for their safety. He would be there soon, and he knew it.

Chapter 11

The Curse

"SHHH . . . someone or something is here!" Rukhsaar asked everyone to take caution. "Stay down. . .dont make any movements. . .let me see. . .it could be Fardad!" Rukhsaar continued.

She slowly looked up and around the bushes. She saw it was just a snake that whizzed by them. "Its no one. A snake passed us by. Keep your eyes and ears peeled, people. We could be ambushed, and our responsibility is to protect Pari."

"I understand. We need to protect the princess because our enemies can use her against us," Ukund said.

"Ensuring the safety and security of the princess is my job. Since were in this together, we need to work together. Weve come too far to lose now. Fardad will be here soon looking for us, and I just hope our enemies come first so we can make quick work of them," Rukhsaar said to Gyasi and Ukund. "But I want to ask you all a favor. Princess Parinaaz is my respon-

CHAPTER 11.   THE CURSE

sibility. If something happens to me or I dont make it, you all must promise me you will take care of her. She cant be compromised again. You all must give me your word!" Rukhsaar continued.

"Dont worry about it. We will protect you and the princess as if our life depended on it. Were all going to get out of this in one piece; we just need to be careful. Were not armed, but were still dangerous, although I wish we had swords and arches," Ukund murmured.

"Dont worry. I have no problems sacrificing myself for you all. I am ready for a fight, and we will turn the jungle into a war zone," Gyasi said. "I know many techniques of survival as we have been trained in this art. These men are no match for me, and I can take them out one by one! Gyasi is ready for a fight!" "How is it possible, and what plans do you have, if I may? Youre ready for a fight, but we need to be smart," Ukund commented.

"We dont even have bombs now, so we must keep quiet. We need to outsmart them and catch them off guard. Then well have the upper hand!" Rukhsaar said. "My friends, I, Gyasi, know how to defeat our enemies. Worry not! The sharp pricks of this tree can turn into swords. So, we can improvise, and they will never know what hit them. It has a poisonous sap that will make them unconscious and then blind. We can take them out fairly easily. Rukhsaars bombs took most of them out, and theyre just a few, along with that evil general. Well teach them a lesson not to mess with us. I remember him calling me a black donkey;

he was showing his true colors. That general will die a coward!" Gyasi pointed toward an ugly-looking tree that had many nail-looking spikes coming out of its trunk.

"Everyone, listen up! Quickly, take some tree roots and spikes from the tree, tie them up with the branches, and create your spears. Their swords will not be any match for us! Come on, lets get to it. We can turn the tides against them. They could be here!" Gyasi said, and everyone followed him as if he was the new commander. He wanted to prove himself worthy of leadership because he had been a slave for a long. He enjoyed his freedom and had transformed from slavery to royalty, becoming the assistant to the special advisor of King Kai Kobad. The special advisor was no one else but Fardad, who was desperately looking for his friends. Princess Parinaaz looked like a warrior. Even though she still possessed her beautiful looks, she had transformed into a fighter, aching for revenge. Rukhsaar had trained her to fight and be prepared for battle at all times. The princess had stayed quiet all this time; she was upset about being mishandled and mistreated by the general and his men. She was worried about Fardad, as they had been apart for a long time now. She kept praying to Yazdan to keep him safe.

Since she was the princess, Parinaaz told everyone, "Everyone, we all need to take care of these annoyances so we can reunite with Fardad. I believe that Gyasis plan is the best approach, and we can get an advantage over our opponents. We need to tackle them first to provide a safe passage to Fardad. Our enemies can be here, so lets get ready!"

They did as Gyasi said and took positions behind the tree trunks and bushes. Gyasi signaled others to stay hidden and not make any noises. They could hear the voices of someone approaching, and the voices were becoming more apparent as they came closer. The enemies were at their gates, not knowing what to expect. The general led his cavalry of six men who were still shaken by the previous attack. They were also nervous but were following orders. Gyasi and the rest were keeping watch and ensuring that they struck at the right time. He had asked them all to wait for his signal and then attack. Somehow, the general and his men were suspicious that their former captives were in the area.

"Come out, you Rats. You cannot hide from us! We know youre here. If you come out peacefully, we will do you no harm. If you try anything funny, well slice all your heads one by one except for our prize– the princess! The general will be very gentle with her!" one man said. The man was trying to irk a reaction from their former captives so they would come out, but they stayed hidden. Princess Parinaaz tried to keep calm and not react, although she was fuming. Another soldier remarked, "We know youre hiding, but well find you. We will make you an offer you wont refuse. Your friend, the man coming to rescue his darling Princess and friends, has been captured, and we will release him if you show your face. Now, you can stay hidden, but within five minutes, we will execute him and leave him lying in a pool of blood if you dont show yourselves."

The general was not speaking but allowed his men to get their enemies out of the shadows. Another man screamed, "Show yourself, or he dies!"

Interestingly, the general and his men called a bluff to lure their enemies out, but they underestimated them. Gyasi knew better than to trust the general or his men. He knew they were setting them up for a trap, so he signaled the others to keep lying low. They had their eyes on the general and his men, and there was no captive with them. Fardad was not captured; otherwise, he would be seen. The general grew impatient, but he didnt want to make any moves until he spotted Gyasi and others. Meanwhile, Gyasi and his friends were standing behind the general and his men.

General Nabuzardan was unaware that he and his men could easily be ambushed but played it safe. He looked pretty serious and thirsty for blood. When the general and his men were in the right position to attack, Gyasi signaled Rukhsaar to make the first move.

Rukhsaar aimed and threw the spear she made toward one man, hitting right on target. The spear went through the throat of the soldier, pinning his lifeless body to the tree; the stream of blood sprung forth from his aorta, and the sound of windpipe resounded in the dark and quiet jungle. One man was down, and that alarmed the rest. The general signaled his men to take cover.

CHAPTER 11.   THE CURSE

General Nabuzardan shouted, "Be careful! No sudden movies. Take positions as they are armed. Dont make the same mistakes again, or the king will eat you all for breakfast!"

Gyasi was laughing inside, knowing very well that the king would never see the general or his men as they would soon be outnumbered. Princess Parinaaz was glad that Fardad wasnt among them. It was time for payback, and she would make sure the general and men get the worst punishment ever. She wanted to put her boots on his neck and show him how not to treat a lady and that too a princess.

They wanted to make their moves carefully. Ukund was sitting on a treetop, and there was one rattlesnake wrapped around the branch. Ukund was a master of capturing snakes as the famed astrologer, Aardburzin, had trained him. He used his spear and pushed one down, and it landed right on the shoulder of one man. As soon as the rattlesnake landed, the man stood and started shouting and jumping. There was complete panic and chaos everywhere. Gyasi, waiting for the right moment, threw his spear and killed that man.

Ukund and the others were evening the odds. They wanted to make them vulnerable enough, so the general was forced to surrender. They had to turn the tide in their favor.

There were only four men left, including General Nabuzardan. He was soon about to be outnumbered by the princess and her friends. Nabuzardan noticed his men were being reduced to corpses, making him angry. His mission would fail, and he would face death from his king. He thought he had to take desperate measures to recapture the princess, but he did not know what to do–seeing his men die made him furious.

Meanwhile, Fardad had entered the jungle and started looking for his friends and the princess. He knew that the general and his men were following them, so he avoided calling his friends by their names. He was moving carefully but swiftly through the jungle and looking for the marks on the tree, but there were none. They must have no weapons with them, Fardad thought. He was worried that they could be overpowered because of being unarmed. He had faith in Gyasi, Ukund, and Rukhsaar because they were trained in combat. They could back each other and contain the situation. He just had to get there in time and help them because the fate of Persia and the world was at stake. Too much time had been wasted, and the generals intervention had already put them behind schedule.

After moving through the forest, he started listening to the shouts and screams. He went toward the voices and saw the general with his entourage from a distance. The general and his men failed to notice Fardad. However, Fardad could see his friends, the princess, and her assistant alive and unharmed. He felt delighted and approached the general slowly from his back. He drew his sword out and waited for the moment. Fardad pulled the generals hair from the back with one hand, causing the general to fall on his back.

CHAPTER 11. THE CURSE

Meanwhile, Fardad used his other hand, putting the sword right at the throat of the general. He dragged the general on the ground and shouted, "Enough is enough! General, its very nice to meet you, and I am warning you right now. Tell your men to drop their weapons because I have no problem ending your misery right now. Let them go, or Ill slaughter him, right here!"

The general signaled his men to drop the weapons, and they reluctantly followed his instructions and put the weapons down. Fardad and his friends surrounded the general and his men and tied their hands using tree roots. Finally, when the general and their men were under their control, Fardad spoke to them, "General, you made a huge mistake ambushing my men. They are not cowards, and we are on a mission to save Persia and have no time to entertain yours and your mens cheap thrills. Now, who do you work for!"

Princess Parinaaz then spoke, "This bastard is General Nabuzardan who works for King Marduk. That king is another wretched pig who wanted to marry me, and my father, the honorable King Kai Kobad, said no. Therefore, he sent the general and his lackeys to kidnap me so that he could forcibly marry me.

General, I wont let you go so easily. I promised you I would shove my boot down your neck and make you wish you and your men never laid a hand on me. You will even wish you are dead! Your king has no right to marry me, and I would love to shove my foot down his throat. If theres anyone I would marry, its my prince here standing right beside me."

Ukund looked at Gyasi in bewilderment, and Gyasi smiled back. Gyasi murmured to Ukund, "My brother, just enjoy the moment!"

The princess shoved her boot down on the generals neck, choking him so hard that he could barely breathe. Rukhsaar said, "Princess, you dont want his death on your conscience. Leave these bastards to die in this forest like the rest. We should move on!"

The princess and the others collected all the weapons of the general and his men because they might need them for the mission ahead. They were relieved that they survived this kidnapping attempt and were happy to leave General Nabuzardan and his remaining men alive to die in their misery.

Rukhsaar then collected everyone and spoke, "Everyone, gather up. We need to get away from here to plan our next moves safely. These few men are no match for us, but I dont want them dying on our hands. Weve committed enough bloodshed, and were not murderers but saviors.

Fardad, glad to know youre alright. Hopefully, we can carry on with the rest of the mission now. We need to retrieve the book of Aardburzin first, and I dont see these bastards having it. So, lets get back to their dead friends and hopefully find it there. Lets make a move for it. We dont have enough time!" The group set off to where they had earlier escaped from, which wasnt too far from where they were. After returning to where Rukhsaars bombs were exploded, they saw that

CHAPTER 11.   THE CURSE

General Nabuzardans wounded soldiers were dead.

Fardad spoke, "I saw these men turn into skull and bones in front of my eyes thanks to a dear friend. Now, lets find my fathers book!"

They found the general mens horses and quickly searched for the book of Aardburzin. Luckily, the book was intact, and Ukund picked it up.

Ukund remarked, "Its here and in one piece! I was so scared because this book is my remaining memory of my mentor. I am so glad that we have recovered from this. We need to now head to High Priest Katir to interpret it for us. Thank you so much, my dear friends!" Rukhsaar then said, "Thats what being friends is all about! Its all for one and one for all. We should talk to Katir right away because we need to know what we face. Our mission is far from over, and I hope we dont have to face such surprises again. Lets collect our belongings and head out."

They took their bags and left the area for the safety of the princess. This little intermission was a lot to process for the saviors, and now they were on their way to get answers from High Priest Katir as instructed by honorable King Kai Kobad. They went farther from the area where they came across a small lake and rested. They checked and confirmed that they werent being followed, and Rukhsaar had asked Gyasi and Ukund to verify that. Then they all sat down behind a large rock to figure out how to move forward.

The relief overjoyed Fardad, Ukund, Gyasi, Rukhsaar, and Princess Parinaaz from this misery. So, they sat down and relaxed. The best thing about this station was that the rock was big enough to hide them and their horses.

Fardad said, "Can someone explain to me what the hell this general was doing in our area? How did he find out about our whereabouts?" Princess Parinaaz said, "I told you they wanted to capture me and take me to Marduk. He wanted to marry me, but I had refused. Then he planned to marry me forcefully and had sent his general to capture me. Now that his general is defeated, he will do something terrible when he finds out. He is a maniac magician and a horrible man."

Fardad said, "Do not worry, my Princess. Nothing will happen to you. We all will protect you with our lives if this cruel king tries to capture you again. We defeated mortal men, and we have magic on our side to deal with magicians too. For now, we need to head to the temple and show the book of my father Aardburzin to the temple priests, especially High Priest Katir. Maybe they could decipher the book and let us know what my father had kept secret all this time. We could all learn something from it. I also feel that going to the Zagros Mountains in search of Abzu before its too late. The fate of Persia and the world hangs in the balance. We need to head to both places. However, I shall go alone to Abzu because I cant put all your lives further in danger. Weve already faced enough trouble being involved in two skirmishes since we got together for this mission. I am very proud of how we worked together to survive the challenges, but I promised the king that I would protect you, Dear Princess. So, for your sake, stay with our friends and let me fight this battle by myself!"

"Theres no way youre going alone to locate the Abzu! All for one and one for all. We came on this mission together, and we will return to the palace together as victors. We need to save our kingdom and the world, and thats why were together. Dear Fardad, my father knew the risks, and he still sent me along for this mission with Rukhsaar and your friends."

The princess continued, "We all will go with you. You saved my life and that of Rukhsaar. I owe you my life, and we are safe because we are together. From now on, none of us will split from this group. You all have to listen to me as I am the princess of this kingdom!"

Observing respect in the eyes of the princess, Fardad said, "I understand, Dear Princess. You all can join me until we reach the Zagros Mountains."

Gyasi then asked, "Why only till there? We will be with you till the very end. This mission is as much yours as it is ours!"

Princess also spoke, "Fardad, your friend is right. We will stay with you all the way because we are a team, and we will back you but never leave you."

Ukund then spoke, "The princess is correct. I promised your father that I would protect you, and I will never leave you. Were in this together, or were not!"

Rukhsaar also added, "Fardad, I will not repeat what everyones saying, but as things stand, we need to stick together. You will do whatever you need to, but we will be with you all the way." Fardad then finally replied to the rest, "My friends, I appreciate the support, and it means a lot. You all are more than welcome to join me until the Zagros Mountains, but I will solely descend into Abzu after that. I cannot jeopardize your safety anymore, my Princess."

Rukhsaar then said, "Dont worry about Pari, please. Fardad, we respect your decision, and we will protect the princess and each other. If you are instructed to go into Abzu, we shall back you at the foot of the mountains and wait for your return. There is a long way to go, and we have much to do. Once we figure out whats in the book, we will head to the Zagros Mountains. Lets lie low here for some time, as its getting dark now. We need to head out in the early morning, as the priests will guide us. These priests sleep early because they have to pray in the morning. I suggest one of us keep a watch while we rest. I warn all of you not to make a move or go anywhere. From now on, were together until we get to the mountains and wait for Fardad to do what he needs to do. If you decide to stray off, we will force you to stay at the temple until the mission is over. We cant compromise our mission or our lives. I hope thats clear to you all."

***

Soroush rushed into his chamber and began to thrash

235

everything inside. He began to boil with intense fury and rage that knew no bounds. He smashed his massive mirror with a bottle of Persias finest wine, and both the mirrors and bottle shattered into tiny pieces. One of the glass fragments reverted and struck on the side of the ministers eyes which cut open and began to bleed. However, his agony was so tremendous that neither did he feel the pain, nor did he wince.

After releasing his entire anger on the lifeless objects, he began to heave greatly like a furious beast and let out a growl.

"I will not let that darned Fardad win! I will do whatever thats in my power to stop him! I dont care what it takes! But I will not let him become victorious!" After saying that, he grabbed a quill, a bottle of ink, and parchment from his dressing table and instantly scribbled a note which read:

"Roxana,

I have had enough! If you truly desire your freedom! Then go kill that bloody bastard named Fardad who has been an irritating thorn in my flesh since day one! I DO NOT want to hear any excuses! Go and kill him! Otherwise, you will remain my slave, FOREVER!"

He took the horribly scribbled note and went towards a cage containing a white pigeon. Immediately, he tied the note to its feet and took him towards the windows. Opening the huge window, he ordered, "Go and give this note to Roxana and come back quickly!"

Soroush released the bird and watched it become

smaller in the moon-filled night sky.

***

In the meantime, Roxana was sneaking cautiously across the jungle where Fardad and his friends stayed. She had followed them all this while very carefully without being seen by anyone. However, she was unable to find them in the hugely dense forest area.

"Damn it! I cannot see that Fardad and those other scoundrels anywhere!" she cursed, delivering a tremendous kick to the trunk of a tree. Instantly, she looked at the ancient banyan tree, which was quite towering, nearly fifty feet tall, and an idea flashed in her mind. And without wasting a single moment, she utilized her skills and began to climb the tree. Finally, after jumping across the branches, she managed to reach the top of the tree and observed the entire forest area with her eyes narrowed. Eventually, she found Fardad and her friends nearly a hundred meters away from her.

"Yes! Finally, I have found those darned nuisances!" she exclaimed and punched the air victoriously.

At that point, she noticed a white dot moving across the horizon. The dot became smaller, and she realized that it was her master Soroushs pigeon. The tiny bird moved closer and landed on her palm.

Roxana let out a wide smile and began caressing the gentle creature generously.

"Azlan! How are you, my tiny friend! Its been so long!" she declared and continued to caress the bird.

CHAPTER 11.   THE CURSE

"Let me do that disgusting rat, Soroushs work, then I will get your freedom too from that evil fart of a minister and take you away with me!" she asserted and blew the white bird a soft kiss on its bald head. Suddenly, she noticed the note tied to its feet. Unfastening it, she unrolled it and read the contents. After reading it thoroughly, she crushed it furiously and began abusing the ruthless minister.

"What the hell does that ass of a man think of me?" She cursed with gritted teeth.

"Fardad and those other bastards managed to tame General Nabuzardan and his mighty army of highly skilled soldiers. How the hell am I supposed to fight them alone?!" she punched the trunk of the tree in frustration. "Anyways, for the sake of our freedom, I will have to think of a way to do it," Sighing deeply, she retrieved a quill from the pocket of her cloak and wrote on the back of the parchment.

"Master Soroush,

Be assured. The job will be done, and you will soon receive the news of Fardad and his friends deaths.

Your Faithful Slave, Roxana."

She tied the note back on the birds feet, and giving it a final kiss; she made her leap across the air to return to Soroush.

"Despite my skill, I stand no chance against these four united. The wisest thing would be to follow them till they reach the temple. Then I can think about killing them." Upon saying that, she began to descend the towering tree and landed back on the forest floor.

***

Rukhsaar had become a general herself the way she was commanding the team. She saw the urgency of the matter, and her battle experiences had taught her a lot. She was a true warrior and proud of it and seemed to have found a fancy in Ukund. She saw in him the same warrior spirit she had. She did not know whether Ukund had any feelings for her but would not ask, as she couldnt distract him or anyone else from the mission.

Ukund had looked back at Rukhsaar and smiled because he became sort of attracted toward her. Ukund had found tremendous respect for her, as Rukhsaar had saved the group on two occasions. She had become a formidable leader, and the princess would never veto her orders.

"All of you rest now until I signal us to head to the temple. I will keep a watch. We need the energy for the rest of our mission."

The rest of them nodded in approval and laid down. Princess Parinaaz took Fardad to the side and laid next to him. The others were too tired to care what the two lovebirds would talk about and Rukhsaar, as usual, kept to herself doing her job as a watchman.

Princess Parinaaz spoke in a low voice, "Fardad, my love, I missed you so much. You know how much I love you. I cant bear to see you away from me at all. I was so scared that something had happened to you because you can expect anything from that general.

239

CHAPTER 11.   THE CURSE

I understand you have been asked to do a personal mission, but we will never leave your sight. You are critical to all of us, especially to me."

Fardad looked back at her lovelorn eyes and said, "Oh, Pari, I love you very much, and I swear I was thinking of you all this time. I just wanted to see you, and the way you told that general about us was incredible. I understand that the rest of them will have some questions, and we will let them know in good time."

Princess Parinaaz then said, "Doesnt everyone know already! Rukhsaar already has an idea, and I thought Gyasi knew too. I think you mean Ukund. Your friend and your fathers student. Why have you not told him yet! By the way, have you seen the way he looks at Rukhsaar? I think your friend has fallen in love with my assistant! Love is in the air!"

Fardad laughed and said, "Oh yes. Ukund and I never had time to talk about you and me. I am sure we will once this mission is over. I was more interested in looking at you, so I never bothered if my friend was in love or not! If you think he has, then thats very interesting."

"Yes, I have noticed it, and they will be an adorable couple. Both have undying warrior spirits and show incredible strength of character, and honestly, they should become one just like us."

"Pari, you are right. I would want my best friend to be happy too, and if he and Rukhsaar want to be together, Id be thrilled for them. I missed you so much.

I want to cherish this moment of us lying down in front of each other forever. This reminds me of the times we spent in your palace garden. Those were special times, and this here, right now, is one of them too. I cant wait to be your prince, and we can be together just like your parents. They are the most beautiful royal couple I have ever seen. You take your beauty from your mother, the elegant queen. Your leadership stems from your brave father. I am genuinely in awe of them and inspired by how they have raised you so perfectly. We have so long to go from here, but I want to spend every moment with you, dear Pari." "Fardad, you have me, and I am yours forever. We shall never be apart because true love shines through the darkest times. We are in this together, and we shall survive. Our love will see us through!"

"Pari, I promise you I will never leave your side. I see us as prince and princess living a beautiful life. Even though this is a very challenging time, we are together through this. I would love to kiss you right now...I...I...I...."

Parinaaz had wrapped his arms around his neck, and so did he to hers. She pulled him close and delivered a sweet and sensual kiss. Both of them were once again in each others arms with lips locked. They stayed in that for a few moments and slowly pulled apart.

"Be careful what you wish for, my Prince, because it will come true. You asked, and I delivered. This is a beautiful and magical moment, and I want you with

241

me in my arms until we leave. Lets enjoy this moment under the stars and night sky."

"Pari, you left me breathless. I was so captivated and overwhelmed by your love. I will cherish this moment and this kiss forever. ..."

"Shhh. ..lets just stare into each others eyes and fall in love a hundred times over! I just want you now, and thats an order!"

"I. ..I. ..your wish is my command. ..."

Parinaaz once again pulled him close, planting a kiss on his lips. They were enticed, and the magic that surrounded them helped them drift to sleep in each others arms. Fardad had become very relaxed because he had been away from the princess for far too long. He longed to be in her embrace and continued kissing her until his eyes were wide shut.

As he drifted off to sleep, Fardad once again went into a trance and heard a voice, which was familiar. He thought the princess was speaking to him in his dreams, but it wasnt her, as he heard closely.

"Fardad, Fardad. .. You must take care of the princess because your union is important for the kingdoms survival. Like you are the chosen one, she completes you. She loves you and worries for you. Protecting her is now your responsibility. I told you, and she will become both the King and Queen of Persia. She is yours forever, but you must ensure her survival and safety. Stay with your team and meet High Priest Katir. Learn what he says and then move with them to the Zagros Mountains. I shall continue to guide you until you find Abzu."

"Yes, I need your guidance, and I will let no one harm the princess. Your prophecy has weight, but I dont care for royalty. I just want her with me." "You are the chosen one to save Persia, the world, and rule the kingdom with the princess. I know all of this is too much to take in right now, but she is yours as long as you protect her."

"Are there more dangers youd like me to know of so I can warn my friends? We were separated once, but we cant afford to do so once again."

"Fardad, stick to the plan, and you will never be lost. . .you need to stay with your team and make sure they do that too. . .and you will succeed."

"I will do so and make sure everyone on my team is safe as dangers are lurking ahead that we must watch out for. Our mission is far from over. Thank you so much for being with us."

"I will call upon you when needed, and this is your time to shine. Stick with your team and fulfill your destiny."

"I will. . .I promise. . .."

"Shhh. . .your princess is with you. . .take care of her. . .I will see you again. . .Prince."

With that, he was out of his dream state and realized that the princess was still holding on to him in an embrace, and he smiled to himself, knowing they both were in each others arms. He was so happy that he had found the love of his life. Princess Parinaaz was the epitome of beauty and the bravest warrior princess

243

he had ever encountered. She took it to the general and showed who the boss was. This was a sight that he had never seen. He was excited to know that she would be the most amazing queen when given that opportunity. It was an incredible sight to behold and one he could never forget. His eyes opened, and he could see the princess in front of him with her eyes closed, looking like a beautiful angel; she was enjoying her peaceful siesta with her future prince. He continued looking at her and enjoying her warm embrace. It was perhaps the calm before the storm. He now knew what he had to do to stay on that course. After some time, the princess slowly opened her eyes. "Fardad, my love, did you sleep at all? Or were you looking at me this whole time?"

"Pari, I did both! Youre so beautiful that I went into a trance, and it happens to me every time were so close. I keep falling in love with you the more were with each other. I promise to protect you, my Princess, my Pari!"

"Fardad, I too am pleased to be with you in your embrace. I wish I could have this moment forever, and I know we will once this mission is over. I want you as my prince, and I know my father would want nothing more than he holds you in such high regard. You are my knight in shining armor!"

"Pari, always and forever. . .I am with you. . .we will be victorious and will have each other and, hopefully, no more missions once Persia and the world are safe from danger."

"Fardad, we will. . .and we will make a move soon. I hope Rukhsaar has rested. . .."

Rukhsaar called out to everyone, "Alright, love-birds and warriors, time to get up! The sun is up, so we should start moving, and the priests will be ready to speak to us."

Everyone else slowly opened their eyes and got up. Parinaaz and Fardad were up and talking, so they both stood up. Parinaaz gave Fardad a quick kiss on the cheek before getting up.

Gyasi then asked, "Rukhsaar, you didnt sleep at all?"

Rukhsaar then replied, "I figured you all needed rest, so I stayed up because I had to watch for trouble. Thankfully, we were alright. The general and his men must have died or retreated to their kingdom."

"He didnt have any men left except maybe two. So, we would easily outmatch them as they had no weapons either," said Ukund. Fardad spoke, "We dont need to worry about them. Lets head to the temple so we can plan our next move. Lets stick together till we get there because we want no more surprises."

Rukhsaar then said, "Thats correct. Lets move. We need to get there before the priests start their ritual prayers, and I figure we have around half an hour, and that should get us there before their prayer time."

Gyasi said, "I agree with Rukhsaar. Lets go to the temple and show the book to the priest before its too late. The rest has done us all good. Lets keep our prizes with us, too, as we will need it."

CHAPTER 11.   THE CURSE

Rukhsaar asked, "You mean their gear? We have their weapons and armor so that it will help. Well carry them with us to the temple, and then well suit up before we head out to the mountains. Its time to move out."

All were still tired but had to go because of the urgency of the matter. They all collected their loot and stored it on their horses and walked with them, and they would be at the temple in 30 minutes.

As they walked, Fardad thought about his conversation in the dream state with the older woman–the oracle. It was great to be reassured that he and the princess would be together forever, but he still had to focus on the mission ahead. Everything depended on him saving Persia and the world. Being the chosen one gave him goosebumps, and it was a lot of pressure. He had to take it like a warrior and a champion and be the chosen one that Persia needed.

While our heroes were returning to the temple to discover the secrets of Aardburzins book, General Nabuzardan and his men were tied up tightly and were starving of thirst. They had a few surprise guests, and they were none other than rattlesnakes, ready to get their dose of human flesh. A few minutes later, screams were heard, and sudden silence...a bloody mess everywhere.

Chapter 12

The Relief

Fardad and his friends made their way to the Urmia Temple to speak with High Priest Katir now that they had retrieved Aardburzins book. They had left behind their former captors General Nabuzardan and two soldiers in quite a fix. General Nabuzardan and his two soldiers had to contend with snakes surrounding them. These were rattlesnakes whose venom bites would kill the victim slowly but painfully. The snakes would bite the arms and legs of all three of their captives. The snakes took hold of the ropes that had bound Nabuzardan and his two men, chewing them away.

All three of them were wounded by the snake bites but broke free and made a run for their lives. The snake bites were causing them an awful lot of pain that would eventually slow them down. They raced through the jungle by going back to where they had initially come from.

Nabuzardan suddenly stopped when he saw tons of

skulls and bones and was shocked. It was as if he had seen a massacre: his entire battalion was no more. He cursed himself for not helping them and leaving them to die. It was their time to repay their mistreatment: they were slowly dying. They did not know the effects of the venom bite, but they hoped they could catch up to their former captives soon.

"This hurts...oh....the pain...men, these snakes were too much!" screamed the general.

"Master, from what I know, these snakes bite you and leave their venom in your bodies, which slowly spreads to all parts of your body and poisons it gradually. We will slowly die from these bites. I dont know if there is an antidote for it, but perhaps those priests at the temple could help us," one of his men spoke. "This pain is too much. I dont even know if we can make it to the temple in time. I am feeling too weak already," said the other soldier.

"Men, we need to make it to the temple fast. Those priests must have an antidote. We need to fight the pain!" The general ordered.

"The venom is spreading in our bodies, Master. We wont last too long. Only Yazdan knows how long we have until we die!" one man said!

"Men, we need to move to survive. Either way, we will die here or at the hands of our king!" The general motivated his men to move on.

"Alright, Master, as you say. Lets move on further!" one soldier stated.

"I swear, I wish we had never let these men rot

here and die! We needed all the help we could get," the general remarked.

"Too late, Master. Were on our own!" his soldier spoke while struggling to move forward."

"If they were alive, they would never let us live. They would make sure we die right here with them!" the general replied.

"Be careful what you wished for, Master. Oh, look...were close to the temple!" one of his soldiers stated with fear.

"It doesnt matter, as were already dying. Move, you two, before we bite the dust just like our fallen comrades."

The general and his men ran for their lives. Fascinatingly, these three men were already poisoned, and time was ticking away. They had to make a run to the temple and perhaps hope to get healed by the priests. The general and his men were in a race against time, as the venom would spread all over their bodies and silently kill them. While running for their lives, the general asked his men, "Any idea how long it takes to be completely poisoned?"

One of the men spoke while trying to catch his breath. "Master, I would say it will take three to five hours, and some say it may take an entire day depending on our bodys strength and resilience to fight the poisons effects."

The general replied, "Alright, the temple isnt too far. We can get there within thirty minutes if we run fast enough."

CHAPTER 12.   THE RELIEF

The men were running as fast as possible and were a few minutes away from the temple. The general and his men remained the sole survivors who needed to get to the priest to find some antidote or cure to be healed from the poison. They didnt have much time as running had worsened the pain and weakened their bodies. They had to get hold of one of the priests for a potion or antidote. They kept shouting, "Is anyone here? Anyone here? We need help!"

Suddenly, one of the temple priests showed up and asked them, "What is going on here? How can we help you?"

The general spoke, "Dear Priest, we have come this way before, if you remember. I had an army with me...I...I–"

The priest saw the wounds on the general and his soldiers and interrupted. "Men, please follow me. You are bleeding...what happened to you?"

"We got bit by snakes in the jungle...those rattlesnakes!" the soldier said.

"Those bites are poisonous...you could die if the poison spreads throughout your body!" the priest warned.

"Is there any way you can help us? We will give you anything you want. Just make sure we dont die!" the general requested the priest.

"I am sorry. We are priests, and we dont take anything to help others. We are here to help, but I cant help you," the priest said.

"Then who can? Take me to him!" the general

asked.

The priest replied, "High Priest Katir can help you. He knows how to heal the wounded with the help of the Yazdan."

"Does he have an antidote or potion to heal us?" the general asked.

"He could; the High Priest is known to heal the wounded. You will have to take your chances. Come with me. Hurry now. Theres no time. If that poison spreads all over the body, then you both could die."

The general and his soldiers followed the priest to High Priest Katirs chamber. Both men were anxious to get treated and escape death. The priest asked the men to sit while he got High Priest Katir.

The High Priest Katir, summoned by the Priest, met the three men a few minutes later.

"General, is that you? What happened to you and your army? I was told that you both are wounded. Oh my! You three have been bleeding profusely, and you will lose too much blood even if you dont die from the venom. Brothers, come and let us get these men stitched up."

The other priests took the men with them to a room where the wounded were stitched. Katir first dabbed some herbs to numb the pain and then applied stitches to stop the bleeding. The general asked, "The antidote. ..." The High Priest Katir silenced him and gently asked him to stay quiet. Katir went to his workroom and came back quickly with a potion. This was the antidote that would heal their bodies from the venom. After taking the stitches off, Katir applied the tonic to the wounds in their bodies. Once the tincture was involved, he put the stitches back. The general wanted to know about the escaped captives, especially the princess. "High Priest, I wanted to ask you about a group of young men and women who come this way." The High Priest Katir then replied, "Please stay quiet...you have not healed yet. Please drink these, all of you, if you want to be completely healed." High Priest Katir might have wanted to keep the identities or whereabouts of Fardad and his friends a secret. He didnt give any hints but requested the two wounded men to drink the contents in the glasses handed to them. The wounded men looked at each other and reluctantly drank from the glasses. A few minutes later, the general and his soldiers were in a trance and felt dizzy. Trying to speak and utter a few words, both lay unconscious.

The High Priest requested his fellow priests to take the men into his chamber. He instructed them, "These men are in a deep sleep, and I have given them the potions so the antidote can heal their wounds. While theyre unconscious, the antidote would do its job of keeping them alive and removing the spread of the venom in their bodies. No one will wake them until they regain consciousness, or I wake them up. It will take several hours till theyre completely healed."

The other priests obliged and nodded in agreement. Once the general and his soldier were in deep slumber, the priests went to the other side of the temple where the High Priest spoke to them, "My fellow brothers, we have a problem here. We accept everyone in our temple as its a haven for the wounded, weary, and those who require our help. Now, we have two groups of people. The first group of travelers is Fardad and his friends, who want us to decipher that book. The second group is this general and his soldiers. I could not leave them to die because they came to us for help. They will be healed, and the potion will take a day to heal them. Its that powerful. Their entire body is hurting because of that venom, and it needs rest, so the antidote works. We can meet Fardad and his friends and help them to be on their way. We need to do this before the general and his men get up. So lets make a move. Fardad and his friends have been given shelter at one of our brothers homes. Two of you stay here, and the rest of us come with me. You need to keep the general and his men here and not give them any hint about Fardad and his friends. Well return to the temple later."

Fardad and his friends stayed at one of the priests homes and recuperated. They sought shelter to hide from the general and his men and to get High Priest Katir to decipher Aardburzins book.

In the meantime, Roxana cautiously sneaked outside the priests home and was keeping an eye on Fardad and his friends, who were kept hidden from General Nabuzardan and his soldiers. She was able to see them clearly from the closed window of the priests tiny house and was waiting for an opportunity for one of them to come out so that she could ambush the person and kill.

"Finally, your time has to come to depart this world, Fardad! And I swear on Yazdan, you will not be able to escape this time! Luck has sided with you enough! Now its my turn!" she declared firmly with gritted teeth and placed her soft palm across the handle of her mighty sword.

The priest housing them was a jolly older man who had dedicated his life to worship and helping people who entered the temple. He was always dressed in a dark blue robe and had a small beard and a light mustache, all grayed up. He wore a small cap on his head, which was part of the uniform of the priests. His house was small but large enough to live comfortably. After all, he spent more time worshipping at the temple than at his home, and that was just a place for him to sleep. He and the other priests had dedicated their entire lives to worship.

There was a knock on the door, and the old priest checked through the small round window structured within the entrance and inquired, "Who is it?" High Priest Katir replied, "It is me, Katir, and the others. Let us in, and we need to speak to our guests, and they have some book he wanted us to see." The senior priest obliged, opened the door, and let the other priests in. He had them wait so he could get Fardad and his friends. Fardad, Princess Parinaaz, Ukund, Gyasi, and Rukhsaar showed up together with Aardburzins book. Fardad was the first to introduce himself. "My name is Fardad. I am the deputy officer of the king, and I want to see High Priest Katir."

Katir appeared before him by stepping out from among his fellow priests. He then noticed that Farad was holding the book. "I am High Priest Katir. We had met before when you came looking for your friends earlier on. I also see that book in your hand; is that what you want us to look at? Is that the book youre talking about?" "Yes! It very much is. My father, Aardburzin, kept it all his life and gave it to my best friend, Ukund, and he has since guarded it." High Priest Katir took the book from Fardads hand and read the contents. Then he called upon one of his assistants and showed him the book. They both looked at each other and then stated, "It is an ancient book, and it contains archaic symbols, and we are unable to decipher it."

Ukund then intervened in the conversation. "It has been a long journey just to reach this temple and meet you, and now youre saying that you dont know how to decipher it! The honorable King Kai Kobad recommended that we visit you, and we risked our lives to get here. We almost got killed, captured, and then escaped to find shelter here. All of this effort was for nothing!"

Roxana, who had been eavesdropping on the conversation all this while, jumped with immense joy.

"Spectacular! The stupid priests are unable to decipher the book! This means Fardad and his friends have failed! Well, at least now I dont have to kill them.

CHAPTER 12. THE RELIEF

I was wrong, Fardad, you are really one lucky bastard to have escaped death so many times!" she chuckled softly, and taking a huge sigh of relief, she removed her hand away from her sheathed swords handle. "I must immediately deliver this news to Soroush! I will gain my freedom without dirtying my hands with an innocent mans blood!"

After saying that, she took out a piece of parchment and began to scribble a note in black ink using her quill.

"My Master,

It is with great joy that I would like to inform you that they have failed in this mission! The priests are unable to decipher the book!

Your Faithful Slave."

She kissed the note and took out her white pigeon from the small cage that she carried, and tied the piece of parchment around the baby white pigeons feet. "Alaana! My darling! Deliver this message to Master Soroush and come back quickly!"

She kissed the tiny pigeon's head and let it loose in the air.

Coincidentally, Gyasi was looking out of the window to see whether anyone was coming or not, and his eyes fell on Roxana. He narrowed his eyes and realized that she was spying on them and decided to confront her.

As cautiously as he could, he moved behind her and placed his arm behind her neck.

"Who the hell are you, woman? And why in the

name of Yazdan have you been spying on us?"

"Keep your dirty hands away from me, you filthy black slave!" she breathed angrily, struggling to free herself.

"Answer me! Who sent you after us? Speak now when you have the chance, or else Ill kill you!" he yelled at her. "This is your last chance, woman. Tell me who your master is, or I will be forced to forget that you are a woman and put an end to your life!"

Roxana struggled to free herself, but all her efforts went in vain as Gyasis grip was too strong. Slowly, she placed her hand in her pocket, and upon retrieving her dagger, she thrust it in the side of Gyasis abdomen. Gyasi let out a roar of intense pain and loosened his grip on Roxana, who pushed him and freed herself successfully. Gyasi removed the dagger from his abdomen and threw it on the ground, and the side of his stomach began to bleed profusely.

"Thats it! Now you have had it!" saying that he sprinted towards her like a raging bull shown red cloth. Roxana, on the other hand, stood there calmly and motionlessly. And before Gyasi could strike her, she swerved sideways and grabbed the side of his shoulder. She threw him on the forest floor as though he were a wild beast. Gyasi slid across the ground and groaned in excruciating pain.

"Stand down, slave! I have no intention to kill you. But I might change my mind if you continue to persist," she warned him in the perfect imitation of a mans voice. Gyasi, however, turned even more furious.

With some effort, he got back onto his feet. He rushed towards her and struck the side of her right shoulder. Roxana winced slightly, and eyeing him furiously, she darted towards him and, performing a leap in the air, she delivered a tremendous kick onto his head. However, Gyasi managed to defend himself by placing his arms in the middle. But Roxana spun in midair and performed another kick, but Gyasi caught her foot this time and threw her on the ground. Gyasi was about to grab her by the shoulder when she grabbed some sand from the floor and threw it on the Ethiopian mans face.

"Bloody witch! He growled and began to rub the dirt off his face like a maniac and coughed horrendously. "I will kill you!"

Without wasting a single moment, the cunning young lady rushed away without uttering a single word.

Gyasi got rid of the dirt completely and went back to the High Priests House. The moment he entered the house, Fardad and his other friends rushed towards him. "Gyasi, my Friend, what happened?" Fardad demanded anxiously as he noticed the horrendous gash on his right cheek.

"Who did this to you, Gyasi?" Ukund asked worriedly.

"Lets get his face washed first," Ruksar announced as Fardad and Ukund took him to the washroom and washed his face entirely with cold water. Gyasi wiped his face with a white cloth and sat in the living room. Meanwhile, one of the priests started to inspect the horrible gash on his cheek, which had occurred when Roxana had thrown him across the forest floor.

"It looks like you were made to slide on the hard ground," one of the priests said and began to clean his wound with a fresh neem leaf that possessed medicinal properties. Gyasi began to wince as they rubbed the leaf against his wounded cheek.

"Easy there," Fardad said to the priest like he could feel his dear friends pain. After they had cleaned the wound, they began to stitch it perfectly using a fine black thread. Once the horrible gash had been stitched properly, Gyasi took a sigh of relief and looked at his friend.

"Gyasi, tell us what happened outside? Who did this atrocious thing to you?" Princess Parinaaz asked politely. "My princess, it was a woman. She had been spying on us from outside, and when I confronted her. She attacked me, and we fought, and finally, as I was about to get her, she threw some sand on my face and scampered away," Gyasi narrated softly.

"I bet it was one of the spies of that evil King Marduk!" Princess Parinaaz proclaimed angrily. "He will do everything to get his hands on me!" At her statement, Fardad gritted his teeth angrily and punched the air.

"Whoever is responsible for hurting you, Gyasi, my Friend, will pay for it with his life!" he declared furiously. Then he turned his gaze towards the High Priest. "Honourable Priest, Katir, is there nothing you can do to help us in any way?" he asked him with

CHAPTER 12.   THE RELIEF

a sort of raging resentment. Those priests were supposed to be highly learned people, and if they couldnt decipher a book, it was a matter of extreme shame and disappointment, according to Fardad.

However, the High Priest was lost for words; he didnt know what to say as he was worried that he couldnt help his guests. These priests knew the ancients and were the wisest in the land. However, even he didnt know how to help them. Katir replied, feeling very sorry and troubled, "Im sorry. This language is long lost from even before you were born. It hasnt been used in so long. It looks to be easily 6,000 years old. Only someone who can communicate with spiritual beings can decipher it. None of us here can read it, and your host is the oldest of us all. He will also see and attempt to decipher it. If he cant do it, none of us can help you with the book. However, we can allow you to stay with us for as long as you want, and we will offer you shelter and protection from your enemies who are looking for you." "Our enemies...they came by here? Did they ask about us?" asked Fardad.

"Yes, three men came by here, and they were severely injured. We treated them, allowing their wounds to heal. They were poisoned by rattlesnakes and nearly escaped death," replied Katir.

Fardad then asked, "Was one of them a general?"

"If you leave your fallen soldiers behind in the heat of battle, its an act of betrayal. Yazdan doesnt forgive. However, they wont be giving you any trouble for some time. Our potion is supposed to heal their bodies and will be in effect for a whole day. So, if the senior priest cannot help you, our advice is to either stay in hiding or continue your mission. If you choose to do the latter, we will provide safe passage, but you will need to leave right away before these men regain consciousness. Even though you are five and they are two, never underestimate your enemy."

"Why did you help the enemies of Persia!" they shouted.

Katir then said, "We are men of peace and believe in non-violence. We dont judge anyone, and we help everyone who comes to our temple. Our job is to heal wounds, even if theyre men of evil because we feel that may guide them to the right path. Anyone can be swayed from evil to good, as it is good in every-one. Even that general has good in him but has been overshadowed by evil."

There was a moment of silence, then Katir gave the book to the senior priest to decipher, and he looked at the pages for a few minutes and turned each one to see if there was any symbol he could study. After the first several symbols, he couldnt recognize anything, and his face turned into frustration and disappointment. He handed the book back to Katir, saying, "Master Katir. I could not decipher it. I have never seen these symbols because they belong to another time. Perhaps someone with the knowledge regarding those times could guide our friends. These are ancient and sacred symbols from some other realm that we dont know of. I am sorry, and I wish I could be of more

261

help."

Katir then spoke. "I dont know what to say. I thought we could help you, and since you had come from the royal palace, we are obliged to carry out the wish of the king and queen we hold so dear to our hearts. I respect honorable King Kai Kobad and Queen Anahita and have advised them before, but this book has puzzled us. I dont know how to advise you, but you should continue with your mission."

Fardad then said, "There must be someone who can help us with this book. You must know!"

Katir replied, "I wish I could tell you, but unfortunately, I dont know."

Fardad and his friends were stunned and started looking at each other. Princess Parinaaz said to Fardad, "Lets go out and have some fresh air." They all came out disappointed with the outcome of the whole journey. Fardad said to others, "Friends, I guess now the oracle is the only way. She has spoken to me. She has asked me to go to the Zagros Mountains in the Abzu to save the kingdom of Persia and the world from destruction. There must be some other path towards which she was guiding,"

Ukund said, "Fardad, you must listen to her. Take her advice and follow it fully. She guides the righteous ones. Maybe, if you complete your mission, she may decipher your fathers book, or you can ask her if she seeks you again. You must leave now if you wish to get to the Zagros Mountains in time." A priest came out and heard them talking about the Zagros Mountains.

"Zagros mountains? But why do you want to go there? "

Fardad thought for the moment and then decided not to tell the priests about his search for Abzu.

Rukhsaar spoke, "We are all going to the Zagros Mountains, as the king instructed us."

The priest became perplexed, but he advised them to go west.

Rukhsaar said, "Everyone must follow my lead. None of us is to separate until we get to these mountains after finding Abzu."

Princess Parinaaz then said, "I am the Princess here, so I say we should listen to Rukhsaar. We need to stick with her to get us out of tough situations, and I would trust her with my life. We need to do this for Persia and the world, and we need to save it and not let it get destroyed by evil."

"Thats settled then. We must head there now. People, lets head there right away. Lets make a move before that general and his henchman wakes up. We need to make do with the gear we have and see if we can buy more weapons from a dealer on the way. I dont think our priest friends keep weapons and armor," Fardad said. The priest guided them until the city gates and then went toward the Zagros Mountains.

***

In the interim, Minister Soroush was seated on his royal armchair inside his chamber. He was intoxicated as he was heavily drinking his favorite red wine. His mind was bursting with anxiety about Roxanas situation and whether or not she had killed Fardad and his comrades.

"This girl is a huge pain in my neck! She doesnt reply back! What on earth is taking her so long! I swear I wish to never grant her freedom and keep her beneath my feet like a mat!" he blabbered loudly.

"Fardad! You bloody bastard! You have been a massive pain in my backside for too long! I swear I wish to fry you like sheesh kebabs and eat you for dinner! I imagine myself biting into your disgusting flesh and chewing it like a lion chews its kill!"

He kept on blabbering and burped loudly. Then, he took another large sip of his favorite red wine and was about throw the golden goblet on the floor when he heard a cooing sound. Immediately his eyes struck the window, and he noticed Roxanas tiny white pigeon, Alaana standing with the note tied to her feet. Instantly, he placed the goblet aside and rushed to open the window. He brought the pigeon inside and grabbed the note.

After reading the note, Soroush burst with bliss and excitement. His entire intoxication went away, and he spoke with sanity.

"Roxana, my dear girl! You have given me the best news ever! That ruddy man has failed@! This means that the entire trust that Kai Kobad had on him will turn into wisps of smoke, and he will be kicked out of this palace!"

Soroush let out a howl of laughter and kissed the

note.

"Master Marduk will reward me now! Well done, Roxana, well done!"

After saying that, he grabbed another piece of parchment and wrote another note to her, which read.

"Lovely slave R..a,

I am thrilled at the news of their failure! And I am ready to grant you your freedom, but you have to do a little work more. Just keep an eye on their all moves and update me from time to time. I am sure he will try some other tricks. Soon the Babylonians will take care of him now, and you be relieved from this job. If he returns to the capital by any chance, I will have him humiliated and kicked out of this place like a donkey!

Your Caring Master!"

He fastened the letter to the white pigeons feet and released it outside the window. Then he drank another goblet of wine and began to hum and dance merrily like a mad man across the chamber.

The priests gave them the clothes of ordinary people so they could blend in with the public while moving out of the temple area. Katir warned them that the general and his man could wake up anytime, so they couldnt take chances. They should not stand out from the crowd or get noticed as royalty. He warned them that they didnt know who came here as they welcomed everyone so others could watch them from King Marduks palace.

Suddenly, Fardad stopped because he had been

CHAPTER 12.   THE RELIEF

thinking for a long time about how they all had been away from the royal palace and the king and queen had no idea about their whereabouts or the fact that the priests could offer only a little help. They had no idea about the general and even the recent tremors. The king and queen had to know to send reinforcements to the temple and provide backup until they returned from their mission to the Zagros Mountains. The king and queen had no idea about that mission too.

Fardad spoke to his entourage, "People, I think we need to inform the royal palace of what has been going on. None of them at the palace have a clue about our whereabouts. I must go to the capital first to inform the honorable King Kai Kobad about the events and the aggression from King Marduk of the neighboring kingdom. He had sent his general to intercept us and capture my lovely Princess. It was as if he knew what our plans were. From what I know of him, he is an evil sorcerer and knows a lot more than we do. He wants to stop us, so the world and Persia are destroyed, and he can build a new world and kingdom to rule. You realize we need all the backup we can get. What do you think? We cant just go through this mission and get stopped by ambushes. With backup taking care of these little surprises, we will move faster."

The princess held a different view, and she said to Fardad, "I am the princess here, and I command you to go to Abzu and see what options are possible and what we can best choose from them. We all will be backing you up till the Zagros Mountains, and I feel that we have a backup in the form of that oracle lady guiding us all along. Now that weve been through all this hell and back, I realize that we could have avoided all these problems if we had given heed to her sayings. If we had acted on her word, we would have been already close to Abzu."

Ukund then said, "Your Majesty, if you dont mind, let me interject here, please. My friend is right. If we do not inform the honorable King Kai Kobad, Marduk can take advantage of the situation and attack the palace and take the king and queen hostage. We cant afford that, and they need to know what is happening. I am sure theyre worried about you as much as all of us. You, more of course, as you are their daughter."

The princess then said, "I understand and agree with the both of you. We are already running short of time and have to move fast; we cant afford more breaks. We need to follow Rukhsaars lead and back each other up to Abzu."

"Gyasi, can you do us this favor, please? You can move faster than all of us and get there in time. You can then send reinforcements our way, and in the temple area so we have enough backup. Do this for your princess, please? Its a request!"

Gyasi looked at Fardad, and Fardad nodded his head in agreement.

Gyasi then spoke, "Anything for you and saving the kingdom, your Majesty! I will get there as fast as I can and inform the royal palace to send in reinforcements. But where are our horses?"

CHAPTER 12.   THE RELIEF

Suddenly, they heard loud noises of something traveling toward them.

Rukhsaar commanded, "Stand firm. It could be another surprise attack!"

They all saw their horses run toward them as soon as she said that. In all the rush and confusion, they had left their horses behind. There was a note on one of them. Rukhsaar opened it and read it out loud.

"You left your steeds, and we sent them your way. May Yazdan be with you. They will get you to the mountains fast, as we have trained them to go in that direction. Your friend, Katir."

Rukhsaar breathed a sigh of relief as Katir had sent the horses their way so they could finally get more momentum. She had borrowed the parchment and ink from the motel owner, and the princess dictated the whole account which Rukhsaar wrote on the parchment. She then sealed the envelope and gave Gyasi and ordered him to go to the capital as fast as possible. She gave him one of the horses to take with him, and he was soon off his way. Now, they were four going toward Abzu.

Rukhsaar, Ukund, Princess, and Fardad loaded their belongings on their horses and started traveling toward the Zagros Mountains in Abzu.

***

Back at the temple, General Nabuzardan and his soldiers were still drowsy. They had been hurt badly by the snakes, and that had taken an enormous toll on their bodies. They could not recover in time to capture the princess and her companions, which was all the time Fardad needed to move out. "Be careful now, Guys. We need to move fast, but watch our tracks at all times. We cant afford any more surprise attacks, and we might face tougher enemies later, so we have to be on our guard at all times," Rukhsaar spoke like a true general. She had transformed into a formidable leader of the group and saved them on various occasions. They all nodded in agreement and moved ahead. Rukhsaar asked Gyasi and Ukund to watch for any surprises behind them while she, Fardad, and the princess would look ahead.

As the team trudged ahead, they saw a nice and pleasant evening, and birds were already flying over their heads and heading to their nests. Though everything looked calm and friendly, the fear of unexpected change lurked internally in their hearts.

The priests were watching General Nabuzardan and his soldiers. It seemed they had healed and were waking up. The men were in a daze and looked around, and they then remembered that they were in the temple and were completely healed.

The general said, "Thank you for your help in healing us. I feel strong as ever!"

His soldiers looked at him and nodded in agreement. The priests acknowledged and left them in the chamber so the three could plan their next moves.

After the priests left, the general said, "I havent given up on my quest to kidnap Princess Parinaaz and

CHAPTER 12.   THE RELIEF

take her back with me to the Eastern Kingdom of Turan. Her friends, those miscreants, had destroyed my plans. They must pay dearly for our misery. I have lost my entire army, and they chased us in the form of the undead while we were trying to survive the snakebites and the ensuing venom in our bodies. Had we not reached here, we could have been dead already."

The generals soldiers quietly listened to their master speaking about his torment, and then one of them said, "We are at your command, Sire. Tell us what needs to be done. I feel as good as new. Their potion is incredible. I cant believe we escaped death, especially after all that bleeding, the pain, and being chased by the army of the dead!"

"Hmmm," Nabuzardan frowned, brooding over about the matter.

"You know what? We made a mistake. We hadnt searched their bags when we captured those imbeciles. They took care of an entire army with those explosive balls that our now-dead soldiers were playing with. We never interrogated them when we had them captured, and we have no clue what the hell they were doing here!" the general continued.

He then said, "I believe that King Marduk knew through his knowledge that the princess was going to visit this temple, and thats why he sent us all here in this direction."

"King Marduk is one mighty king. He knows so much, but he never tells us anything more than just what we need to do," the other soldier exclaimed.

"Hes not only just a mighty and resourceful king, but he is also one of the most fearsome sorcerers in our lands. You better not cross him. We cant carry on like this, and we need reinforcements. Lets go back to our kingdom and speak to him. If he gives us the knowledge we seek about our former captives plans, we can then strike harder with a much stronger battalion," Nabuzardan said.

"I dont think he will be happy to see us go back empty-handed, Sire."

"What choice do we have, you idiot? We cant just sit around here at the temple while those no-good do-gooders go about playing saviors of our lands. We have to face the music, taking whatever comes our way. We deserve it because we failed. Lets make a move. The longer we stay here, the faster our enemies will complete their mission, and we will suffer a fate worse than death."

"And what is that, Sire?"

"Its a lifetime of living in our kings hell where well be burned to a crisp and be reborn and continue suffering!" "Oh my! Then, lets move!"

"Lets go. We can ask the priests to help us get two horses. So, well be on our way. Well also ask them about our enemies if they came here, and I doubt these priests will tell us if they even came here."

"How about we threaten to kill them?"

"You imbecile. We are strictly forbidden to do any such thing, and our king has told us not to harm them lest you forget they healed us!" "Yes, youre right, Sire.

271

CHAPTER 12.   THE RELIEF

Lets go. We are behind you."

The general and his soldiers were in no mood to face the wrath of King Marduk, but they had no choice. Without an army and weapons, they were of no use. They dreaded the journey back home and meeting their supreme leader but took a few deep breaths and went to the priests to bid them farewell and one final thank you. They had no idea what would happen to them, but they swallowed the bitter pill of failure and decided to head back.

Chapter 13

The Adversary

T HE journey back to King Marduks palace was very stressful. They had left the palace with a massive army but returned with just three, including the general. General Nabuzardan had underestimated their enemies. For a while, their enemies were captured, but Rukhsaars bombs were a bit too much for the army and allowed them an escape. Since then, the tides had turned, with Fardad and his friends gaining headway. Now that they were moving towards the Zagros Mountains, the general and his two soldiers are returning home with nothing to show for. They feared the wrath of their king and had no choice but to go home and inform their king. General Nabuzardan was a seasoned veteran soldier of King Marduks army and was a man who feared no mortal man.

He didnt like snakes, and his recent run-in with them was not at all welcoming. He would bravely face any punishment other than death. He would plead forgiveness and beg for another chance to capture their enemies but would not retreat. He has spent a lifetime in the kings army and had gone up the ranks from an ordinary soldier. He had learned the art of war and was thus crowned general not that long ago. King Marduk had specially asked the general to embark on this mission to capture Princess Parinaaz and had put his trust in him to do the job.

Before the General had left for the mission, the king had said, "General, you are to intercept the princess and capture her and bring her back to me. My sources and spies tell me she has left the palace with some friends and is heading towards the Urmia Temple for some work for her father, King Kai Kobad. He wanted the princess and forcibly marry her, and the only way to do it was to capture her. King Kai Kobad and King Marduk were mortal enemies since the princess rejected his advances. King Marduk was a powerful sorcerer and magician, and he could strike terror in the hearts of men and the undead. He offered no mercy and was ruthless. Whoever disobeyed him would suffer his wrath, and clearly, General Nabuzardan feared precisely that. The general hoped the king would offer him some salvation, considering he has been a loyal servant for a long time.

The journey back home was a few days, and the priests were pleasant enough to give them two horses, so they didnt have to walk all the way. The general sat on one horse, and the other two soldiers sat on the other. Their wounds had wholly healed earlier thanks to Katirs potion. However, it would not help them against King Marduks magic and sorcery. The king ruled over the Bactrian Kingdom and always wanted to conquer Persia. He had set his sights on taking down King Kai Kobads army but had first tried allying marriage to Princess Parinaaz but had now sought vengeance. The general knew he wouldnt be getting any love but was a loyal soldier. He did what he had to do and would face wrath because he had no choice and had to inform the king.

While the general and two soldiers were moving towards their home kingdom, another journeyman was venturing home too, back to the Persian capital. That man was Gyasi, who was traveling swiftly back to inform the honorable King Kai Kobad about the status of their mission and what they found about from High Priest Katir. A lot was going on in his head, and time was running out. He was constantly worrying about his friends and prayed for their safety. He was galloping fast and thinking back to his time spent with his friends. It was an unbelievable adventure.

He had formed a fantastic bond with Fardad and then, after meeting Ukund, Rukhsaar, and Princess Parinaaz. He and Ukund failed to bond so well earlier on but became close as the mission went on. He also realized a deeper bond with Rukhsaar and Ukund, but it seemed the others didnt notice. He also respected Ukund more because he cared about Fardad a lot. Fardad was very important and a vital part of this mission, plus he helped Gyasi gain his much-needed freedom. He owed Fardad his life, and thanks to their friendship, he was now a member of the royal palace, too.

He went from slavery to royalty, which was a giant leap for him, as he had spent years in slavery and did not know his family. Fardad was his family, and he would give his life to him. Gyasis mission was to inform the king and arrange an army to back his friends and prevent an assault from the evil King Marduk and his army. The task was far from over, and Gyasi was as worried as the other friends he left behind.

He was no stranger to following orders, so he listened to the princess and followed through. However, this time around, he was doing it to help his friends, which was part of his mission. Gyasi was afraid of the future and worried about his friend Fardad. The task he has undertaken was dangerous and could cost him his life. Therefore, he had to inform the honorable King Kai Kobad that his future son-in-law and prince of Persia needed further help and that enemies could outnumber him and his friends. It would take Gyasi a day or two to get back to the Kingdom, so he doesnt plan to stop for breaks unless his horse gets tired.

While Gyasi was speeding back to the Persian capital, his friends were shuffling forward to the Zagros Mountains. Their trip would take some time, but they stuck together and moved decently while looking out for enemies. Ukund and Rukhsaar led the way, with Princess Parinaaz and Fardad behind them. Mostly, the journey was tranquil, as each of them was concerned about getting the mission done in time. They had all been tired of the journey despite resting in a few places, such as the temple they were at before.

However, these breaks didnt help them overcome their overall tiredness because they were mentally exhausted. The mission had taken a significant toll on them because they had to escape death and capture frequently. They wanted to get now the job done and go home. However, they were unaware of the dangers that lay ahead. The evil King Marduk would get a rude awakening from his general, and when that happens, all hell will break loose.

For now, they were safe as they moved along. It was very much the calm before the storm. Fardad was amazed that the Princess was always by his side, despite the danger they would face later. She could have quickly gone home with Gyasi but stayed with her friends and out of love for her future prince. This was the unrivaled dedication both Fardad and Princess Parinaaz had for each other. They would stick with each other through thick and thin. They loved each other enough to give their lives to each other. That was the power of their love, and there was no way each of them would lose their sight. Their survival was crucial for the missions success. The missions success meant that Persia and the world would be saved from destruction, and any evil plans by enemies would be destroyed.

Ukund and Rukhsaar also knew that they were in it till the very end. The two of them had formed a liking towards each other but had never expressed it to their friends. Ukund was very fascinated by Rukhsaars bravery. She had saved the friends from very tough situations and close encounters. She also bravely led them and had the makings of a brilliant military general. She was more strong-willed and courageous than her male counterparts, being a woman.

Despite her tough exterior, she still had the heart of a woman. She also wanted to feel loved and love someone the way her princess had found her man. She had seen that man in Ukund. Ukund had joined the mission as Fardads best friend but now had become an able leader in his own right. He had now become the righthand man of the warrior lady Rukhsaar. She had spent her life in the palace and trained to be a formidable soldier and personal assistant of the princess. She was her best friend and her bodyguard. She would give her life for hers if it meant preserving her life.

Now that she knew the princess was safe, she kept wondering if Ukund would take a fancy to her, just like she had done with him. Ukund would constantly keep a straight face and was very good at hiding his feelings and emotions. However, more recently, theyd exchanged quite a few smiles and glances with each other. As they moved ahead, Ukund broke the ice and the silence and spoke to Rukhsaar, "How far are we from our destination?"

"We have to keep moving forward until we get to Abzu. The priests suggested this path would lead us there, and I strongly feel that these are coordinates to a map or directions to Abzu. You kept mentioning that Aadburzin is a famous astrologer, and since this is his book, these have to be coordinated. I am also very interested in astrology, so this is fascinating. We dont know how to follow these coordinates until your best friend speaks to that Oracle lady, and I believe she holds the key to unlocking the coordinates in the book. Your friend can only tell us when she contacts him."

"I hope its soon; otherwise, wed get just following this path. Theres a long way to cover, but I feel when the time is right, the oracle will contact him." "I believe the oracle speaks to Fardad in his dreams, so we may need to take a rest stop and hope for a miracle!"

"We are fine for now. If there is an urgent matter, the oracle will contact Fardad. We should follow the path and find a place to rest, and hopefully, we will find one further down this path."

"The horses will need rest, too. Well stop a little way ahead. Its just the four of us now, and well need to back each other. Hopefully, our other friend will get to the Persian capital in time to inform the king. We need all the help we can get."

"Hell get there in time for sure. Fardad trusts him, so will I. By the way, Ive never seen a courageous woman warrior in my life. Your bag of tricks saved us several times!"

"I enjoy taking out enemies by surprise, and thats my specialty. These bastards dont deserve any mercy. If they lay a hand on the princess or my friends, I will make sure theres hell to pay."

"Youve got so much fire in you, Rukhsaar! Its unbelievable. Ive never seen so much fire in a woman!"

"You know Ive been waiting for someone to extinguish it with love!"

"Quite direct, arent you, Rukhsaar!"

"Yes. I dont enjoy playing mind games or riddles. I say what I feel, and you were direct too!"

"Thats how I like my women, and not that Ive been involved in one before! I just like it when women dont beat around the bush so much!"

"I like my men the same way, not that I have been with a man before, but I do like you. There, I said it!"

"Yes, we can be like fire and water, and I can extinguish your fire. I do like you too, Rukhsaar. Its been an honor and a privilege going on this mission and in battle with you."

"The mission is far from over, so we shouldnt be distracted. However, this journey requires a delightful conversation, so I welcome this! That being said, Id love to know you more. So, Ukund, tell me about yourself?"

"I thought you knew, but I will give you a refresher. I have been friends with Fardad since we were kids. I looked up to his father like my own, and you know Aadburzin was a famous astrologer. I told him I would protect his son after hes gone, so that brings me here. I am honoring the word of my best friends father, and you are here to protect the princess, so were both the same."

"Yes, I knew about the friendship, and now it all makes sense. I wondered why you had that astrologers book, and he left it in your care, and I believe you knew he was going on a mission he may never return from."

"Aadburzin asked me to keep it a secret and that he may not return, but he was doing a favor for the Persian king."

"I see. I can connect the dots, so that famous astrologer got us together on this mission. Did he tell you what he was going to do?"

"Aadburzin never spoke of it because he didnt want me to or his family to get worried. I also didnt have the habit of asking him questions, so I didnt."

"I am sure he was going on a noble cause for the king, and now we must finish what he started. I see a small village coming up, and lets move towards it and rest. I hope we can have the oracle visit your friend and guide us further."

"I like that idea. The horses would need rest, food, and water. We should stop when we get to the village, and we also need answers so that rest will help." "Yes, we should be in the village area in like 10 minutes."

That said, the four friends were about to make a stop at the village. Ukund and Rukhsaar had finally confessed their love to each other. Fate had brought these four together, and new relationships have formed.

While the friends were nearing the village, General Nabuzardan had entered his kingdom area. He felt home drawing closer. He signaled his men that they would need to stop soon and take the horses to the palace. Finally, the castle drew nearer, and the fears of the three men heightened by a big notch. They were dreading the meeting with the evil King Marduk. The general kept himself calm as he was used to facing his fears.

One soldier told the general, "Sire, I do not wish to see the king. Please speak on our behalf."

The general replied, "Even if you dont, he will still punish you because he knows everything. I will speak to him as I am his General. I suggest you stay out of sight so you dont aggravate him more. I know what to expect. If you thought those snake bites were poisonous, then you must not underestimate his magic. He will burn us crisp and eat us for supper. Whatever will happen will happen. Lets move on. Well be reaching the palace soon."

In a manner of minutes, the general and his men were at the palace. General Nabuzardan entered the Bactrian Kingdoms Royal Palace. His men went to their quarters and left the general to speak to the king. The guards informed him that King Marduk was strolling near the river going through the palace.

"Welcome home, General Nabuzardan. King Marduk wishes to meet you. He informed us to let you know when you return. We got wind that you were on your way back. We shall not ask you about your mission as the king would want to know why you came back empty-handed. He has been very anxious lately. He is on his regular stroll near the river. You may find him there and speak to him," said one of the palace guards.

General Nabuzardan had gotten more anxious and worried about his life. Several fears were going through his mind. He had returned home with a small fraction of the massive army he had left the palace with. The failed secret mission of kidnapping the princess was a blotch on his career. He had to answer why so many men under his command could not hold on to the princess or care for her friends. He had to face the king and go towards the river.

General Nabuzardan walked over to the king and bowed to him. The king was walking back and forth but stopped in his tracks when he saw his general and was a bit surprised to see him empty-handed. He thought the captives had been sent to the prisons. He would soon get his answers. The king was a tall figure with a gold crown on his head and a cape on his back. He held a long staff in his hand, which had magic powers. He wore silk robes and looked majestic in his appearance. He looked down at the general, who was nearly half his height.

"General, I have been expecting you. I hope you didnt come back empty-handed and have taken our esteemed guests to their respective chambers if you know what I mean."

"Your majesty, I am so sorry for not coming sooner. We captured the princess...."

"Thats splendid. Have you asked the palace guards to treat her well? I shall soon meet my future queen."

"Your Majesty, we had her with us...."

CHAPTER 13.   THE ADVERSARY

"Yes, you did, but now she is at the palace. You and your men deserve a reward. Did you come back with all your men, or did you face any resistance from the princess and her friends?"

"Your Majesty, we faced resistance, but. ..."

"You brought the princess. I dont care about the men, and we have enough soldiers. What about her friends? Did they come?"

"No. the friends escaped. ..."

"You mean, they retreated?"

"Yes, they did. Your Majesty, the Princess..."

"Good, we dont have any need for them. Greetings to our esteemed guest."

"Your Majesty, please wait. You must hear me out!"

"General, head to your chamber and speak. We can talk later. Rest. You came from a long mission, and you shall be rewarded."

"My Lord, the task you sent to me has not been fulfilled!" General Nabuzardan said in a broken voice.

"What do you mean? Let me go to the chambers."

The king rushed to the chambers and asked the guards where the princess was?

"Lord, the general came empty-handed with just two men!"

The king turned around, fuming, but he blasted fireballs from his staff towards the guards before he left. The guards ran for their lives, knowing the king was in a horrible mood.

"General!!!!! You did not bring back the princess!!!!

How could you? You had an entire army? You just returned with two men! I am appalled by your performance. You have failed me!"

King Marduk turned and looked at his most trusted general. He held his staff in his hand and wanted to shoot but kept it aside.

He moved forward, kicked Nabuzardan, and growled, "What a shame! I was not expecting this from you, Nabuzardan! I trusted you and made you general because I knew you wouldnt ever fail me! How could you! Now you must face the everlasting punishment of dwelling in my hell where you will burn, crisp, and die and be reborn, and the cycle will continue. You will suffer for eternity for failing me! You and your men against a pathetic group of people protecting the princess, and still it wasnt enough!? This is unbelievable! I dont need a general because I can do this myself. Now, it is time for you to face your fate!"

General Nabuzardan kneeled and begged for mercy.

"Spare my life, my Lord, and please hear me out! Give me a chance to explain! I beg you!"

"You have five minutes. If you dont wrap up your story, you shall be toast, and so will your two men!"

"I tried my best and even had captured the princess pretty easily. Unfortunately, one lowlife young man had tricked us and rescued the princess. I later searched for her but couldnt locate her. Not only that, one of her friends had a bag of tricks that took us by surprise. As you know, some of our men got too overconfident and learned a terrible lesson. She had explosive balls that blinded us and took several of us out.

When the dust cleared, they had escaped. When we tried to capture them again, we were outnumbered, and they retreated with the princess nowhere to be found again. We went back to the Urmia Temple wounded because of bites from rattlesnakes. Had we not reached the temple in time, the priests would not have healed us. We knew that the mission had been over because we were without our army and clueless about where those imbeciles left with their princess. This is why we returned here to the palace to explain our failure and await further instructions. My humble apologies. We failed you, and we deserve your anger and wrath. Please dont send us to that hell. We deserve another chance. If you allow me, we will recapture the princess. This time, we will go with tricks of our own!" "Your time is up. Who was that man you talked about? Does he have a name?"

"Lord, its Fardad!"

"Fardad, son of Aadburzin? Yes, I know of his father, the famous astrologer. He was on some secret mission, and I had my minions take care of him. Now, his son is finishing his fathers unfinished business. We will take care of him and his peasant friends. You want a chance, General. This is your final chance. Dont fail me!" "Lord, what would you want me to do?"

"I will cast a spell that will send a deadly disease to all of Persia. Everyone, including the king and queen, shall die. You will lead an army of the dead to the Zagros Mountains in Abzu, and no mortal man has ever gone there."

"I have never heard of that place, my Lord."

"Of course, you numbskull. How would you? Its an ancient land full of magic and unlimited power. The son of Aadburzin is heading there. You must head there immediately with this powerful army of monsters and undead and take out our enemies. Dont let that man climb the mountains! Dont fail me, and as for your two failed soldiers, they will burn in hell!"

"Lord, spare them please, as you spared me. Give them a chance. ..."

"Silence!!! Begone now; dont interfere in my affairs. It will help if you take your leave now. Theres no time to waste! If you fail me, you will join them too. . .now begone!"

The general left to get his gear from the armory and saw the guards escorting the two soldiers while they were screaming, "Save us, save us, general!" Only screams were heard a few minutes later, and the general walked off feeling hopeless. He had another chance for redemption, and he would not return to the kingdom until he achieved success.

Chapter 14

The Shaking

GYASI reached the palace door at Takht-e-Shah. Even though he was tired, he reached the daarbans (guards) standing at the main entrance.

"I want to see the King immediately. Its urgent," Gyasi shouted to guards.

The guards immediately recognized Gyasi, and he was promptly escorted to the kings chamber, where he waited for the honorable King Kai Kobad. The king had been away from the palace on his hunt and was informed by the palace guards that Gyasi had returned and wished to speak with him. Gyasi was waiting with bated breath because he was worried about his friends. I dont know where to begin. Theres so much to say, but I will tell His Majesty everything.

King Kai Kobad entered the chamber, and Gyasi stood up in respect.

"Your Majesty, I bring to you news from my friends at the request of your daughter, Princess Parinaaz."

"Gyasi, make yourself at home. Tell me if my

daughter is safe."

"Your Majesty, the princess is doing very well. My friends have ensured her safety."

"Thank you so much. I am glad that they are safe too. So, I understand you have urgent matters to discuss. Tell me. How can I be of assistance?"

But before Gyasi could say anything, Queen posed a question, "Where are Parinaaz and Rukhsaar?" the queen asked.

"My Queen, they stayed in the north as they figured it was better to stay in that region," Gyasi informed.

Soroush looked cunningly with one cocked eye and began to scan Gyasi. Then immediately, he stood up like a roaring tiger and pounced on the Ethiopian man. "Where is your honorable friend Fardad, Ethiopian? He is supposed to be accompanying our dear Princess Parinaaz! Where is he then? Gone hiding, eh? Too scared to do anything? Soroush roared in a mocking tone.

"Soroush!" growled King Kai Kobad, which made all the courtiers shiver profusely. "How dare you raise your voice in front of me? Your king is right here! And you dare to raise your voice in front of me! You know very well that I can have you ruthlessly punished for your insolence!"

Soroush turned into a scary cat at King Kai Kobads roar and timidly begged him for forgiveness.

"I sincerely apologize, my King."

Gyasi looked at him distastefully as though he were

a piece of trash and replied, "Wise Minister Soroush, Fardad is now traversing the northern region with the princess," Gyasi explained in a dangerously sarcastic voice, yet not meeting his eye completely. He was pretty nervous as he did not want to reveal the oracle dream story to the king and his courtier. He feared they might call Fardad a lunatic. But he knew in his heart that Fardad was a man of his words–something which Suhrab might not know.

"What did the High Priest Katir say?" Soroush asked rather timidly this time.

"Sire, High Priest Katir, couldnt offer us any insight into the contents of Aardburzins book. He told us that the symbols in the book are ancient, and no one in the temple could understand them."

"Thats indeed disappointing!" Soroush said in a sadly sarcastic tone.

"So going to the north towards the temple doesnt bring any benefit." Soroush turned and said while looking at the king and queen. "Therefore, my king, I would like to humbly request you to call back Princess Parinaaz and Fardad, who knows in what condition our sweet princess might be in, and what all conditions she might have to bear and what all places she might have to spend the nights in, and there might not be any proper food too!" he cried, sarcastically placing his palm on his chest in a mocking expression of dreadfulness. "Why force her into embarking further on a pointless journey now?"

But before King Kai Kobad could take any deci-

CHAPTER 14.   THE SHAKING

sion, Gyasi intervened quickly.

"There is something I would like to inform you, my honorable King, and that is why I been sent here. There is a clear and present danger to Persia!" Gyasi said. As Gyasi uttered these words, there was a huge murmur amongst the courtiers, and Suhrab turned and looked back at him and said, "What sort of danger?"

"Your Majesty, there are spies in Persia. Thanks to Yazdan, we escaped. My friends and your daughter are now safe, but we were captured before. They tried to torture us, but we thwarted them and escaped. Moreover, my King, we spotted the secret spy mission roaming near Urmia. They traced us and tried to kidnap the princess. But we were saved by my Lord Fardad, and that is why he and the princess stayed in that region and sent me to inform you urgently," Gyasi informed.

"Spies from where?" the king demanded furiously.

"My lord from Babylon," Gyasi said.

"It has to be that darned magician king Marduk! By Yazdan, that evil monstrosity of a human wont leave my daughter!" the king shouted in rage.

"What is our army doing, Suhrab?" the queen asked worriedly.

"My Queen, Ill inform the Persian army to be alert!" General Suhraab said with a bow and left.

"Is there anything else I need to know? I shall send some of my men in their direction to provide them support in case they encounter trouble," the king asked Gyasi. "My Lord, there is more. King Marduk had sent his General Nabuzardan to capture Princess Parinaaz. They ambushed us, and we were temporarily captured but escaped thanks to Rukhsaars bombs. We had an advantage when we encountered the army later, as many of their soldiers were fatally wounded. We tied them up and then left for the Urmia Temple. We did not see them after that, but we believe the general is alive and has possibly returned to his king. If that is the case, they can launch an attack on Persia. I would highly advise you to get your men ready for any attack or cut them off before they reach the capital."

The queen remembered how things changed. When Parinaaz refused the marriage proposal, Marduk felt betrayed, and thats when his animosity began. He warned King Kai Kobad that he would deliver vengeance.

"Oh God, that evil king wanted to marry my daughter against her will, and neither was her father in favor of it nor I. He is desperate to see us fall and would do anything to get back at us and have forcibly married the princess. I will get the men to stay on guard, and we can station more men on the capital borders. We will send another team to help my daughter and your friends," the queen said.

"Thank you for bringing this to my attention. You better get ready to move. I will get a team of soldiers ready to go with you on horseback," the king said. "As you wish, Lord. We will move fast toward the north, but we dont know what King Marduk is planning. We have to be prepared for possibly anything." "He is a sorcerer who will do all evils he can do to harm us. We have to do the best we can. We dont have magic powers, but we have a strong and brave army. So, dont worry and move on ahead. Well do our best here," Soroush said.

"But the question is how Marduk knew the princess is heading towards the north?" Gyasi said, and the entire court was in silence.

"My Lord, I wont let you down. I shall be on my way," Soroush said in a nervous tone and looked at Gyasi.

"I am going to ask my generals to go with you to a battalion. Time is of the essence. Lets move!"

***

Back at the village, Fardad and his friends had found a motel to rest. They had stopped to take some time off and got some food as they had a long journey ahead. They werent sure if they were heading in the right direction.

Princess Parinaaz and Fardad went on a short stroll and talked things over. The lovebirds were in a reflective mood and wanted to talk about how things had gone on so far and the mission at hand.

"Fardad, my Love, I feel like where we get lost if we go in between these mountains. The jagged peaks and sharp edges tower over us as if were bobbing under the surface of the earth and couldnt see the top of the mountain. Each peak towers higher than we do, and were not ready to climb these mountains. Theres a lot of confusion," the princess said.

"Pari, I know weve been through a lot, and theres still a massive challenge lying ahead of us. We will prevail. But Princess, I request that you, Rukhsaar, and Ukund stay here in these mountains until I find the way to Abzu. That oracle lady has said that I do not need to climb over the mountains," Fardad replied. "You know climbing mountains was my desire. From my palace windows, I always wanted to reach the snow-capped peaks of Alburz mountains, but now I realize it is not that simple," Parinaaz laughingly said.

Fardad smiled; he was quiet and worried as well. Leaving the princess in the mountains was also not safe.

There could be beasts here, he thought.

"My Princess, dont you worry about that. I dont remember what the older woman told me when I reached the Zagros mountains. But surely, I will recall it back," Fardad said.

"I am not worried. With you by my side, we can conquer anything!"

"Thats the spirit. Lets head back to the motel so we can meet up with the others."

The two of them then headed back to the motel to catch up with the others and plan their next move. Rukhsaar and Ukund discussed their subsequent actions at the motel while waiting for Princess Parinaaz and Fardad to come back.

"Ukund, we should move out soon. I dont want

to spend another night here waiting for the oracle to give Fardad a premonition. I fear that King Marduk will send another spy mission to capture the princess in the Zagros Mountains. I suggest we get ready to move out when our friends return."

"Rukhsaar, I agree. We dont know if were heading in the right direction or not. We cannot stay here longer. Its too dangerous, and besides that, Fardad has forgotten half of his dream,"

"Ukund, we will move in the direction Katir told us. If the older woman wishes to contact Fardad, she can, without him going into a dreaming state." "I dont know what the next appropriate step should be. However, you have raised a fair point: we cant sit here and let our enemies catch up to us or get to the mountains faster than us."

As they were talking, Princess Parinaaz and Fardad walked in.

Rukhsaar spoke, "Glad to see you both back. We need to make a move now."

Fardad then said, "I have not been contacted by the oracle yet. Are you sure we shouldnt wait for her to contact me?"

Rukhsaar firmly stated, "I dont care, honestly. The lady contacts you with her will, and we dont have time. Fardad, we need to move, and she hasnt even contacted you for some time. She could have contacted you if she wanted to. You want us just to sit around and wait for her?"

"I am not saying that. We dont know if were even

heading in the right direction, as the High Priest took a hunch by sending us here. Were here, and the plan was to wait for her to contact me," replied Fardad.

Rukhsaar tried to calm herself down as much as she could. She then spoke, "Fardad, we will move in the direction we were advised. If she wants to contact you, she will. I understand your concern, but we dont have time. We arent safe here, and who knows what that evil king could do knowing Parinaaz wasnt captured."

Princess Parinaaz then intervened and said, "Rukhsaar is right. I trust her, and so should we. Gyasi should have gotten in touch with my father, and I am sure my father would send help our way or do something. Fardad, we cant take our chances. What if we stay the night here and the oracle doesnt contact you? Then what shall we do? We have three days, and then we should move out from here. Fardad, trust me. Were doing the right thing."

Ukund then chimed in with his feedback, "I second what the ladies have to say. We should move. My friend, the oracle, will contact you, but we need to move fast. We have been pushed back already. Remember, we are on a deadline. Lets all move out now."

Fardad finally agreed by saying, "Alright! We will head out now, and hopefully, the oracle will contact me within three days."

The four of them grabbed their gear, mounted their horses, and moved in the same direction. Ukund paid the motel owner and asked him if he knew Abzus location. He told them that legend has it that Abzu was in the direction they were going. Other than that, the owner had no clue. The motel owner had people ask him previously about it, so he had some idea. The four friends headed out in the same direction.

***

King Marduk was on his horse, looking at a disciplined army of thousands of men. The mens heads were down, and they were looking at the ground. There wore metallic armor on their chests and metallic helmets on their heads. The men were not sweating and were not breathing, though they were all standing. Also, even though it was hot, they were not sweating. General Nabuzardan felt proud as he stood near the kings horse in front of the massive army.

King Marduk spoke to the general, "General, now you must not return as a failure. This is my most powerful army, and you are commanding it. I will not give you any leverage to fail, and if you do, you will be eaten by them!"

"My Lord, I promise you that those low lives will pay the price, and we will destroy their temples and the capital. I will bring back the heads of their king and the queen, and you can display them as you wish–"

"You fool, I want their daughter. Do you think I care about those royals? If I see them, Ill burn them to a crisp. They will not be spared, but their daughter shall be my queen. Now, you must move. I will watch your every move, and I will take matters into my hands if you fail. Persia will now bear my wrath! Now, move!"

General Nabuzardan took the mace and struck it on the ground. The entire army did the same, and the earth shook as he did so mechanically. The men lifted their heads and shouted. The men had rotten flesh on their faces as if they had been raised from Dakhma—something left by birds and vultures.

General Nabuzardan moved out of the Babylonian capital with his heavily armed battalion on a mission where failure was not an option.

I hope my king hands over control of Persia to me. I deserve this much for serving him for so many years. I have been his loyal servant and soldier. I have led his armies into battle and earned some great victories. I deserve this much. If my king crowns me as the new king of Persia, and every man, woman, and child will obey me. I will have my redemption for all I have suffered in the last mission. The humiliation. The horror. Now, I will not let anyone steal my glory. This is my army, and I am its commanding officer, Nabuzardan thought.

***

Fardad and the princess, Ukund, and Rukhsaar were galloping fast towards Zagros mountains, hoping that the oracle would contact him somewhere down the path. He was worried as he could see the light in the sky turning into darkness slowly. Fardad, while moving forward, started praying to Lord Yazdan to show him the light. They could hear the wind rustling through the trees and the low growl of a wolf howling in the distance.

"We need to look for the shelter. There are wolves here," Rukhsaar said, and all looked at each other.

Fardad looked at the sky. To his far left was a blushing pink, and it was clear that it would be darkened soon.

Ukund took a stick from the bushes and sketched the zodiac on the ground. He was doing his calculations, and then he turned to Fardad and said, "We should stop now." Ruhsaar had climbed up some rocks, and she was traversing the place for the likely place to spend the night.

Parinaaz, looking at the skies, stopped and asked her friends to look toward the sky.

"My Friends, war is about to begin in Persia. I know this is a sign. The skies have turned dark. Evil King Marduk has cast a darkness spell, drowning the light, and he wants to slow us down. This is also a sign that war is about to begin. He sends his forces to the capital; otherwise, the skies would never turn this dark. The time for deliverance is here. I hope theyre ready for battle. It seemed as if King Marduk had cast a spell on the entire land where it would all be entirely engulfed in darkness," Ukund said.

"Control your nervousness, Ukund. The King knows what to do. We must continue with the mission. We have sent Gyasi to warn him, so he must know by now," Rukhsaar said.

"Parinaaz, we will move, but the darkness will slow us down. Lets keep moving down this path and see where we take."

The group resumed their journey.

***

The priest in the army looked at the skies and said to General Suhraab, "War is upon us. The skies have turned dark: the evil king has sent his army to the capital." "I can sense it. However, we must move forward and fight them before they reach the capital. We will be victorious. Lets pray to Yazdan for success." General Suhraab replied, "You are right. War is upon us, and we will go to the north to stop the entry of Babylonians into Persia. The fate of Persia lies in our hands."

"I hope your friend knows what we are doing," Soroush looked at Gyasi and spoke.

"I know Fardad will do whatever is good for our kingdom, but we need to get to him as fast as we can," Gyasi said.

"We must stop the Babylonians," King said.

"Were moving as fast as we can. May Lord Yazdans blessings be upon us all!"

King Kai Kobad and General Suhraab took a battalion toward the north. It would not be safe for the queen to stay at the capital, so they sent her to the south. Queen Anahita was without her royal robes and was disguised as a commoner. The palace guards had gone to each house in the capital and asked the people to either leave or stay inside hidden as the capital was on the verge of war.

***

Rukhsaar led her friends toward Abzu, but the Oracle had not contacted Fardad yet. Rukhsaar signaled her friends to keep moving because they were surrounded by darkness. Suddenly, the road became narrower, and it seemed as if they were on the right track. Rukhsaar signaled forward, saying, "My friends, the road is getting narrower, and I feel were moving in the right direction. Lets keep moving! I also think that the oracle will contact Fardad once we get closer. Oracle, where are you? Fardad thought.

The group kept moving toward the single road as the darkness enveloped the entire area. However, the road was the only way to go so that the darkness wouldnt be a hindrance.

Suddenly, they found a cave in the rocks.

"This could be the den of wolves!" Rukhsaar said.

"Quickly, we must gather some twigs and start the fire!"

They started the fire, and Rukhsaar made a fireball using cloth from her sleeve and threw it into the cave. Luckily, the cave was empty.

They went inside, and Ukund made a sigil on the entrance to protect them. Ukund said, "Fardad and I will fulfill the duties one after another. The princess and Rukhsaar should sleep first."

The princess and Rukhsaar slept. They were too tired and had only a few minutes to enter into a deep slumber. Ukund made some tinctures from the herbs he collected along with the bushes nearby and made a soothing tea.

After some time, Ukund started feeling sleepy and went deep asleep. Now only Fardad was awake, and he started dizzy too. Within minutes he found it utterly difficult to remain to awaken and while saying, "Ukund...Ukund drifted into sleep," Fardad saw the dream. There were wee clouds all around him, and he heard an echoing voice, "The time is now to light the darkest hour....Only you can light the darkness!"

"I hope what you say is true....," Fardad said.

"You need to reach Abzu and save Persia," the voice said.

"How do I save the kingdom? I dont even know how to get to Abzu."

"You leave your friends and go alone from onwards ...."

"How do I go? I dont know the way!"

"Utter the Glorious Name of Lord Yazdan, which I am pronouncing."

Fardad heard an echo in his head, and he memorized the Great Divines name.

"Once you utter the name. Its echo will wake the Holy Simurgh Bird from its hibernation of 6000 years. The Bird Simurgh will appear and lead you to the entrance of Abzu. "Wake up now, and you will light the way in the darkness... you shall find what you seek."

Oracles voice kept diminishing until there was complete silence.

"Oracle, Oracle. . .wait, wait. . .!"

A few seconds later, Fardad fell to the ground on his side. Fardad opened his eyes. While his head was still on the ground, he found many wolves at the cave entrance to his horror.

Fardad stood up and shouted with full force. His friends woke up as well. The girls shouted, and quickly they took their quiver and arrows and started throwing arrows. Ukund and Fardad took their swords out. But the wolves were too much for them.

Fardad suddenly recalled the great divine name, and he pronounced the name. His breath turned into a vortex, and all the wolves were taken by it, and they were thrown centrifugally out. The mountains started shaking, and a loud sound was heard.

They all came out of the cave and found that the Zagros mountains were still reverberating. There was echoing, and then behind the mountains, the light started emerging as if some fiery storm was coming out of it, and then appeared a gigantic bird in the sky. Suddenly, they heard a sound, and a colossal creature hovered over them.

Ukund cried out, "Everyone, take cover. We could be under attack!"

Parinaaz said, "I dont think its threatening at all. Its huge but is not looking to attack us. Everyone, dont make any sudden moves or intimidate the creature. It may be here to tell us something."

The bird came down and landed near them.

"Simurgh!"

They all shouted in surprise.

"The oracle told the truth!" Fardad shouted with happiness.

"By Yazdan, what is this being!?" Rukhsaar looked at it with her jaws dropped.

"I have never seen such a creature in my life! Its magnificent!" Fardad said.

The creature was a massive bird who landed in front of the group and announced its arrival, saying, "My Friends, dont fear me. I am not here to harm but help. I am here for the chosen one to fulfill his destiny. Please appear before me so we can save the world."

They were stunned that such a magnificent bird could speak. It had long white wings and a short eagle-like beak. It had a soft and padded seat for someone to sit on, and it seemed like it could only hold one person. Ukund recognized the bird from one of the drawings in Aadburzins book. He quickly took out the picture, pointed at it, and saw the uncanny resemblance.

"If I am not mistaken, we are in the presence of the great Simurgh! My master Aadburzin would always tell me that Simurgh would save us, and I could never understand what he meant. Now, I know that I am standing in front of the legendary Simurgh! The one you seek is my best friend Fardad, son of my master Aadburzin. He is standing next to me."

"Very well, so it is you, Fardad. Its indeed a pleasure to meet the chosen one. You are correct in stating that I am Simurgh and shall take you to the cave of Abzu and save Persia," Simurgh spoke.

"Yazdan is with us," Parinaaz said.

"I know, Pari. Thats why I am so relaxed. I just was disturbed by the quick conversation with the oracle. She just asked me to reach Abzu through the Simurgh." "We shall. Trust Yazdan!" Fardad said.

"Of course, always trust in Him."

"Because you are the chosen one. I am at your service. Persia is under attack, and if we dont move fast, we wont have a kingdom or even world to save," Simurgh said.

Parinaaz asked the bird, "Is my father safe? Is he? I am the daughter of–"

Simurgh cut in and said, "Honorable King Kai Kobad...you are Princess Parinaaz. Your father is safe. He has escaped the palace with your friend. The former slave Gyasi."

Parinaaz then said, "I am so glad he is alright. Do you know where they are headed?"

Simurgh replied, "I believe they are headed north, which means they could be coming here. Thats all I know."

Fardad suddenly remembered that he had left his mother behind. He asked Simurgh, "Can you tell me if my mother and Queen Anahita are safe? They were at the palace when we left." Simurgh let out a smile and said, "The fine ladies are safe. The king had already sent them away before the invasion began. You will see them again once youre victorious. You dont need to worry about them now."

Fardad and Parinaaz breathed sighs of relief, knowing that their respective mothers were safe. The final battle was upon them, and they had to stay strong for their loved ones.

Fardad and his friends climbed over the Simurgh, and the giant bird flew into the sky.

***

General Nabuzardan and his dead army were heading towards the Persian capital. They had come in from the Kingdom of Babylon in the west. They crossed the dark forest and met the Persian army battalion.

"Weve been given orders by honorable King Kai Kobad to ask you to surrender and stand down. None of you will be hurt. There is no need to go to war," The Persian Commander Kamran commanded.

General Nabuzardan smiled ferociously and said, "No one asks Nabuzardan to surrender. You dont know who youre talking to, and your men are no match for us. Why dont you surrender and let us take over, and we promise not to hurt you? Otherwise, your fate is sealed. This army will devour your men and your people. I suggest you stand aside and clear the path so we can move on. Your king is now King Marduk will deal with Kai as he pleases. After all, he is the father of the beautiful princess who has won our kings heart."

CHAPTER 14.   THE SHAKING

"Shut up, Nabuzardan, Commander Kamran roared. We are given orders not to let your army pass for any reason, and were ready to lay down our lives to protect Persia and the king and even his princess. Go through us if you wish to pass. We will not let you go or negotiate with your king." "Gladly. At my command, my dead army will move in. Charge!"

General Nabuzardans army effortlessly broke through the barricades near lake Urmia. The Persian soldiers were powerless against them. They showed some resistance, but to no avail. The army of dead was too strong for them. The rams were blown throughout the kingdom, signifying that the land was under attack.

***

Fardad was in a complete trance after seeing Simurgh and riding on him. Its long wide wings and beak resembled the eagle but were perhaps easily 20 times its size with a long tail perhaps used to deflect attacks from enemies. Fardad waited for Simurgh and was hoping the rest of the mission would go very smoothly. Princess Parinaaz and Fardad looked at each other and smiled, knowing they were near their destination. Rukhsaar suddenly felt something uneasy. She had a fear of heights and was holding tight on Ukund.

Ukund asked her, "Is everything okay? Were almost there now."

"I dont feel good at all. Theres a sick feeling in my stomach. Dont tell the princess."

Ukund laughed and said, "We should be happy now. Yazdan is sending the Simurgh for our help. I am now sure all will be fine."

Rukhsaar smiled and said, "You keep me sane, my Love. Well win and will shine this darkness with our light."

They continued charging toward the mountains, following the path. Each of them was marveling with awe at the sight of the magnificent mountain range. Finally, the bird landed near a cave.

"Now, I shall go alone. Give me the book of my father, Ukund," Fardad said.

Ukund took out the book and gave it to Fardad.

Fardad looked at his friends.

"My Love, weve gotten this far. Its unbelievable. The mountains are incredible, and well get there with you. Just look inside your heart, and you will be guided. My father would tell me stories about the noble princes of the past who would look into their hearts and seek guidance. Just close your eyes and touch your heart. Youll know what to do!" Parinaaz motivated her love.

"Fardad, trust your instincts. I believe in you!" Ukund said.

Fardad then said, "I believe you all. Here goes nothing!"

He closed his eyes and touched his heart. Parinaaz embraced him while his eyes were closed. He kissed Parinaazs hand a few minutes later and spoke, "Ill be back soon!"

CHAPTER 14.   THE SHAKING

Ukund then asked, "So, what do we do while you are away? Shall we stay here and wait for Gyasi and the king?"

Simurgh then replied, "I believe you should stay here and wait for him. Once the mission is over, he will reunite with you. You must stand guard for any enemy attacks."

"Fardad, go ahead. Fulfill your destiny. We shall wait for you here. If I am correct, Gyasi and the king shall be with us soon. We need to give them safe passage and protection," Rukhsaar said.

"My love, my darling, this is your time to shine. You can save us all. The kingdom and the world depend on you! May the blessings of Yazdan be with you," Princess Parinaaz said after she gave Fardad a hug and a kiss.

Ukund embraced his friend and wished him well, "Go on, my dear friend. I am so proud of you today. You remind me of your father. This is what you were born for. You will be the hero of Persia. Go now. The fate of Persia and the world is in your hands!"

"Thank you, my friends, and my love Pari. I shall be back soon. Simurgh, you stay here with my friends."

"The blessings of Yazdan be with you," Simurgh said.

"What do I do when I get inside? Where do I go? What must I do?"

"You shall see the signs. Just go inside, and you will be guided. Dont worry. You shall not be lost."

The mythical bird had played a tremendous role in

keeping Fardads heart at ease, despite the surrealism of all that was happening around him. If there was any chance for him to again share the joy and slight worry that he had experienced, he would love to have it happen again. Fardad looked at his friends, who beckoned a reassuring smile in return, and Fardad entered the cave.

Chapter 15

The Abzu

Back in Babylon, King Marduk got word through spies that the Persian capital would soon be taken. The Persian army was no match for General Nabuzardan and his army of undead. The news was circulating that the king had left the capital.

"Kai Kobad, that coward. I knew that imbecile Kai Kobad would escape. He would never stay behind to surrender like a man. He didn't even stay back for his people. Persia is ours, and the so-called honorable king is on the run. That fugitive won't be out of harm's way too long. He has nowhere to go as his kingdom is mine! His daughter will return to a kingdom that is not even hers. I will finally make Parinaaz mine! She will not be able to resist the power of my magic. I will hypnotize her and make her fall in love with me. My conquest of Persia will remain incomplete until I make her my bride and my queen," King Marduk screamed aloud in victory.

He continued, "I have achieved victory but not my

revenge. I shall send a curse to the Persian kingdom and the world. This curse shall turn everyone into mutants, and they shall hunt down the traitors and fugitives. After all, today is the day of the grand festival. I shall first send this curse to Lake Urmia, where my newly-formed army of mutants shall hunt down my enemies. They will crush them, and vengeance shall be mine! No one and nothing can stop me now. Hahahahahaha!"

***

General Nabuzardan's voice was echoing in the gorge. He said, "This is our time. I have done my very best, and this mission will be flawless. We are an unstoppable army now. No force or army can bring us down. We will camp here and move on tomorrow!"

The Babylonian army started making camp for their commander. That was the only tent in the middle of the field.

General Nabuzardan slept and saw in his dream that his army continued forward. It wasn't too long before the invading army reached the heavily guarded barricades. General Nabuzardan's army crushed the guards and broke through the gates. Everyone else retreated, but the army of the dead captured those who were left behind as prisoners. The general went to the throne room, sat on it with pride, and screamed loudly with joy!

"Persia is ours. My lord, you shall be proud of your loyal general who has finally brought you glory.

We have conquered Persia, and next, we will take over the world! Men, take your positions and guard the gates. One of you head back to Babylon and inform our king of our conquest! We will become the rulers and masters of the world soon enough!"

This was truly a momentous moment for General Nabuzardan. He had captured Persia, the land of his ancestors. This was no small achievement. No, on the contrary, scribes from all across the world would revere him as the conqueror of Persia. The people would sing songs about him long after he was gone. Most of all, he had accomplished something that his peers could never have dreamed of. It didn't matter who he did it, for, in his mind, he was the conqueror and the next potential king. This was a stature that General Nabuzardan at a time would've felt impossible to achieve. However, times changed dramatically, and he sat on the throne celebrating his victory. He had achieved something that couldn't be accomplished in multiple lifetimes, let alone one. So, obviously, his confidence was through the roof, and in his mind, he had nothing more to accomplish. Nabuzardan was enjoying his dream.

***

The festival near the Fire Temple was truly something out of the world. It hosted tens of thousands of people who came from different parts of Persia and all across the world. It was truly a sight to behold as you could find anything you desired. The festival was undoubtedly the personification of opulence. And, perhaps, its most endearing quality was that it welcomed people from all classes.

It didn't have any restrictions based on the individual's ethnicity, culture, or religion. On the contrary, it welcomed people from all walks of life and allowed them to celebrate as intensely as possible. The festival was truly the stuff of legends, and the grandeur of the event perplexed and awed everyone in the known world. The festival occurred on the outskirts of Lake Urmia. The organizers made sure that the river was visible on all sides. That is why they ensured the boundaries were spread out as far as the eye could see. At the same time, the boundaries were decorated with sigils and symbols of the ruling dynasty. The majority of these decorations were fashioned from copper.

However, there were certain pieces of pottery that had a fine, bronze touch to them. Gold was, of course, heavily present in most items in the festival. It was a norm for women to wear gold bangles, earrings, rings, and copper hairbands. In fact, the women had donned so much jewelry that, from a distance, their faces and upper body were not visible. And, surprisingly enough, the women used to wear these ornaments without any worries whatsoever. They knew that the festival was the one day in which everyone celebrated wholeheartedly.

There was no need to fear bandits or thieves since the festival itself held a spiritual significance. The people understood that they would be punished swiftly if they committed any vile acts on that day. The king wouldn't even need to carry out this sentence. Instead, the long arm of nature would have its way and cast down the transgressor harshly.

Hence, naturally, no person dared to carry out any selfish agenda and celebrated life with the rest of their brethren. To tell the truth, the overall experience of the festival was totally divine—one could easily get lost in the ambiance and its sheer intensity. Not to mention, the area covered by the festival was so immense that if a family or couple didn't stay close, they would be lost and probably end up on the other side of the lake.

Because of this, entire families consisting of children, teenagers, adults, and senior citizens used to walk closely together and would call out each other's names every five minutes. This helped the families and couples keep track of their loved ones and enjoy the festival without fearing any uncertain situation. As soon as people entered the festival grounds, their eyes would immediately focus on the several trays lined up on the east and west side. These trays had multiple-colored herbs and spices. And, each of these herbs carried some benefits for the human body.

At the same time, the guests also had the privilege of seeing musicians, magicians, jugglers, fire eaters, and other entertainers in action. These entertainers put on quite a spectacle for their audience. The festival also had several competitions based on the art form. All the entertainers would compete with one another, and the winners of each tournament later played in the king's court.

It was a huge honor playing in the king's court, and every performer would go the extra mile to win the bout. The competition would get pretty intense at times, but the local guard prevented the situation from escalating. The guards deployed in the festival were originally military personnel, and they ensured that every person stayed in line.

In addition to the festival's significance, the thought of an armed guard breaking one's spine was also pretty threatening for troublemakers. Due to these measures, people waited and made their presence known throughout the year. In other words, the festival was truly heaven on earth.

***

The ground was shaking terribly. Princess Parinaaz commanded her friends, "Find cover, stay low. This could be an earthquake!"

"Or Marduk's horrible spells!" cried Ukund.

The ground trembled, the trees shook, the wind howled. The air all around was dark, filled with mystery.

Everyone took cover and was holding on to trees until the shaking stopped. The tremors were felt all over the land.

They were behind the rocks and saw a large army is coming in.

"Persia is under attack," Rukhsaar said.

"I hope Gyasi reached the palace by now," Ukund said.

"They will not go unharmed," Rukhsaar said.

"They will be stopped in their tracks. At least a quarter of their army will fall from their horses and vanish in the dust. Our arrows will bore their chests."

"Your speed will not stop the Babylonians from moving towards the capital," Ukund said.

"Be quiet!"

"King Marduk has miscalculated King Kai Kobad."

"For them, troops were expendable. They were merely tools needed to accomplish a 'greater' goal. So, naturally, he didn't care about their welfare. Instead of feeling sorry for his men who were willing to die at his command, they are just pushing them towards death. Just because the princess didn't marry king Marduk!" Rukhsaar said in a sad tone.

Back in the Abzu, the group finally breathed sighs of relief since the tremors got over. Simurgh said to all the friends, "You are a brave group of friends who have fought for Persia and the world. You have been willing to lay your lives which is commendable. Always remember that good always prevails over evil. The evil king Marduk will fail because he has underestimated all of you. You will be victorious."

Ukund did some calculations and claimed that the day was the birthday of the mighty Zoroaster.

"It will become a curse for Babylonians!" Ukund said.

CHAPTER 15.   THE ABZU

***

Fardad entered the cave. Sometimes it felt as if the cave's walls were moving, but sometimes they seemed to shift within their own place. Despite the oddity of it, the cave felt more welcoming. He then stepped inside and started walking. He kept walking until he found a dead end. He then heard a rumbling sound underneath the floor. He looked around and wondered what was going on.

Is this some kind of trap? He thought. The rumbling increased further to the point that Fardad lost his balance and fell down. Suddenly he saw an opening on the floor ahead of him. A spring rose suddenly. He couldn't make sense of what was going on, but after observing the spring for some time, he realized what it truly was. Fardad saw the holy spring had crystal clear water. The clarity of the water was unlike anything he had seen before. His reflection was clearer than anyone had ever seen in any river or stream. The smell that came from it was of perfume. A strange thing, considering water never had any smell associated with it. What was odder was that, unlike most springs, this one did not show any kind of source. How could the water be sprouting and be so clean in a cave, to begin with? If anything, most of them would be plagued with mud and earth. This spring was tremendously large as well.

Most springs didn't stretch far than a mere few meters. This was spread across the entire ground and seemed to be growing more as the moments passed. When it first sprung, Fardad had plenty of distance from it, but when he spent a few moments merely taking in its appearance, the water was closing in on his feet. This spring even sprouted water in an oddly controlled manner. There was nothing messy in its splashing nor out of place. The water poured out with perfect precision, glimmering its clarity to Fardad's eyes.

Is it a dream? He wondered. The thought had been rushing through his mind many times and seemed to be getting stronger. Fardad tried to step forward, but the spring seemed to have detected him trying to approach.

The water was closing in on his feet, but the young man waited, wondering if the tremors would return. Perhaps one touch of the liquid would drop him further deep into the earth, and he would have no way out.

The scented perfume of the water began to fill his nose more. The aroma was enough to drive one's sensation on fire. No scent maker could create what this water emitted at that moment. The flowers of the world could not come close to it. The spring spread its supremacy of scent by merely flowing everywhere.

He looked at it for a few minutes, wondering the purpose of the water. Without warning, in the deafening silence of his surrounding, He heard a voice, "Drink the water, Fardad!"

"Is anyone there? Who's speaking to me! Show yourself?"

CHAPTER 15.　　THE ABZU

Nevertheless, Fardad took some water from the holy spring in his hand and drank it. He took a few gulps and felt an incredible sensation in his entire body. As he drank more of the water, he realized that it made him very strong. The young man was quite tired and drained for some time, but the exhaustion began to fade with every sip of the crystallized water. The source of life seemed to be giving him the strength that he had craved for so long. His mind became clearer, and a flow of energy ran through his veins. He felt the strength in his bones and muscles. The tired arms and legs began to feel as if they were growing. The mere touch of the water to his lips also led a hint of music to travel on course to his confused mind.

Unlike the voice from before that was repetitive and slightly authoritative, the music was soothing and slow. From the plucking of strings to a serenading harmony, his mind no longer worried. He could feel powerful inside, and he had never felt this way before this.

The ground that it had made wet had no stain on it. It was almost as if the water had not even touched the earth at all. The aroma that it had scattered across the place now also began to subside. He realized that the holy spring was reserved for him, and now that he had drunk from it, he would have to move forward.

It suddenly turned to pitch dark, and Fardad got a bit scared. He didn't know where to go. He kept shouting, "Is anyone there? Oracle? Are you here?"

He heard no response as there was complete and utter silence. He had no idea what to do because he was completely blind. The tremendous glow overtook the shining lights from above that provided some hints of brightness that the spring carried. Now with both gone, there was nothing but darkness. Here Fardad seemed to be facing mythical creatures and objects. There could be a possibility that something from his nightmares could emerge from a corner. If it did, he would have no means to defend himself. The darkness was bound to keep him at a disadvantage, and he began to feel more nervous as the moments passed.

Fardad took a deep breath and began to calm himself. The water may have granted him strength and helped him recover from his exhaustion, but it had not prepared him for the unexpected. After a few minutes, he saw illumination from inside the cavern. A few seconds later, he heard those same sounds again in his head. "Chosen One, come forward. I want to see you." These exact words repeated themselves in his head, and he shouted back, "I'm coming forward. Is that you, Oracle?"

He couldn't hear anything back but moved forward. The grass was not only a sight to hold, but its touch put no strain on his feet. He felt the strands tickle him a bit but nothing bothersome as such. He let his hand feel the earth as he walked.

It was good to be among nature after enduring what felt like ages in the maze before. Fardad followed the voice's instruction but couldn't see anyone in sight

CHAPTER 15.   THE ABZU

until he came across a visible being. He saw an old lady coming his way. She had long white hair and was glowing brightly. She looked like a beautiful sorceress, and age hadn't impacted her beauty at all, it seemed.

He wondered who or what it was. His mind kept telling him that it was the oracle, but he wasn't convinced. She took different forms in his sleep meetings with her, but this may have been her full-bodied form. The grey in her hair did not seem aged but strong. There were not many wrinkles on her skin either, and her eyes flashed emerald green. She wore robes made of perfect silk that stretched far on the ground. Its reddish color, along with streaks of blue, made it clear that her clothing was rare.

Blue was not an easy color to find within the lands of Persia even then. So, how this woman garnered it either highlighted the tremendous skill of its maker or something supernatural.

In her hand, she carried a thin staff. There appeared nothing intimidating or strong about it, but Fardad was not going to take a chance. He made sure not to make any trouble.

Now much closer to Fardad in proximity, the woman placed her hand on her chest and smiled. There was something quite friendly and nostalgic about it. As if meeting an old friend after many years.

She called on to him, "Wait there, Chosen One. It's an honor to meet you. I have been waiting for this moment for a long, long time."

After a few minutes, she caught up to him and

spoke, "I know you're wondering if I am the oracle. I am indeed the oracle, and you have tons of questions for me. Do not worry, choose one. I will answer them all for you. I would advise you to hold on to them. Now, you must take my hand. We need to move fast. That water you had was the holy water, by the way. It has made you immune to all diseases and evil spells."

As instructed, Fardad stayed quiet and took the oracle's hand, and followed him into what seemed like another maze. He kept following her with his hands clasped on hers. Unlike the maze from before, the surrounding structure was not made of rocks but the trees themselves. They swayed to the direction, which guided both to their destination. This maze carried no feeling of tension or worry. Instead, it seemed to be easier to walk through, and Fardad didn't find himself feeling scared. The presence of the oracle in front of him kept him at ease. If she truly was who she claimed to be, then there was no longer a threat to worry about. He would be protected as long as he stayed in her company. He noticed a strange thought, considering that his entire surrounding boasted of security. She then left his hand and moved ahead and stood facing him. She once again signaled him to stay quiet. A few seconds later, a massive blast of light illuminated from her, and light bolts came out from her, leaving Fardad spellbound. He had no idea what was going on, but it seemed like some transformation was taking place. The bolts flew everywhere, and Fardad wondered, What was going on?

CHAPTER 15.   THE ABZU

The oracle then chanted loudly, "Rise, Spandarmaz, rise!"

It seemed like she was calling on some inner power, and the word Spandarmaz was very familiar. The woman floated off the ground and held her arms high. The sigh of her levitation caught Fardad off guard. He had known mythical beasts flew and knew angels were able to do the same; to see it in front of his eyes was something he was not prepared for.

The bolts of lightning flashed at a faster frequency and its energy emitted in all directions. Fardad worried about what were to happen if one of the bolts had struck him.

To his surprise, not one but plenty came at him, but they didn't hurt him in any way. Instead, they simply passed through. Fardad could not believe his eyes. He looked back at the oracle, whose appearance began to change. Her long silvery hair began to shorten. Her delicate face became more stoic and sharper. The thin body she carried herself in was now becoming larger and masculine.

A few minutes later, the transformation ended. The oracle was nowhere to be seen, and a man was standing in her place. Fardad was surprised and bewildered as to what had happened.

The man took a few steps toward him and then started speaking. He had this glowing aura around him that made him look larger than life. He stood at least seven feet tall and had a very low baritone voice. He was wearing a white robe with a cape on his back.

He had an angelic crown on his head, and he seemed like a mirror image of the drawings that Aadburzin had made for Fardad when he was young.

"I am the angel Spandermaz, and you are the chosen one. I came as the oracle in your dream state and your mind, but in truth, I am Spandermaz. You are, therefore, that destined clairvoyant and savior of Persia and the world. Now, I understand you have numerous questions for me. I wanted you to wait till I take on my original form, so now is your chance. You can ask me now or forever hold your silence."

"Spandermaz, I thought you were a figment of my imagination. I thought it was all make-believe stories that people would tell their children. In fact, I didn't consider the Simurgh a reality until I saw the legendary bird in front of my eyes. I was asked to come here to Abzu, all alone. What makes me so special? What is the meaning of all of this! I would love it if you could explain all this because there is so much confusion in my mind. I don't even know where to begin. Does Parinaaz play a role too?" "Fardad, son of Aadburzin, you are doing what destiny has written for you."

"I am looking for someone to decipher the book of my father. This book has ancient symbols and references that no one but my father could understand. Even the temple priests couldn't decipher the book. Can you help me?"

Fardad took out the book from his bag and handed it to Spandermaz.

The Spandermaz took the book and said, "The

book has served its purpose. The book is no longer needed."

Spandermaz threw the book in the air, blasted a ray of light from his hand, and destroyed it to the shock, awe, and dismay of Fardad. The remaining pieces were all tossed into the water, which was issuing from the ground.

Fardad asked, "Why did you do that! That was my father's book!"

"It held secrets for so many centuries! All of them are gone!" "The book of your father had empty pages. He kept it there just to make you understand that life is not controlled by planets and stars. We made it a deception for people by creating symbols on it just to bring you here to Abzu. You drank the water, and now you are immune from all diseases and evil spells. Now you go back."

"Go back where?"

"To the temple at Lake Urmia. Babylonians have attacked Persia. You will see things that you will not like, but you must follow your heart." Spandermaz spoke, "Fardad, underneath your feet in the water are the holy sands of the Abzu. Take a fistful of sand into your pockets. You will be guided to use them when the time comes."

Fardad took the sand and put it into his pockets. When he stood up, the angel said, "Now go human and save your land!"

Spandermaz came closer and placed his hand on his chest, which illuminated a unique glow of its own.

The brightness and illumination were so high that Fardad closed his eyes. When he opened them, the angel Spandermaz was not there.

Fardad could sense that he was very close to the end of his quest but had goosebumps. He was alone for the second time on this mission and could feel the weight of the world on his shoulders. It was a very overwhelming feeling. He was the only man who could save Persia and the world. He was terrified but willing to go all the way for the sake of his loved ones, friends, and the people of Persia.

Chapter 16

The Sands

Gyasi and King Kai Kobad were heading north. The king told Gyasi, "I fear that a plague has been unleashed on Persia. The evil King Marduk had been planning this attack for a long time. We must reach north as fast as possible. Hopefully, we'll catch up with my daughter and her friends and decide our next plan of action." Fardad hopes you are fine and reached Abzu by now, Gyasi thought. "Marduk will not make things easy for us. He must have cast one of his evil spells, and Yazdan knows what the hell he may have unleashed." "Lord, we are going as fast as we can. We will be there. I must assure you that Persia is still in safe hands. We will win the kingdom back. Once we save our friends and Fardad completes his mission, Persia will once again be ours, and the world will be safe from Marduk's sorcery forever. We need to end this evil once and for all." "I hear you loud and clear. Let's keep moving. I am confident we will be there very soon. I love your spirit, young man. When we

CHAPTER 16.   THE SANDS

return, I shall make you a general in the royal army."
"It will be over. Trust Yazdan. He is watching us.
For Persia!!!!!" Gyasi, King Kai Kobad, and the army
kept marching forward as their friends were bracing
for battle.

***

Marduk's mutants were moving over the Zagros
Mountains like ants. These people had deformed faces
and were utterly brainwashed. They would be uttering
some gibberish and were in a complete trance. Their
faces resembled the army of the dead that General
Nabuzardan had led into the Persian capital. They
were under a spell and were moving aggressively over
the Mountains.

In the interim, Soroush lay inside his tent. The
stupid minister had nothing to worry about the attack
from King Marduks army. He had simply retreated
to the camp while the rest of the kingdom was busy
assembling against Babylonians. Nevertheless, he was
pacing hither and thither as he waited impatiently for
his slave Roxana. "Where could that stupid girl be?
Why in the name of Yazdan is it taking her so long
to return! Could it be that she disobeyed me and
escaped?" he muttered worriedly under his breath.

As he was cursing her under his breath, he heard
a woman's voice. She was asking permission to enter and arguing with the soldiers stationed. Soroush
immediately went out, and he turned his eyes imme-

diately to find Roxana there. Instantly, he let out a yell of glee and pulled her inside.

"My dear master!" she said, bowing to him as she entered his tent.

"Oh, my lovely Roxana! I missed you so much!" he expressed and gave her a hug. "What took you so long, Dear Girl!?"

Barely recovering from the shock of the affection bestowed by the cruel minister, Roxana replied, "Master Soroush, the entire kingdom will soon be attacked! Babylonians are everywhere! The entire nation is going to the dogs! So I had to sneak in very carefully to get back to you!" she blurted out hurriedly.

"Calm down, my lovely girl," he said, and kissing her palm, he offered her a glass of wine.

"Here! Drink it up! You look really thirsty,"

"Thank you, Master, you seem to be very kind today," she remarked, gulped down the red wine quickly, and wiped her mouth.

"Master," she began, looking at him hopefully. "I did as you instructed!" she said with a smile and removed her white veil. "Yes, You did, my dear girl, and I am so proud of you!"

"Master Soroush! I have done everything you have ever asked me to do! So, as you promised me a long time ago, would you grant me my freedom now?" "Roxana, my dear beautiful girl! I would like to offer you something even better in return for your loyalty!"

"Master Soroush, forgive me, but I do not wish to have anything else. Kindly just grant me my freedom," she said in a low and desperate voice. "My dear Roxana. I grant you your freedom, but I would like to make you my wife," he declared, looking at her intensely. "My Master-" she broke off as Minister Soroush gave her a rib-cracking hug.

"Yes, Roxana. Ever since I have had you, you have proven to be an efficient and loyal slave. If your loyalty as a slave was so substantial, then I imagine how faithful and loyal you would be as a wife!" he asserted, and after letting go of her, he placed her at arms length and kissed the back of her palm sweetly. "I have fallen in love with you, my gorgeous Roxana, and so, I would like to take you as my bride. We will flee this nation and settle in some faraway land, completely away from all the evil! Only you and me!"

Roxana was amazed to bits at this proposal of marriage from her master and looked bamboozled. "My master....I...."

"Please say yes," he insisted and held her hand. "There is no woman fit to be the mother of my future children but you! I want my children to have your beauty, strength, courage, loyalty, and intellect!" These words had an immense effect on the slave girl; no one had ever said anything like that to her ever before, and so she melted drastically. And eventually, Roxanas expression of bewilderment turned into a warm and loving smile, and Soroush got her reply in her eyes. Moreover, she began to blush deeply and turned her head aside to hide the redness on her face. "Excellent! Lets get out of here then!" he announced, and they came out of the tent. There were Persian soldiers all around. They took two horses and started galloping towards the mountains. The Persian soldiers were mostly tired and were indulged in cooking eating, and some were busy in other works as thus far there were no signs of Babylonian around.

After galloping horses for several hours, Soroush and Roxana were in the mountains. They wanted to rest to start their journey again. Suddenly, they saw a few shadows moving towards them. A mob of Marduks zombies was chasing them. They tried to take another path, but unfortunately, they were surrounded by the mutants. "Mutants! I am Minister Soroush! The spy of King Marduk! So I order you to clear my path and let us go!" he commanded proudly.

However, those soulless creatures saw nothing but fresh meat in front of their eyes. They continued to surround them from both sides. Roxana retrieved her sword and began to fight the zombies; she swished her sword skillfully and sliced the heads of the filthy creatures; however, their heads seemed to grow again the instant they were beheaded. Nevertheless, Roxana continued to battle them desperately whilst holding onto her beloved masters hand. But all her efforts seemed futile as the mutants grew back everything and more of them appeared. Finally, Soroush and Roxana began to back away in fear as death was coming closer. "Master, perhaps we have come towards the end! We are going to die, but I have no complaints from this ruthless life as it has given me the chance to die with the man I love!" Roxana whispered emotionally as she clutched Soroushs hand tighter than before.

"You love me too, Roxana?" Soroush asked her serenely.

"Yes, I do, master," she replied with a tear trickling down her cheek. The love birds stared into each others eyes, and then something happened that turned Roxanas world upside down. In that desperate moment, the selfish wart Soroush showed his true colors and detached his hand from Roxanas. "Master?" she said blankly in shock.

"I am really, really sorry, dear Roxana; indeed, I love you truly... But I love myself even more. And I am not ready yet to leave this world. And besides, you wanted freedom, right? So I am merely granting your wish!"

After saying that, he pushed her towards the advancing group of murderous creatures and escaped through a tiny lane between two shops. The beastly creatures tore through the young girl's flesh, and her gut-wrenching screams echoed across the entire city. Meanwhile, Soroush was running across the lane and cheering loudly that he had managed to save his life; however, as he was about to come out of the lane, he noticed another mutant coming from that side. Within a fraction of a second, the zombie struck mercilessly and slit his throat, causing a splash of blood across its soulless face while the rest of the zombies feasted on the deceptive ministers dying body.

***

The friends could hear the loud thuds near them as the mutant armies moved closer. They all looked at each other, wondering what was going on, and they were puzzled as to what was happening.

Rukhsaar figured out what was going on and commanded them, "Take cover. I fear the evil king has launched a curse, and there's an army moving towards us. Please don't make a move until I tell you. I have enough bombs in my arsenal to get us a safe passage. We'll make it out of this, I know it!"

The friends took cover and waited for Rukhsaar's signal to attack. For now, they were outnumbered, but Rukhsaar's surprises would give them an advantage. They had to survive for Fardaad, and hopefully, they will have back up soon in the form of King Kai Kobad, Gyasi, and their army. The friends were on a collision course with the mutants, and this time, Rukhsaar's smart bombs may not save them. These mutants seemed to possess more power than mortal humans and would not die too easily.

If Rukhsaar and company don't put up a strong resistance, they could mutate too, and that would make things very difficult for Fardad. They had to fight and resist until their backup arrived.

Rukhsaar pointed towards the charging mutants, "There they come! Everyone, take your positions. We are about to be under attack and could possibly be captured. Don't attack till I signal!"

CHAPTER 16.   THE SANDS

Ukund then stated, "Friends, we will survive this. We will not give up or surrender!"

Rukhsaar then said, "I will never let them harm our princess. I swear my life on this!"

Parinaaz then spoke, "Don't worry about me. We are three, but our combined might and determination will pull us through. Rukhsaar, let us know, and we will strike." Rukhsaar then said, "Alright! Brace yourselves for impact. They're coming toward us!"

The mutants soon surrounded the three friends and were hungry for human meat. Rukhsaar whispered, "Don't make a move until I tell you so. Keep your weapons intact at all times."

The mutants were getting closer to them. Rukhsaar screamed at them, "You boys want to play! Catch!"

She threw the smart ball bombs from her arsenal, hoping to cause a distraction to create an escape as they did before. However, the mutants were too strong. Their hands extended and destroyed the bombs before they could explode.

"Looks like I spoke too soon. These mutants are too strong. These were just people enjoying the festival. Marduk cast a spell on them!" Rukhsaar said alarmingly. Ukund said, "Don't make a move. We're not finished yet!"

Rukhsaar said, "Are we? Do you have any bright ideas because I don't! I can't waste more bombs, but we need more men. The three of us will be captured!" Parinaaz then shouted, "Just stay together. We will survive! I know it!"

Rukhsaar then said, "I wish you were right, princess, but these mutants are too strong! We will be captured unless. . .."

Simurgh let out a huge scream of anger in the form of a call. The call sent shockwaves toward the mutant enemies, pushing them back, and knocking them unconscious. Simurgh flapped its wings heavily and created further shockwaves to stop more mutants from attacking. As expected, they were retreating.

Suddenly fire arrows were launched towards the mutants. They were distracted, and Rukhsaar looked around and heard a very familiar voice! "Did anyone miss me!"

They saw that Fardad had come out of the cave, and he was throwing arrows. His friends rushed toward him. After drinking the water of Abzu, he felt stronger and more aggressive. He was full of jest and panache, and he said to them, "We must go to the temple. Persia is in danger!"

His voice had an echo, and his friends realized that he had changed.

"Were you able to get the book deciphered?" Ukund asked, holding Fardad's hand.

Fardad looked at him and said with empty eyes, "No."

"What!" they all exclaimed.

"So what happened inside? Did you meet the oracle?"

'I met the angel of Yazdan, and he informed me that I must go back to the temple as I can save Persia.

CHAPTER 16.   THE SANDS

That's all that I know!"

"Hurry up, and we have no time to waste."

Upon saying this, Fardad ran, and his friends followed suit. They climbed the magnificent Simurgh again, and the bird flew across the sky. When they reached cloud level, they could see the Babylonian army marching towards Lake Urmia. They were already in Persian territory, and their maces had the heads of the Persian army.

"Oh Yazdan, save us," uttered Parinaaz.

Chapter 17

The Fire

Upon arriving at Lake Urmia, Fardad got a huge surprise. He realized that there was a festive atmosphere all around him. He then remembered that this was the day of a famous and grand Persian festival. He figured that the date was the 6th of Farvardin in the Persian Calendar, and the temple was super crowded as it was the Birthday of Zarathushtra (Zoroaster).

When he entered the festival, Fardad saw the priests doing fire rituals. Fardad was riding on Simurgh, and the people around them were all mesmerized and shouted in joy at the sight of the legendary bird. All of them were in awe at the sight in front. The fact that Simurgh had arrived on such an occasion gave hope that better things were to come. Some of the priests gawked in shock, unable to believe that this was happening.

So many years had passed since they kept believing in the prophecy, and some began to doubt whether it would come true. There stood, the mighty bird flapping its wings that blew winds that caught them off

CHAPTER 17.   THE FIRE

balance.

None of them would ever think they would have seen Simurgh in their lives, but it finally happened. Fardad was looked upon as a mighty hero, and Yazdan had sent them to bless the festival. The people that surrounded the priests were also enraptured with joy. The dancing rituals were paying off, and the answer to their prayers had now come. Their dancing became more enthusiastic with the bird's presence, and they chanted louder than before. Their belief gave them strength, and Fardad, himself, felt the zeal of the surrounding energy consume his home. Whatever doubt he carried was erased.

He then hopped off Simurgh and began to walk towards the temple. Everyone around him cleared his way because they considered him the reincarnation of Zarathushtra. Some of them blessed him with prayers as he passed by. A few even patted his back. Fardad was moved by their gestures of kindness. He himself had doubted his own abilities, but now in the company of strangers, he had found trust and faith.

People all over shouted, "All praise to Zarathustra." Fardad was surprised to be honored like the great Persian sage. So many of the festival attendees surrounded his legendary bird companion. Simurgh was enjoying the attention as Fardad continued their way toward the temple. Plenty of people tried to feel the feathers of the mythical bird. Simurgh didn't mind at all. In fact, he held his neck high with pride. The people loved him, and he was to make sure that he and Fardad were able to succeed.

***

As Fardad walked through the temple, he heard a loud sound resembling a ram's horn. That sound was music to the years of everyone at the festival, but they had no idea that no joy would be coming of it. It was an ambush in the form of a surprise attack. The temple pilgrims panicked as they saw a massive swarm of zombies making their way toward the temple.

The ground began to shake, and the once silent hall was now echoing with the sounds of help and panic as many tried to make a run for their lives. Fardad turned to face the incoming attack. Simurgh flew in, shoving countless zombies to different sides. They were helpless against the might of the mythical giant. Fardad realized that the lives of the temple pilgrims were under threat, and he had to do something. Simurgh noticed the influx of invading zombies and flew in front of Fardad and the pilgrims making a barrier between them and the zombies.

Fardad shouted to everyone, "Everybody come behind Simurgh and me, and you will be safe. Prepare to defend yourself against these zombies. They will not spare your lives as these zombies are mutants that devour us, mortals. We shall protect you as long as you stay on our side. Don't make any sudden moves, please. As long as the legendary Simurgh is among us, we shall be safe!"

CHAPTER 17.   THE FIRE

Everyone around him listened attentively and followed his orders as they thought the orders were coming from Zarathustra himself.

Marduk wanted to kill all, no matter who was in the temple or outside. However, he didn't know that his mutants would meet their match in the form of Simurgh. The battle was red hot, and the mission was far from over. Fardad had to contend with the mutants and then proceed with the mission. Some of the pilgrims got very scared and decided to flee the temple to protect their lives despite orders from Fardad to stop. There wasn't much Fardad could do as the mutant archers shot them down with their arrows. Simurgh and Fardad were unable to protect them there.

Fardad cried to Simurgh, "I'm so sad that we couldn't protect them. I wish they stayed back."

Simurgh screamed, "Fardad, get inside the temple now! Don't worry about me! Just go!"

Fardad replied, "No way I am leaving you to fend for yourself. These mutants aren't going to stop coming!"

"You're wasting time. I'll hold them off till you're back. Just go inside now. The priests are going to be at the fire. That's where you need to throw the sands. Leave now!"

As Fardad was about to head inside the temple, he saw a familiar face in enemy lines.

"Is that Marduks general? Nabuzardan?" Fardad asked.

"I believe it is. He has led an army here. This

means Nabuzardan is back."

General Nabuzardan spoke with pride to his men, "What you all see before you right now is the legendary Simurgh. I never thought I'd see the day I'd come face to face with this bird. This is one incredible moment for me. I want the bird to be captured alive. Legend says that whoever drinks its blood he would live thousands of years without aging."

"We can win over them if we destroy their temple," Nabuzardan commanded his army as they prepared the catapults.

Simurgh looked worried. Despite all the powers the mythical bird carried, the enemy was now gaining more and more. If his flames and shockwaves could only kill the mutants for a short time, it wouldn't be long before they overpower everyone all together. The bird continued to fight as hard as it could, but it was slowly becoming apparent that his powers were no longer serving their purpose. Whatever it destroyed would only be resurrected, and he would find himself in the same cycle over and over again.

Fardad couldn't believe his eyes. Simurgh was getting exhausted due to repeatedly firing his shockwaves and fiery breath. This was taking a huge toll on the bird, and Fardad could see it was getting weak. His friends were now ambushed from all sides, and the mutants were attacking innocent people, eating them alive. It was a massacre. Fardad was crying, seeing headless innocent people being thrown around like dirt with their heads displaced. He couldn't bear to

CHAPTER 17. THE FIRE

see the sight of innocents being slaughtered left, right, and center.

Fardad couldn't understand how evil forces would attack a temple. Worst of all, he couldn't do anything but watch this massacre transpire in front of his eyes. He could see the destruction of Persia happening right in front of his eyes. The entire civilization was being demolished, and the evil forces were winning. He started feeling that his world had crumbled around him and he was sinking in deeply and unable to push himself out. He felt like a failure because he was the chosen one destined to save the Persian civilization and the world. He could no longer believe he was the chosen one as his friends were in danger, and so many pilgrims at the temple were just becoming meat for mutants.

Suddenly, a vision came and stood in front of him, and it was Spendermaz, "Fardad, you can save Persia! Go in the temple!"

"What?"

"Go, Fardad. Go!"

Fardad ran inside the temple because he had no choice. The fate of the Persian civilization was in his hands. He could hear Spandermaz tell him in his mind, "Run, Fardad, run!"

Fardad kept running toward the fire and saw the priests encircling the holy fire and chanting their mantras for protection from the Babylonian army. These priests had no choice but to pray to Yazdan because the enemies had gained a foothold against the peacekeeping forces of Persia. Fardad saw a very familiar face, and he never imagined he would run into that man again.

"Throw the sand on fire!" Spendermaz said.

Spendermaz gave a baffling instruction, but Fardad had no other option but to do it.

Fardad moved forward with both hands inside his pocket. The people stepped aside as soon as they saw the Simurgh rider was coming toward the holy fire. Fardad went close enough, and with a loud pronunciation of words, "With the name of Yazdan, I throw it."

He threw a fistful of sand in his hand toward the fire. The sand particles all went in the air, and people and priests were mesmerized by the sparkling sands. The sand particles started hovering over the fire like honey bees and then fell on the fire. The fire, which had been burning since time immemorial, was suddenly extinguished.

There was a great shockwave, and everyone surrounding the fire, including Fardad, fell to the ground. The shockwave spread across the whole of Persia, and all fires were extinguished.

The priests got very upset upon seeing the fire extinguisher. They were furious, shouting, "Blasphemy! Hunt him down! Kill him!"

They thought Fardad had come here to bring destruction on the day of the festival. He was sent by the Babylonians and not Yazdan. Everyone around Fardad, including people and priests, ran toward him with their daggers out and began to attack him.

CHAPTER 17.   THE FIRE

Fardad quickly stood up, ran out of the temple, and he came out. Then, the priests and people inside the temple followed him.

Chapter 18

The Verdict

ADRENALINE and the thirst for blood fueled through the priests veins, and now they were ready to do what was necessary. Fardad wondered whether they had the slightest sense to know that by killing him, they would lose all their chances to live through the chaotic ordeal. Katir came in between them and pleaded with them to stop. He held his open palms in front and stood strong in the hope of intimidating the incoming priests before they took action. Katir understood the zealousness of the priests. Despite their claims of being peace lovers, they were, in actuality, people. Like most who would get scared in a time of crisis, their fuming blood was getting the better of them. There was no hint of tolerance or understanding left in their minds.

All that rattled in their heads was the urge to kill and hope that they could live to see another day. Some, in fact, might have even thought that killing Fardad could save them from the trouble they were

CHAPTER 18.   THE VERDICT

in.

Katir being the high priest knew better. He had spent years following the faith and had worked his way to becoming one of the most well-respected and high priests of the kingdom. Throughout his life, he had witnessed people, despite being kind or good, immediately turn themselves in to the most selfish and cruelest of monsters. In times of war and crisis, it was a common thing for people to give in to panic and make impulsive decisions that caused more harm than good.

Having seen this happen many times, Katir promised always to keep his mind intact. He was not one to let emotions get the better of him. He had witnessed terrible consequences, and it was only a few moments away from the same mistake to repeat itself.

If the priests managed to hurt or, worse, kill Fardad, then not only would one life be taken, but the whole of Persia would fall in corruption and destruction. One tried to lunge ahead, but despite Katirs age, he was able to catch him in time and push him away back to the others. The priest fumbled to the floor while the others watched in surprise. Never before had any of them seen the high priest display this form of strength before.

Another tried his luck but found himself overpowered by Katir again and was tossed to the side. The high priest was not necessarily gifted in fighting and did not carry as much strength as he did in his youth, but he was smart in how to avoid and counter an incoming opponent.

Luckily for him, the priests that were now filled with rage also did not carry tremendous fighting skills. Most were old men simply holding knives in their hands. Their only chance of getting their task done was a lucky strike against Fardad. Now that Katir had managed to throw two of them to the side, one more wanted to try his luck. Their eyes were now filled with rage and confusion. Fardad knew now that they were becoming desperate and needed to vent their anger on someone. They had seen the man who they felt was to blame and were now ready to take the matter into their own hands. Fardad had priests behind him and the Babylonian army in front. He looked at the sky and said, "Save me, God!"

Suddenly the catapults threw huge stones at the temple, and the temple was destroyed. Fardad was panting near lake Urmia. He was barefoot, looking towards the temple. It was no more there. His dream came true.

The Babylonians jeered with joy as the temple was destroyed.

"Now they are defeated," Nabuzardan said to his army.

"Launch a full-scale attack. Eat them all!"

The priest saw that they were surrounded from all sides by Babylonians, and they had little chance to escape.

"You are with the Babylonians to destroy our temple!" the priests shouted in rage.

"Your blood will make Urmia redder now!"

CHAPTER 18.   THE VERDICT

***

The blood-thirsty priests advanced towards Fardad furiously. Despite the High Priest Katir stunning some of the priests, he couldnt possibly defeat all of them. Therefore, three priests attacked together, and Katir battled them, throwing one of them onto the side, but the other two slashed his back with knives, and he screamed in pain. However, he managed to turn around and kick the knives out of their hands, and pushed them back on the ground. Katir began to moan in pain but continued to shield Fardad like a bodyguard.

"Dont you dare come any further!" he warned weakly as he placed his hand in front of Fardad. The slash on his back had made him weaker, and he was unable to fight any longer. Fardad admired him greatly for his courage and silently prayed to Yazdan to save their lives.

Suddenly, an arrow came rushing through the sky and struck Nabuzardans horse which neighed loudly in pain and threw its master on the ground. Fardad looked onto the source of the arrow, and his eyes gleamed with joy as he saw his love Princess Parinaaz and friends Gyasi, Ukund, and Rukhsar riding towards them along with the entire Persian army.

Gyasi, on the other hand, aimed a large spear at one of the zombies and struck it so skillfully that it pierced the zombie directly in its heart. "Grow that back, you vicious monster!" he growled.

One mutant jumped and landed on Gyasi.

Gyasi managed to grab the mutants throat and threw him onto the side. He then sprinted towards the zombies who were advancing towards the Persian army, and after grabbing their shoulders, he shoved them onto the ground.

Ruksar and Princess Parinaaz kept shooting arrows at Nabuzardans human soldiers, who died instantly on the ground.

King Kai Kobad himself was galloping on his horse like a mighty warrior and began to slice the heads of the zombies.

Ukund descended from his horse and ran towards Fardad. "Whats going on?" he roared, and upon retrieving his gleaming sword, he moved forward.

"This man Fardad isnt the enemy! He was merely trying to save us from these zombies and the hostile army!" Ukund shouted at the priests.

However, the priests still did not believe Ukund and thought that Fardad was putting on a faade.

"No! Dont spare him! He is not even a human!" one priest yelled.

"He brought the curse here," another priest added.

However, just as it seemed that the person was winning, a major twist came during the battle as some of the soldiers (who had gotten involved in fighting the Persians personally) rushed back to the catapults on the command of General Nabuzardan. The catapults were fired in Fardads direction and one of the massive rocks that was fired crushed the Persian soldiers surrounding him. The other rock was rushing toward him at lightning speed and was meters away from a collision when a massive flap of wings was heard across the sky as the mighty Simurgh arrived. The humongous bird flew between the rock and Fardad, and upon collision, the rock was crushed into pieces and spread across the ground.

Fardad was overjoyed to see Simurgh and rushed toward it.

"Simurgh, you have arrived!" he said with an exhilarating smile.

"Yes, Chosen One. It is my duty to protect you and Persia!" he declared firmly.

Fardad climbed the Simurgh, and the priest ran to stop him but failed. The hostile priests were frustrated and yelled furiously.

"That damn bird! We wont let him go!" Babylonian soldiers noticed that Fardad was on Simurgh in the sky, and they catapulted rocks at the bird! "Lets see how many can it crush!"

More and more catapults were loaded with heavy rocks and fired instantly.

"Watch out!" screamed Fardad as the rocks came crashing down. Simurgh looked up, and after flying in zig-zag motion across the air, it sank its razor-sharp claws across each and crushed them to tiny pieces.

Nabuzardan and his men got frustrated at Simurgh thwarting all of their attacks and just didnt know what to do. In addition to that, Simurgh swooshed through the ground and cut off all the zombies into pieces with its claws.

***

Nabuzardan was confronted by General Suhrab, who stood in front with his sword extended towards him.

"You cannot go back to Babylon, you spineless wart," General Suhrab asserted.

"Go to Dozakh (Hell)!" Nabuzardan growled, "I will have you ripped apart, Persian!"

After saying that, Nabuzardan called upon his mutant soldiers and ordered them to kill Suhrab. The blood-thirsty mutants began to surround Suhrab. Two of the zombies pounced on Suhrab, who swerved aside to avoid them and went rolling onto the ground. He got back on his feet and was about to strike the zombies when one of the enemy soldiers sneaked from behind and slashed his back. Suhrab yelled in excruciating pain, and his eyes widened. He turned around slowly and was about to slice his sword when the man delivered a kick on his chest, and he went falling toward the ravenous zombies.

Suhrabs horrendous screams shook the earth as his body was being mutilated by the ruthless monsters who piled upon him and slaughtered the courageous warrior who died a martyrs death. The thunder roared more viciously after Suhrabs demise as though enraged by it.

The vicious Nabuzardan laughed at the brave soldiers blood-curdling demise and looked at his army proudly.

"Excellent job!" he praised proudly.

***

As the battle brewed between Nabuzardan and the Persian army, a sort of miracle happened as the clouds began to cover the clear sky slowly, and a roar of thunder echoed across the horizon. Within a few moments, a downpour started, and the moment the rainwater hit the zombies, they began to shriek loudly and run helter-skelter as though the raindrops were burning their skin.

Fardad looked at the sky with a massive beam on his face and raised his hands, "Yazdan! You have showered your blessing upon us in the form of rain!" Then he looked at one of the shrieking zombies, and raising his sword, he struck its head off and noticed that it didnt grow back. The entire Persian army witnessed this miraculous sight, and after roaring loudly, it began to attack the mutants.

***

Some distance away, King Kai Kobad was fighting Nabuzardans soldiers on his horseback. The kings horse neighed loudly and tumbled one of the soldiers on the ground. It then proceeded to trample his chest, and the crushed soldier puked a splash of blood.

"Bastards!" Kai Kobad shouted and galloped his horse through the zombies and began to behead all the weakened mutants with his sword. The zombies had become extremely weak due to the rain and hence were unable to even defend themselves properly, let alone attack. As more and more rain showered all over the battleground, the ground became even bloodier as various heads and torsos lay butchered across the field.

The rain halted, and the sky cleared as all the zombies were wiped out. The forces of Marduk were getting killed one after another, and the Persian army was on the verge of victory.

"Sir! It seems like we will lose this battle horribly! We must do something to gain the upper hand again!" he suggested while pulling the arrow from his generals shins.

"Yes! If we lose the battle, we will either be killed horribly by these pathetic Persians or will die mercilessly at the hands of King Marduk if we manage to return home!"

"What should I do, General?" he asked, hoping for his general to come up with miraculous solutions. Nabuzardan looked around and witnessed his soldiers getting either slaughtered or running away from the battlefield and getting captured. As slowly as he could, the Babylonian general began to sneak out of the battlefield.

***

In the interim, the Persian army had disposed of the last of the Babylonian soldiers, and King Kai Kobad raised his sword in the air.

CHAPTER 18.   THE VERDICT

"My loyal and brave Soldiers!   On this day, we have attained victory over the ruthless Babylonians and their monsters by the blessings of Yazdan, who showered rain at the right moment! And although we have had to bear the heavy losses of our loved ones, we shouldnt think that they died for nothing. Rather they gave up their lives so that we could live and be victorious. They laid down their lives for us, and so, lets keep them alive inside our hearts! Hail the almighty Yazdan!"

Kai Kobad praised his entire army, including Gyasi, Ukund, Parinaaz, and Rukhsar, who raised their swords and praised their Lord Yazdan.

***

Fardad had landed on the ground, and he looked around and couldnt see Nabuzardan anywhere.

"Where the hell is that bloody Babylonian general?!" he exclaimed.

"General Nabuzardan is trying to escape," Simurgh informed him.

"Lets go get him then!" Fardad said, and he jumped onto the mighty birds back, and it quickly rose in the air.

Nabuzardan was limping away as fast as he could. His leg was wounded, and so he couldnt run properly. His fearful mind was flashing intensely.

I need to escape this place as quickly as I can and go into hiding! He thought in desperation.

"If I fall into the Persians hands, they will hang me, and if Marduk finds out that I am alive, he will have me slaughtered! Oh Lord, help me!" Nabuzardan was on the brink of escaping when he noticed a gargantuan shadow on the ground closing in toward him. Looking above, he noticed Fardad zooming across the sky on Simurgh and coming for him.

"Where do you think you are going, General?!" Fardad yelled on top of his lungs with a victorious relish in his voice. "I didnt think that you were going to be such a coward!"

Instantaneously, Simurgh lowered its altitude slowly and moved toward the Babylonian general. Fardad moved towards the edge of the birds back and, placing his hand in the air, he grabbed Nabuzardan by the collar and lifted him up, and Simurgh flew higher.

"Let me go! You filthy piece of Persian dung, let me go!" he bellowed, struggling to free himself from Fardads grip.

"Now, you shouldnt be so stupid, General!" Fardad mocked sarcastically while clutching the collar of his black robes. "If I let you go, you would meet your death on the ground!" The moment Fardad said that, Nabuzardan came to his senses and stopped struggling, and the mighty Simurgh flew higher across the horizon.

***

The priests stood in front of King Kai Kobad at the palace in Takht-e-Shah. King Kai Kobad was looking at them sharply like a furious lion. While Fardad, Princes Parinaaz, Ukund, Gyasi, and the High Priest Katir, stood on the side.

"Begin!" Kai Kobad commanded, and one of the priests commenced his speech.

"Your Majesty! This man named Fardad committed the biggest crime that even an enemy would think hundred times before committing!"

"And what is that may I ask?" Kai Kobad demanded coolly.

"Your Highness! He intentionally extinguished the holy fire at the Urmia Temple!"

The moment he made that statement, all the ministers and the kings subjects began to chatter amongst themselves and looked quite angry.

"Moreover," the priest continued, clearing his throat, "He was on the side of the enemy who attacked us and destroyed the temple! He should be punished severely! We priests believe that he should be sentenced to the most gruesome death any criminal has ever been given in the history of Persia!"

Immediately, Parinaaz and Gyasi shouted at the priest in a fit of fury.

"That is so not true!" Parinaaz claimed, "Father, it is true that Fardad extinguished the fire at the Urmia temple but only because he was instructed to do so by the oracle whom he had encountered at the cave!"

"Yes, your Majesty! Princess Parinaaz is absolutely right! My friend, Fardad, was told by the oracle that the blessed Sands of Abzu should be thrown in the holy fire and that would place an end to the indestructible enemies!" Gyasi supported Princes Parinaazs statement.

"Yeah, right!" the priest mocked Gyasi and threw him an extremely dirty look.

"If what you utter is right, then why in the name of Yazdan didnt it destroy the enemy?! Go ahead, tell us why?"

There was a moment of silence as nobody, including Fardad, held the answer to this pressing question. Ukund, who was quietly listening to the argument all this while, moved forward and bowing before the king. He made the simplest and wisest statement at that point, "Your Highness, before I say anything, I would like to clarify that I am not speaking here as Fardads friend or comrade. Rather I am speaking as a common man and Persian."

He then turned toward the priests.

"Respectable Priests! We had come to you for help because we obviously held the belief that since you all were men of God, you were supposed to be the wisest, most pious, and the most sensible people of this country. However, your beastly and inhumane attempts to kill Fardad after the temple was destroyed shocked me immensely and made me reconsider my opinion about you all. Dont you realize that the most important thing in these desperate times when the entire Persia was under attack was to save the lives of people and not the temple? And thats what Fardad did! His actions were all meant to save every Persian present on the battlefield that day!"

"Yes!" Katir voiced his agreement as he emerged from the crowd. "My fellow Priests, do you want to know why Fardad was ordered to extinguish the holy fire of Urmia? It was because the almighty and all-wise Yazdan wanted to show the innermost nature of us humans. He wanted to show that even the most peace-loving, non-violent, and empathetic priests like us, who are willing to show mercy even to our worst enemies, can turn into beasts when our lives are at stake!"

Katirs words had the most profound effect on his fellow priests as they finally realized their mistake and hung their heads in shame. And before the king could even ask them, they moved toward Fardad and asked him for forgiveness for their insolent and beastly be-havior. The kind-hearted Fardad smiled generously and forgave them all instantly.

King Kai Kobad ordered the Babylonian General Nabuzardan to be brought into the court. A few mo-ments later, Kai Kobads soldiers dragged Nabuzardan, who was bound in iron chains, into the court. Far-dad and the rest stared at him distastefully as though something horrible had entered the hall. "Nabuzardan!" called the king. "You are a ruthless war criminal who has murdered thousands of innocent lives and tried to destroy Persia. In addition to that, your King Mar-duk has destroyed the lives of countless innocent men and women by turning them into soulless mutants! Thereby, for all your evil and murderous acts, I, King

Kai Kobad of Persia, sentence you to death by execution!"

Nabuzardan listened to the charges and his death sentence with no remorse whatsoever. Rather he looked extremely pleased with himself for committing these barbaric acts of war.

"You Fools!" he roared, making the entire place shudder. "You have no idea what you have brought upon yourself! You have no earthly idea about Master Marduks powers! He will slaughter each and every one of you without batting an eyelash! You havent defeated his army but rather dug your own grave!" You all will receive a dogs death, and he will marry your daughter on the pile of your corpses!" Nabuzardan began laughing like a maniac, and a burst of vile laughter echoed horribly across the entire palace.

"Soldiers!" ordered King Kai Kobad, fuming furiously with anger but controlling himself. "Take him away... before I lose control and do something!"

The soldiers dragged Nabuzardan like a wild beast that needed to be controlled and took him away. A deafening silence spread across the entire palace as the Babylonian generals venomous words still rang in the peoples ears. However, to get his people out of the trauma, King Kai Kobad announced rather exciting news.

"My People! On this glorious day, we have crushed the danger that lurked across our beautiful city. I would like to make a delightful announcement. Today, I announce the marriage of my beloved daughter,

CHAPTER 18.   THE VERDICT

Parinaaz with. . .."

He paused for a moment and, smiling gracefully, said, "The Nakhsat of Persia and my successor, Fardad!"

The news filled the entire palace with immense exhilaration and joy. Fardad and his friends widened their eyes in amazement and looked at him with intense glee and excitement.

"I would request Fardad to come forward!" said Kai Kobad, and Gyasi and Ukund backed him to do so with huge beams on their faces. Fardad moved toward Kai Kobad, who took out the crown from his head and placed it on Fardads while Parinaaz stood beside him. The entire palace broke out with cheers and glee as they gave a round of applause and chanted along with Gyasi and Ukund.

"Hail to the new king of Persia, Fardad!"

Amidst the cheers, Fardad noticed his mother, who had tears of joy in her eyes, and without thinking about anything, he moved toward her and touched her feet while she lifted him up and pulled him into a tight embrace.

"You finally fulfilled your destiny, my Son! Your father would have been so proud of you!" she exclaimed as she wiped the tears from her eyes. "Yes, he would," Fardad said and hung his head down.

"What happened, my Son?" his mother inquired worriedly.

"Nothing, I just. . . I just wish that he could be here to finally watch it happen. . . ." Fardad sighed in melancholy.

"He is here, Fardad!" said his mother and placed her hand on his chest. "He rests within you... and will stay with you... till the very end!"

Fardad and Parinaaz got married in the most magnificent ceremony that Persia had ever witnessed. The entire city was splendidly lit up for the celebration, and kings and queens from various kingdoms across the world were invited as well as the noble priests from all parts of the country, who showered their blessings upon the adorable couple. In addition to that, Ukund was appointed as the general of the Persian army.

Moreover, he and Rukhsar too tied the knot in a small, fabulous ceremony a few days later. Gyasis fortune lit up as well, as he was appointed as the commander-in-chief of the Persian army along with being the Foreign Affairs Minister to the new king of Persia, Fardad.

In the meantime, Nabuzardan met his end and was executed in front of the entire kingdom, and his head was hung on a branch of the tallest tree in the Takht-e-Shah to serve as a warning to people. Immense peace and joy began to spread like wildfire across the Takht-e-Shah and, eventually, across the entire Persian Empire.

***

In the interim, the evil King Marduk sat silently on his throne in Babylonia. He began to tap the side of his throne calmly while his ministers looked

365

CHAPTER 18.   THE VERDICT

at him in terror and confusion. With Soroush killed and Nabuzardan executed, he had no other choice but to take the final step.

"Your Lordship!" called one of his ministers as he moved forward and bowed before Marduk. "What are we going to do now?" he asked while shivering slightly in fear. Marduk began to laugh wildly at this question. And when his laughter ended, he grabbed a dagger and threw it at the ministers chest, which led to his instant death and sent shivers across the spines of the other ministers.

"What are we going to do, eh?!" Marduk growled angrily. "What the hell can you all do?! Shall I tell you?! Absolutely nothing! You all are spineless pieces of rat scum! Bloody useless donkeys upon whom I am riding!"

King Marduk spat on the ground in disgust and got out of his throne and began to walk towards the large window onto his right and turned his gaze towards the gloomy dark clouds outside.

"Now, whatever needs to be done, will be done by me! All the horses, generals, and spies have made their moves. Its the kings turn now! Fine then! I will go to Persia myself....and meet the chosen one!"

King Marduk laughed coldly, whose echo tore through the gigantic walls of his palace and struck the horizon like a bolt of lightning.

About the Author

Nassim Odin holds PhD degree in Aerospace Engineering and he teaches engineering. He likes to read about the pyramids and ancient civilizations.
https://www.nassimodin.com

The Sands of Abzu
— book blurb —

Long before Alexander, in ancient Persia, there lived an
energetic young man known as Fardad who was a gifted
clairvoyant. An unanticipated whirlpool of the fate made him
the grand-vizier of the mighty King Kai-Kobad. As the Kings
appointed minister with the princess on his side, Fardad has to
enter the caves, ascend the mountains, flight the manticores to
get to the clues to decode the book of astrology. He must reach
the legendary place called Abzu, which lies hidden deep
somewhere in the Zagros mountains of Persia. Will he be able
to reach there and fulfil his duty and bring back the code?

Printed in Great Britain
by Amazon

35505124R00212